Also by Jodi Compton

Jodi Compton

HAILEY'S WAR

First published in Great Britain by Simon & Schuster UK Ltd, 2010
A CBS COMPANY

This paperback edition first published 2010

1 3 5 7 9 10 8 6 4 2

Simon & Schuster UK Ltd
1st Floor
222 Gray's Inn Road
London WC1X 8HB

www.simonandschuster.co.uk

Simon & Schuster Australia
Sydney

A CIP catalogue record for this book is available from the British Library

ISBN: 978-1-84739-376-0

Printed in the UK by CPI Cox & Wyman, Reading RG1 8EX

Dedicated to the memory of
Stuart Compton, 1921–2009

Author's Note

Hailey's War is a work of fiction and takes the usual liberties with the nonfiction subjects its story touches on. I drew on multiple sources in researching all of these subjects. However, I want to note that Hailey's reflections on the history of the Golden Gate Bridge are largely derived from Tad Friend's article "Jumpers" in the October 2003 issue of the *New Yorker,* a fascinating piece that also inspired the documentary *The Bridge.*

HAILEY'S WAR

prologue

The moon rises over the mountains of central Mexico, a nearly full moon in a sky the deep blue of an hour past sunset.

Get up.

I'm lying on a slope just down from a rural highway, lying in a mix of slate and grass and dirt that is damp with blood. There is dirt in my eyelashes and blood in what little of my hair I can see. There isn't much pain, but I'm very, very tired.

Get up or you'll die here.

My memories of what happened are inexact. I remember driving on a narrow highway through the mountains and into a dim tunnel with rough stone walls. Then this, looking up at the mountain ridge and the sky. I don't know how I got from the tunnel to here. It seems impossible, but I think I was shot.

I search my memories for some explanation. A rough voice: *You're one of our most promising cadets. I hate like hell to see this happen to you.*

No, that was too long ago.

A younger voice: *Pack up just what you need, I'm getting you out of L.A.*

That's not it, either.

I'm so tired, I just want to close my eyes. Except for that moon. It's getting brighter and higher, like God lifting his lamp, looking for his lost sheep.

I think the highway is up the slope, above me. If I were nearer to it, someone might see me. It might make a difference.

I get to my hands and knees, swaying, and put the waxing moon in my sights.

On your feet, soldier. You can do this. You're made outta this.

Then I stand up.

Part I

one

"Do you ever think about Jonah?"

"Jesus, is that my Bible? I haven't opened that thing in years. So you're talking about the guy that was swallowed by a whale?"

"Yeah."

"No, I'd have to say I don't think about him. I wouldn't think you would, either. I didn't take you for particularly religious."

"I'm not. That's my point, though. When you're not raised religious, you think of Jonah as the swallowed-by-a-whale guy, like Noah is the ark guy. But when you actually read the Book of Jonah, it's not what you expect."

"You read the whole book?"

"It's three pages long."

Morning in San Francisco. Jack Foreman, tall and thin, in his early forties, with a premature streak of gray in his light brown hair, was across the room, already dressed at quarter to eight, already having cleared away last night's Ketel One bottle and two glasses, showered, dressed, and fixed and consumed breakfast and an espresso. He was now scanning the headlines of both the *San Francisco Chronicle* and the *Los Angeles Times,* and at the same time keeping an eye on CNN with the sound off. I was still in his bed, naked, with my hair half raveled in the braids I forgot to take out last night, reading his Bible for no particular reason other than that it had caught my eye while Jack was still in the shower.

"The thing that's strange about the story is, Jonah doesn't seem to be scared of anything, even when he should be."

"No?"

5

"No. The story goes that God tells Jonah to go to the city of Nineveh to preach, and Jonah doesn't want to, so he gets on a ship for Spain. God sends a violent storm, and the ship's crew is scared. But when they go down to the hold to find Jonah, he's sleeping."

"Yeah?"

"*Sleeping*. Through a storm that has veteran sailors scared. So they wake him up and tell him, 'We're pretty sure we haven't done anything to anger our gods, might you have done something to anger yours?' And Jonah suggests that if they think this is the case, maybe they should throw him overboard."

"Huh."

"They're way out at sea. Jonah's effectively asking to be *drowned*. The crew says no at first, but later they decide he's right, and they throw him over, and then comes the whale part that everyone knows about. That's what it takes for him to finally decide that maybe he's in trouble. He prays to God—it's kind of a pretty poem, by the way—and God intervenes, so the whale spits him up onto dry land. And then he does go to Nineveh, and everyone in Nineveh really gets with the program, from the king on down. They repent in a big way. And Jonah isn't happy about it. He gets mad. He goes out in the desert and argues with God about destroying Nineveh."

"He wants Nineveh destroyed?"

"Yeah, but the bigger point is, he's arguing with the God of the Old Testament, the all-powerful white-beard guy who used to strike people dead. Doesn't that seem a little insane? Shouldn't Jonah be a little more afraid?"

"You think Jonah was suicidal."

"No. I mean, not necessarily."

"Then what's your theory? You sound like you've been putting a lot of thought into this. You must have one."

"No, sorry. I'm just a bike messenger. I don't get paid enough to theorize."

"Hailey . . ." he said, his tone a change of subject in itself.

"I know. You're ready for work. I've got to get up and dressed and out. I'll hurry." I was already sliding his Bible back onto the bookshelf.

Jack was a newsman for the Associated Press, a Midwestern transplant to California by way of, apparently, everywhere. Photographs on the far wall of his studio, Jack's own amateur work, attested to the width and breadth of his reporting career. Fellow reporters, editors, photographers, and other acquaintances looked out from pictures taken in the world's capitals and war zones, places Jack had been a correspondent.

He and I had crossed paths several times at the courthouse, where he covered motions and trials and I, a bike courier, dropped off and picked up legal papers. But we didn't get to know each other until the Friday night I'd literally backed into him in a tiny, crowded Asian grocery. When, after a few minutes of conversation, he asked me if I wanted company for dinner, I surprised myself by saying yes. Maybe it had been so long since I'd seen a guy who was neither a metrosexual nor a pierced and dreadlocked bike messenger that he had been exotic to me.

He was the first guy I ever slept with who wore boxer shorts. I didn't tell him that, our first night together. Guys have lost erections over less.

Now, as I was pulling on my long-sleeved thermal shirt and cargo pants, Jack said, "Are you hungry? There's bagels."

I shook my head. "I'll eat later." It was my day off, and a small plan for the morning was forming.

I sat on the floor to put on my boots. When I looked up, Jack was watching me.

He said, "Every time I see you lacing up those boots, I think I'm sleeping with an undercover DEA agent."

Bates Enforcers, heavy-soled black lace-ups with a side zip, draw a lot of attention.

"They're comfortable, is all."

Jack had never seen the gun. It was a .38 caliber Smith & Wesson Airweight, easy to conceal. Just five shots, but the kind of trouble I was likely to get into was the up-close-and-personal kind, and if

I couldn't get out of it with five rounds, I wasn't getting out of it at all.

I stood and gathered up my single-strap messenger bag, putting it over my shoulder, when the newspapers on the counter caught my attention.

"Are you done with this?" I asked, indicating the *Los Angeles Times* Calendar section, its front page dominated by a profile of a young white hip-hop producer. "Can I have it?"

"Sure," Jack said.

I slid the section of the paper into my bag, then walked ahead of Jack into the entryway, where my bicycle—it was my private transportation as well as my livelihood—leaned against the wall.

We emerged into the cool gray of June in San Francisco, me wheeling the bike and Jack holding the keys to his old Saab. He stopped for a moment, tapping a cigarette out of a pack, his first of the day. While he lit up, I looked downhill, toward the rest of the city. Jack's studio was at the edge of Parnassus Heights, and the view was fantastic.

It's hard to find anyone who doesn't find San Francisco beautiful, and I couldn't argue. I had been in San Francisco nearly a year. I had ridden every inch of its neighborhoods, the storied ones like Chinatown and North Beach, the quiet ones like the Sunset and Presidio Heights. Late at night, I had watched the lights of great containerships as they ghosted into the port of Oakland, across the water. I had seen this city in the rain, the sun, the fog, the moonlight, on moonless evenings illuminated by its own city lights. San Francisco seemed to pose for you endlessly, proving it could look beautiful under any conditions. People came from all over the country and paid exorbitant prices to own or rent a tiny part of San Francisco.

Only a philistine could stand on a hill, look out at San Francisco, and wish she were seeing the overheated sprawl of L.A. instead. But I did.

Jack had gotten his cigarette going; I could smell the fragrant-acrid smoke from behind me. I turned back to him and was just about to say, *I'll call you sometime this week,* when he spoke first. "Hailey?"

"What?"

"When you say you're going to get something to eat later, you mean later this morning, right? Not late this afternoon?"

"Yeah," I said, baffled. "Why?"

"We had a lot to drink last night, but I didn't see you eat anything. You're getting thin."

"Jack, my job burns, like, eight thousand calories an hour. I couldn't do it if I wasn't eating enough," I pointed out.

He was not appeased. I said, "Something else on your mind?"

He said, "You treat yourself with a certain amount of disregard, Hailey. I've known you for six months, and how often in that time have you been injured on the job? First those stitches in your eyebrow, then that thing with your wrist—"

"That was an old break. The bone was weak," I argued. "Look, I'm a bike messenger. I've been the top-earning rider for my service nearly every month since I hired on. I couldn't do that without taking some risks. There's a lot of competition."

Jack closed his eyes briefly, then said, "You don't want to be the most reckless bike messenger in San Francisco, Hailey. That's like being the town drunk in New Orleans."

"I didn't know you cared."

"You ever think about school?"

"I thought I mentioned that before," I said. "I did a little school back east. It didn't work out."

"And you can never go back?"

"What's with you today?" I asked him. "The thing I like most about you is that you're free of all the middle-class rhetoric, and now suddenly you're doing a guidance-counselor thing."

Jack sighed. "I'm not trying to make you angry."

"I'm not," I said, relenting.

"Really?" He threw down the cigarette and stepped on it.

"Really. I'll call you tomorrow. We'll get together, I'll eat a whole pile of food. You can watch."

Besides, I hadn't been lying when I said I was planning on having breakfast. Just not right away.

I didn't own a car, which wasn't supposed to be a problem in San Francisco. It's said to be one of the world's great walking cities—fairly compact, with temperate weather and beautiful neighborhoods. All true, but even so: forty-nine square miles. In my first weeks here, I'd chronically underjudged the time it was going to take me to walk places. Now, of course, I had my bike—an old silver Motobecane, very fast, with drop handlebars and paint rubbed off the top tube where someone had probably kept a chain wrapped around it.

I'd been a messenger for eight months, long enough to develop the cyclist's long, flat ellipse of muscle in my calf—I didn't have that even back east in school, when I'd thought I was in the best shape of my life. Now a short, easy ride brought me to my destination, the Golden Gate Bridge. Ever since I'd come out to San Francisco, it had become something of a habit of mine to come up here when I didn't have any big plan for my day.

If you've driven in California and visited the Bay Area, the bridge you most likely drove on was the Bay Bridge. It connects San Francisco to the East Bay. It is heavily trafficked, double-decked, beautiful in an industrial way. But it isn't an icon. The Golden Gate Bridge is, largely due to its location: It serves as a kind of borderline between the enclosed waters of the Bay and the open water of the Pacific, between the American continent and the rest of the world. It is open to cyclists and to pedestrians, many of whom are dazzled tourists. In its most mundane sense, it is the bridge between the city and the Marin headlands. But to twenty or more people a year, it is the bridge to eternity.

The Golden Gate Bridge is America's foremost suicide destination.

The first suicide off the bridge was a WWI veteran who appeared to be out for a stroll until he told a passerby, "This is as far as I go." That was three months after the bridge was opened; it was still in its infancy. Sometimes I wondered: If that man had stayed home and stuck his head in an oven instead, would it have changed the bridge's destiny? Without his precedent, would the next person and the next have reconsidered, until it was understood that jumping off the Golden Gate just wasn't done? There are other bridges in America that are as accessible and potentially fatal but have virtually no history of suicides, apparently because it just didn't become a tradition.

Psychologists know there is a contagious aspect to suicide—not merely the destructive impulse itself, but also the where and the how of it. In Japan, they've had to close public attractions because they've become magnets for suicides. One person jumps into a volcano and more people get the idea. In other countries, the authorities intervene. In America, land of the individual destiny, not so much.

Cops who try to prevent suicides up here will tell you that they'll see a pedestrian with that end-it-all look and ask them if they're thinking of jumping. The pedestrian denies it and the cop has to take their word for it and move on. Then they'll look back and the guy is just gone. It's that quick. You don't even hear anything. I know, I've seen it, too.

I asked a patrolman once how he recognized someone with the suicide look. He told me, "You'll know it when you see it." And I do. It's in what they're *not* looking at. Unlike the tourists, they're not looking at the city skyline or the Marin headlands. They're looking at the water. Or at nothing, because all their attention is directed inside, replaying the past and seeing the bleak endless nothing of the future.

That's the thing I don't understand: How exactly do they choose their spot? What says to them, *This far but no farther*? I've never asked a potential jumper how they choose their spot. It's too flippant, and when I'm up here, I'm very, very careful. It's probably the most careful I ever am.

There was a man standing by the railing ten feet ahead of me. He wasn't even a particularly hard guess. He was pretty obviously homeless, skin leathery from sun and wind and maybe drug use. He wasn't looking at anything in particular, and he was too caught up in his internal weather to notice me approach.

The men were usually easier than the women. They could usually be softened by a young woman taking interest in them. The women were sometimes hostile. They told me that *someone like you* couldn't understand their problems. It was never quite clear what they meant by *someone like you*.

"Hey," I said quietly.

He was a big man, maybe six-foot-six, with shaggy hair and a shaggy beard. I could imagine him, at a happier point in his life, dressing as a pirate for Halloween, scaring little kids and then making them laugh.

"Are you hungry?" I said.

He looked at me flatly. "No," he said.

So much for the easy way, getting him off the bridge first, under a pretext. I said, "I thought you might want to get something to eat." I paused. "You know, instead of jumping."

He blinked, startled.

"I'm sorry to be so blunt," I said, "but that's the plan, isn't it? Jumping?"

"So what?" he said, and it wasn't hostile. He was probably too depressed to get really angry anymore. At least I hoped so. He was big enough that even if he wasn't in shape anymore, he could still pick me up and throw me off the bridge without much effort. I thought of the edged ripples of iron-colored water below, of Jonah's prayer: *You cast me into the deep, and all the flood surrounded me.*

I said: "I'm not here to tell you I understand all your problems or that everything's going to be okay. But I'm hungry, and I've got enough money to buy two breakfasts. If you're hungry, too."

And then, at the worst time, my cell phone began to ring. I really should shut it off when I'm up here. I knew who it was: work. Someone had called in sick, or just hadn't shown up. I was needed. And normally I'd have answered, except that right now the guy in front of me was about to make a life-or-death decision and I couldn't just say, *Hold that thought, I have to take this.*

The man in front of me was curious: "Don't you want to answer that?"

"Not really," I said, and it stopped ringing, going into voice mail. I persisted: "What do you say? Breakfast? And you leave the bridge alone at least one more day?"

He nodded slowly. "Yeah," he said. "Yeah, okay."

I'd like to tell you that Todd's story—that was his name—was original and fascinating. It wasn't. I'd heard it before: A good and happy life in an average way, until the onset of a chronic illness, exacerbated by drink. He went on disability until the money ran out. His marriage failed. He was unable to pay child support, so his wife saw no reason for him to know where she'd moved with their two kids. He'd stayed with a buddy until the buddy's wife wouldn't have it anymore. That left no one to care that he was standing on the bridge, ready to jump.

Todd and I made a plan for him that involved having only one drink and going to the VA to look up the brother he hadn't seen in twenty years, but who just might take him in. To level the playing field a bit, I told Todd part of my story—the part about going east to school and why I came back. Without that, the potential jumpers usually looked at me like some idealist who'd read a few too many inspirational books. Like if I weren't doing this, I'd be at the mission feeding the homeless, or in Africa doing medical work.

In someone else, what I did on the bridge would be philanthropy. For me it wasn't. A shrink would probably have a field day with it, trying to put the pieces together, how it fit with the reason I came back from the East Coast, and the reason I had to leave L.A. Those are two different stories, by the way. I'm getting to that.

I hadn't left Todd behind at the diner for more than three minutes when my cell rang again, and with a stab of guilt, remembering the call I'd ignored on the bridge, I immediately brought the Motobecane to a stop.

"It's me." Shay Clements was the owner of Aries Courier. "Fabian just radioed in. His crank's busted, he's stranded on Market Street. Can you go meet him, pick up his packages, and make his drops?"

"Yeah."

"Like, right now?"

Shay wasn't being pushy. A courier service stood or failed on its on-time performance, and that in itself gave me a twinge of confusion: The hour that had passed between the phone call on the bridge and this one was far too much time for Shay to wait. But there wasn't time to wonder about that. "I'm on it right now," I said. "I'm literally standing over my bike."

"Thanks," Shay said after giving me the intersection where I was to meet Fabian.

"It's no problem," I said.

And it wasn't. This was my work now, and I did it with the great humility life has taught me since I washed out of the United States Military Academy at West Point, just two months before I would have graduated and become a second lieutenant in the United States Army.

two

My name is Hailey Cain. I'm twenty-three and have one of the most popular
first names for girls of my generation. Every year in school there were
half a dozen Hailies or Haleys or Haileys in my class.

I'm Californian in a way that a lot of people are Californian: I was
born somewhere else. My father was Texan, my mother from West
Virginia. I was born in an off-base hospital near Fort Hood, Texas,
where Staff Sgt. Henry Cain was stationed at the time. I missed being
born on the Fourth of July by one day; my birthday was the fifth.
Maybe I was born to be a failed patriot.

I take after my father in looks; I have his straw-blond hair and
open face, except that mine is marked by a port-wine birthmark high
on my right cheekbone. In my one photo of him, he's a big guy, shoul-
dery, and I have a similar mesomorphic build at five-foot-seven. My
only really good feature is my full lips. In high school, reading
beauty-magazine articles about the power of a sultry movie-star
gaze, I'd wished I could trade my good lips for thick double-fringed
eyelashes. My cousin CJ had waved that off, saying, *Guys don't fan-
tasize about how* eyelashes *will feel wrapped around the johnson.* CJ
could get away with saying outrageous shit like that because he had
never fully lost his Southern accent, and it gave everything he said a
good-old-boy innocence.

After Texas, my father was posted in Hawaii and Kentucky and
then Illinois, where he died in an accident, a truck rollover on the
base. I was eleven at the time. The Army's death benefit wasn't going
to keep my mother and me solvent very long; Julianne had never been
what you'd call a career woman. So we went to California, where her

sister Angeline had already moved with her husband, Porter Mooney, and their four kids.

Porter was a guard at the federal prison in Lompoc, and the Mooneys had a big falling-down house outside of town that re-created the way they'd lived in West Virginia. There were always half a dozen cars in the yard—Porter and his oldest son, Constantine, were mechanics par excellence. They didn't just fix up cars and trucks; they worked on farm equipment, too, when people brought it to them. Be-hind the house was a half-acre of kitchen garden, and a dozen chick-ens roamed the yard. Angeline sold the eggs they didn't need at the farmers' market, along with sunflowers from the garden, and she gave piano lessons to local kids. There were always people who would sneer at how the West Virginia Mooneys lived, but the fact that six people got by comfortably on just one full-time salary and a few sidelines shamed the debt culture that most of middle-class Cali-fornia was mired in.

When Julianne and I arrived from Illinois, bereaved and nearly broke, theirs became an eight-person household. Porter and Ange-line's two oldest kids were almost finished with high school, and I never got too close to them. And the baby of the family, Virgil, was only starting first grade. But the middle son, my cousin CJ, he was a different story.

CJ and I were the same age, almost literally. We'd been born ten days and a thousand miles apart, and never met until I came to California. We were in the same grade and same class in school, and if it hadn't been for that, I would have been friendless pretty much until high school. I was skinny and unprepossessing, self-conscious about my birthmark, shell-shocked over my father's death, culture-shocked over my arrival in California.

I was used to moving—all Army kids are—but Santa Barbara County was different. People hear the words *Santa Barbara* and they think of wealth, and that was certainly true of the city itself, with its gleaming white Mission-style architecture and streets generously lined with bougainvillea. But where the Mooneys lived, east of Van-denberg Air Force Base, was mostly rural, and yet more racially and economically diverse than an outsider would have thought. In the halls of my new school quite a few of the white students, and some black, were the children of Air Force personnel or staff at the federal prison. Many others were Latino, the sons and daughters of agricul-tural workers, some of them undocumented. In this working-class mix moved the well-dressed children of winemaker families, new money that had recently gravitated to what was becoming a hotbed of viticulture. Old California was here, too, in the kids with Chumash blood, the Indians who originally settled the area. Our high-school salutatorian was a Japanese boy whose family had farmed its acreage for generations—all except for those years spent in an internment camp during World War II.

Put another way: There's a certain kind of white person I like to tell about my first real kiss. It was with a classmate in the seventh grade who was black. *Awww, isn't that great,* I can almost see the lis-tener thinking. Then I tell the rest of it. The next day, three girls cor-nered me out behind one of the portable classrooms at the edge of the school grounds. They were black. Their leader was a girl who'd been the boy's best friend since childhood and felt that she should have been first in line to get that kiss. Her two friends had held my arms while she gave me a pretty good beatdown.

And that's all I say. Usually, it's clear that the listener wants there to be more: some throat-clearing rhetoric about how I understand the social tensions that led to et cetera cetera cetera, or maybe that the girl and I had become friends later in high school. When I don't say any-thing like that, sometimes people look uncomfortable, like I've said something racist, though they can't identify exactly what it is.

The truth is that the girl and I didn't become friends, but by a year later, if either of us thought about the incident at all, we remembered it as just girls fighting over a boy. It could have happened between two black girls or two white girls, but it hadn't. The difference between the way middle-class educated people thought about race and the way people like me lived it was like the difference between what was in surgical textbooks and what happened in an Army field hospital.

When I say that the only thing that made those early years bearable was my cousin CJ, though, I don't mean that he knew everybody at school and introduced me around, easing my way into social success. The Mooneys had arrived in California only a year before Julianne and me, and though CJ would later become Californian in a big way, it hadn't happened by the time I got there. In sixth grade, CJ was already six feet tall, but too skinny, with rawboned hands. The other kids found his Appalachian accent incomprehensible and his first name laughably Southern. I never used it; I always called him CJ, which he liked.

CJ had one advantage over me, though: The other kids learned pretty quickly that he could fight, and they left him alone. I served my fistfight apprenticeship a lot more slowly and painfully. To his credit, CJ never jumped in and fought my battles for me. He understood, the way an adult wouldn't have, that I had to earn my respect myself.

If nothing else, though, CJ's friendship soothed the pains of early adolescence. At school, we ate lunch together when the longtime Californians and the Air Force kids were branched off in their cliques. After school, we halved the time it took us to do homework by splitting the assignments and copying each other's answers. It was probably that joint arrangement that kept CJ's grades up in junior high. It's not that he wasn't bright—he was—but his studies had never interested him much.

What interested him was music. CJ's mother had started teaching him the piano when he wasn't yet old enough to read, and though he was good at it, by junior high he rarely played, considering the piano to be a feminine, Victorian instrument. But he did love music, black music in particular—blues, gospel, and jazz. Even at thirteen, if he owned a CD by a white artist, I didn't know what it was. He was forever slipping his headphones over my ears so I could appreciate something about Miles Davis or John Lee Hooker.

In the insecurity of youth, I'd felt I deserved my outsider status, but often I wondered why the other kids didn't see the CJ I knew. He was kind and funny; he was smart. And he was an excellent kisser. That part, of course, I would rather have died than let the other girls know that I knew.

Yes, I've heard all the jokes about the South and kissing cousins. But most people I know have at least one I-didn't-know-any-better incident in their early sexual history. CJ and I had just been experimenting. It wasn't like we'd had anyone else to practice on.

I'd started things, one night when we were outside on a sleeping bag after dark, waiting to watch a rocket launch from Vandenberg. Offhandedly I told CJ that I'd never kissed with an open mouth, and I wanted to learn. CJ said that I'd get a chance soon enough and to be patient. Patience had not been my strong suit, so finally he relented and showed me. And kept showing me. Those satellite launches got delayed a lot. It wasn't like there'd been anything else for us to do.

For about a year after that, making out was just something we did when we had time and privacy. It was mostly kissing, except that when I started getting my breasts, I let CJ cup them in his gentle, long-fingered hands. And the summer before we started high school—I admit there was a bottle of Jack Daniel's involved in this— he let me touch him down low. He was hard, and when I wrapped my hand around him, I was amazed at how it felt, so powerful and yet vulnerable, all at once.

Then CJ rolled away from me, breathing hard, and said, "We probably ought to knock this shit off."

And I said, "Yeah, I know."

So we stopped. We were going to be in high school next year; it was time to put away childish things. No big deal.

In high school, we drifted apart a little. This was partly because Julianne scraped together the money to move us out of the Mooney home and into a rented house in town. But what really set CJ and me on different paths was something that happened to me in a book-store, a few months before I finished eighth grade.

I was looking for a present for Julianne's birthday. I knew she didn't want a book as a gift, but I was mad at her for moving us out of the Mooney house, where I'd felt comfortable. In theory, Julianne and I had moved "so Hailey can have her own room." In reality, it was so she could have privacy to entertain the Air Force guys she liked. I hated the house—it was cramped and Helen Keller could have done a more tasteful job on the color scheme—and disliked most of the men she dated. I missed the Mooney house with its warmth and life. So there I was, browsing, when I passed a display of educational books and a thick volume caught my attention.

It was *Wheelock's Latin*. I wasn't interested in foreign languages, but even so I picked it up and ran my finger along the words inside— difficult, opaque, more than merely foreign, almost alien—and somehow they dazzled me. This, I thought, was the language of ancient soldiers and empire builders, of discipline and honor. And it seemed to me that it was somehow my birthright, because of my father, who had been in my eyes a warrior. By the time I left the store, I'd not only bought my mother's birthday gift but also the *Wheelock's*, and it wasn't long after that I understood that I would someday apply to West Point.

That's a pretty big leap in logic, I know. The ideas that you have at thirteen rarely stand up to the test of time. But they're very powerful in the moment; you feel things at that age with an intensity that few people can still access in adulthood.

Those feelings also run pretty hot and cold. I studied the Latin text voraciously for about five days before casting it aside in frustration. But I started up again when I began high school in the fall, and worked at it more slowly and patiently. When it was time for my appointment with the guidance counselor, and she asked me what I thought I might like to do for a living, I told her about West Point. Her eyebrows inched toward her hairline, and I couldn't blame her: Nothing in my life that far suggested any latent achieverhood. To give her credit, she didn't voice her skepticism. Instead, she asked me if I'd thought about the Air Force Academy in Colorado—remember, we were in Air Force territory. I told her to fuck off the way fourteen-year-olds tell adults to fuck off—"I'll think about it"—and she nodded and then did something to my file that switched me from graduation track to college preparatory.

She explained the drill: four years of math, four years of English, three years of science, two years of foreign language. I asked her if there was any way I could get credit for studying Latin instead of the Spanish, French, or German our school offered. Her eyebrows made that same ascent and she said she didn't see how that would work, and besides, for a military officer who might be stationed overseas, French would be a much more useful language.

I spited her by enrolling in Spanish instead, and on my own time I studied Latin. By the time I was a junior, the principal was sufficiently impressed with my resolve that he signed off on the deal that let me out of study hall twice a week to bus over to the community college to take Latin classes there.

It's hard for me to explain what Latin means to me. My guidance counselor had been right: It wasn't at all useful to a military career. But to be fair, I think Latin got me into West Point, because studying it was how I learned I could do difficult things. Hard things had happened to me—my father's death, most of all—but Latin was the first burden I picked up of my own choice.

It has to be said that I wasn't squeaky clean in high school. I got in some fights, and I got in some backseats. I can't say I don't know what a meth high feels like. You have to grow up in a small town to understand. On Friday and Saturday nights, things go on in farmhouses that would shock the ghetto. But I was always in homeroom with my schoolwork done on Monday morning, so the adults around me never knew. That's something that all smart kids figure out pretty early on: As long as your grades are good and you don't smoke or wear heavy eyeliner, the authority figures around you generally don't look any deeper than that.

Don't get me wrong, I wasn't a delinquent. I didn't start fights, but I didn't back down from them either, so I had some pretty good scraps with girls I wasn't even sure how I'd offended. Some of it was about my plans for the future, I guess, my grades and West Point ambitions. Some people will tear you down for no reason other than that you're trying to build yourself up.

And the sex? I never actually went all the way, not back then. Like many girls, I protected my reputation by making the distinction between giving head and giving it up. If my generation didn't invent the idea of "oral sex isn't sex," we'd popularized it, and I wasn't reluctant to show a guy I liked him in that way.

And maybe on some level I was competing with CJ, who was going through my female classmates at a truly amazing rate. Because while I was becoming somebody different, my cousin was, too.

All the Mooney kids adapted to California—their accents softened, and they called the freeway "the 246," not just "246," and so forth. But it was CJ who went native in a big way. In his freshman year he'd started going to the ocean with friends who had driver's licenses, and the sun and salt water brought out gold lights in his reddish-blond hair, which he let grow out to his shoulders, smoothing out the tightness of its curls. He traded in his checked flannel shirts and dark-blue jeans for T-shirts and faded, ripped Levi's and casually unlaced basketball shoes. Though I could always spot him in the halls because of his height, sometimes I barely recognized the skinny country cousin I'd first met.

In our second year of high school, CJ got his driver's license, and not long after he bought a twenty-year-old silver BMW that he'd seen advertised "for parts" and rebuilt it from the ground up. He also won a starting spot on the baseball team, where he vexed opposing batters with the deep sinker and nasty screwball that Porter had taught him.

I don't know if my cousin ever had the kind of life-changing moment that I did in the bookstore, but he told me a story about the time when, as far as he could tell, school turned around for him. It was in the middle of that sophomore year. CJ was getting books from his locker when a pretty black girl, a new transfer from Oxnard, took in his height—he was six-three then, on his way to six-five—and said teasingly, "Do you hang off the end of your bed?"

CJ had winked at her and said, "Only recreationally," and not only had she laughed, the kids around her had, too.

By the end of that week, CJ and the girl from Oxnard were going out, and suddenly the entire female population of our school discovered, seemingly all at once, the aphrodisiac qualities of a Southern accent. CJ, of course, was happy to help them enjoy that discovery.

By our junior year I saw very little of him on weekends, not just because he was out with girlfriends—though he often was—but because once he got his car running, he could go to Los Angeles without waiting to ride along with friends. CJ wasn't antisocial, but his interest in L.A. wasn't the same as that of his friends. They went to surf and drink around campfires on the beach. CJ went to sweet-talk his way into L.A.'s music venues, the eighteen-and-over or twenty-one-only clubs where the new hip-hop acts debuted. All the money he earned repairing cars for his father went either to gas money or to two-drink minimums. He kept his grades up just high enough to stay on the baseball team, but that was all.

Teachers sighed and shook their heads about CJ Mooney, but there was no animus in it. The guidance counselor, she of the mobile eyebrows, saw that he'd inherited the Mooney gift with cars, put him on the graduation track, and loaded his schedule with shop classes.

They didn't see what he was. Back then, none of us did.

Sure, it was obvious that he loved music. But in high school, what kid doesn't? Even the fact that he was a white boy in love with black music didn't raise any eyebrows; that was a story older than Elvis Presley.

Then, after our junior year, he dropped out of high school and moved to Los Angeles to try to find work in the music business.

Even in poor and rural areas, that doesn't happen so much anymore. It caused a stir. At school, the teachers were shocked, the baseball coach cursed the loss of his best pitching arm, and the girls went into mourning. But his parents took it hardest. Several Mooneys of their generation had dropped out, but they'd made damn sure none of CJ's had. They were convinced he was on the road to ruin: just seventeen, talented but with no marketable skills, in a town that ate gifted youth for breakfast and sent them home broke and failed. Both Porter and Angeline called me, asking me to talk to him. I said I couldn't; it was his life. Secretly I believed what everyone else did—that in a year or two CJ would get disillusioned and come home—but I couldn't be disloyal enough to say it aloud.

After that, CJ's parents regularly asked me for news about their son. It wasn't that he didn't call them, but they thought I was getting the true, uncensored news of his life in L.A. "Really, how's he doing down there? Is he working?" they'd ask. And I'd say he was getting by, because I didn't want them to know the truth: Unable to get even the lowest-level job in the music business, CJ was supporting himself by dealing pot.

On the night before I left for West Point, I slept on the floor of his flophouse room, just like he'd done in my bedroom so many times before. He tried strenuously to give me the bed, but I said no, tomorrow I was going to be in Beast Barracks, and if I couldn't tolerate sleeping on the floor, then the outlook was pretty bleak. CJ gave up, but joined me about halfway through the night, dragging a blanket down with him to nestle companionably behind me. I shouldn't have let him, but I was secretly glad for his nearness, because it was the only thing that kept me from spending the night wondering what the hell made me think I could cut it at the United States Military Academy and deciding that it wasn't too late for me to stay in California and go to community college.

The next morning, CJ drove me to LAX. Standing in the departures drop-off zone, he'd joked, "Look at you, baby, you're the pride of the Mooneys, and you're a Cain. That hardly seems fair." Then he'd turned serious, pulled me close, and said, "I am so very proud of you, baby."

I wanted to tell him that I was proud of him, too, the way he lived life on his own terms. But I couldn't, because it would have sounded condescending. He was right: I was the standard-bearer of our family, making my place in the world, and he was the black-sheep underachiever, going nowhere. In that moment, our paths in life seemed set in stone.

Funny how four years can change everything.

Four years later, I was getting off a Greyhound at the downtown L.A. depot, with no commission in the Army, no college degree, less than two hundred dollars to my name, and no place to live. It took the last of my pride to do it, but I called CJ at his office. By which I mean I tried to. I left several messages with a cool-voiced receptionist ("Yeah . . . his cousin Hailey . . . he'll know who you mean") and stood for two hours in the Southern California sun by a pay phone, tired and out of sorts, itching with impatience when passersby stopped to use the phone and tied it up. The next day I'd have a pretty bad sunburn.

Finally the phone rang. I only had to say, "Hello?" and, to my vast relief, I heard that familiar half-Appalachian, half-Californian drawl: "Where are you? I'll come get you."

His first words to me in person, as he was jumping out of the same old silver BMW, were, "Shoot, I am so sorry, baby. My people didn't know who you were."

"I know," I said against his cheek, already enfolded in his long arms.

That was the month that CJ was in *Vanity Fair*'s music issue. In the photo essay of that year's most influential figures, he was labeled "The Prodigy" and was photographed standing on a gritty hotel rooftop, the sun behind him sinking into layers of L.A. atmosphere, the camera angle low enough to make him look seven feet tall. He's turned away from the camera, an abstracted visionary.

At just twenty-two, he had become one of L.A.'s most sought-after producers. No one doubted the depth of his understanding of hip-hop or his respect for it. Some people who saw him in deep concentration, listening to something only he could hear over headphones, said they'd looked at his eyes and thought at first that he was blind.

He had also taken back his name, in the liner notes of the two CDs he'd produced and on the Grammy he'd won. The name Cletus Mooney now commanded respect throughout the music industry.

Practically the first thing I asked him, that day in L.A., was which name he wanted me to use.

He said, "Whatever you want to call me is fine." He checked the traffic before pulling out onto the street. As he did so, he said, "What's wrong with your arm?" He'd noticed the cast on my wrist.

"Broken bone," I said. "I fell. It's no big deal."

"You're not out here on some kind of medical leave, are you?"

"No," I said. "I . . . CJ, I'm not going back."

I could see his confusion, and in a moment he articulated it. "You mean, you graduated early?"

He knew that wasn't it, but denial is like that. Often there's a short detour on the way to the unhappy truth.

"No," I said. "I'm not going to finish."

"Are you serious? Baby, what happened?"

"A lot of people wash out," I said tiredly. "I warned you about that before I went. Do we have to talk about it?"

"No."

"I'm okay. I'll be okay."

"I know you will," he said finally. "Sure you will."

I'm not sure what I was expecting from the place that CJ, with his newfound wealth, would call home. Maybe a retro-Rat-Pack condo with a wet bar, or a beach house in Malibu.

Instead, he drove us up into the hills outside the city, an ascent so steep and fast it reminded me of taking off in a plane, to an area of no particular repute, where acres of land separated the houses and amateur spray paint on the road warned: SLOW! CHILDREN AND

ANIMALS. On the way, his cell phone rang so incessantly that he finally shut it off.

His driveway wasn't even paved, and as we pulled up in a cloud of dust, I looked curiously at the home he'd chosen. It wasn't big, but somehow rambling, built of weathered wood, with old sash windows with little scrapes on them from many cleanings. A live oak tree bent toward the roof as though it wanted to enfold the whole house. There was a deck with a hot tub in it, but no landscaping. The grass that surrounded the house was natural. A Volkswagen Corrado, clearly in mid-repair, stood at a small distance. I observed all this with a growing sense of familiarity.

For as shy as he'd been about bringing people to the Mooney home of his adolescence, CJ had chosen to re-create it here. It wasn't until I'd known the adult CJ awhile that I understood. He had to live a certain kind of life down in the city: the velvet-rope-and-VIP-room life, riding in Navigators with the talent and their entourages, getting drive-thru from In-N-Out Burger after midnight and washing it down with Cristal. But when he was ready to buy a home, CJ chose a place where he could be who he really was: someone who listened to baseball games on the radio while working on cars with his hands.

"Nice," I said. It was inadequate.

"I took just about the first thing the agent showed me," he said. "I just wanted someplace quiet." He watched a red-tailed hawk wheel overhead a moment, then went on. "Look, I'd like to stay here tonight while you get settled in, but I have dinner plans, and actresses can be touchy about things like broken dates."

"My, an *actress*. Aren't you something?"

"Hey," he said, "I'm gonna ask you to think twice about how you talk to someone who walked away from a meeting with two very big record label executives to drive across town to the Greyhound station to collect your stranded ass."

"I know," I said, chastened.

He smiled at me in the old way I remembered, eyes crinkling. "I'm glad you're here," he said. "It's going to be good, having you around."

"Thanks," I said, "but it's only for a while, until I get on my feet."

"No hurry," CJ said.

"No, I understand that you bought this place so you could have some privacy," I said.

He looked at me as if I'd said something incomprehensible, and said, "Not from *you*."

I lived with CJ a month, long enough to find three part-time jobs—none of them particularly interesting or challenging, but the checks cashed fine. When I'd saved enough, I put down money on a tiny studio in town. CJ tried to talk me out of leaving, and I was reluctant, too, but I couldn't have a life that was just an offshoot of his. And I wasn't going far, just down into the city. So he yielded and helped me move.

I wouldn't realize until later—when I had to leave—how much Los Angeles had gotten under my skin. Mostly I'd sat out the long-standing Love L.A./Hate L.A. debate. When I'd chosen to go there after leaving West Point, my decision had been fairly arbitrary. I didn't have roots in Lompoc anymore. Julianne had moved away during my plebe year at West Point, and even the Mooneys, CJ's parents, had done something quintessentially Californian: They'd sold their real estate at a profit and bought a bigger, cheaper place out of state, in Nevada's Washoe Valley. But L.A. was the nearest big city to where I'd grown up. My feeling had been, *I suppose if I'm from anywhere, I'm from here.*

Later, if you'd asked me why I liked it there, I'd have given you everyone's general paean to L.A.: the open streets and the palm trees and the laid-back vibe, et cetera cetera cetera. The truth was simpler: L.A. just felt like a place for people like me, young people raised on high-fructose corn syrup, long on energy and short on a sense of history.

I doubt I would have approved if I'd moved straight there after high school. I'd gone to West Point to test myself against hardship and privation, to see how little comfort and pleasure I could get by on. But I came home in a very different frame of mind. Then, I wanted what I called *omnia gaudia vitae,* all the pleasures of life, and L.A. was the place for that. Vietnamese iced coffee, British Columbian marijuana, Colombian cocaine, French film noir, Israeli krav maga training—you could get it all here, and if it was all imported, like the water supply and the workforce and even the iconic palm trees, who cared?

I told CJ when I moved into town that we'd still see each other all the time, and we did. He opened the doors to the West Hollywood clubs he was always waved into, and I spent many nights drinking and dancing, sometimes in his immediate company, other times only knowing that he was somewhere in the same vast and densely packed venue. I wasn't ever lonely. CJ's circle of friends, friendly acquaintances, and hangers-on was enormous, and they were always willing to share space at their tables, their drugs, even their bodies. I left footprints on the windows of a few Navigators and Escalades owned by guys I didn't know very well.

Some mornings I dreamed of the clean citadel of West Point and woke up first disoriented, then unhappy. I chased that feeling away with strong coffee or a joint, or sometimes a hard workout.

I attained something of a reputation in CJ's crowd as that mostly quiet girl with the birthmark and the occasional hair-trigger temper. From time to time CJ had to drag me away from a vending machine I was trying to bust up for taking my money or a bouncer twice my size I felt provoked by. Sometimes CJ had to wrap his arms around me from behind and negotiate over my shoulder, telling people that I was on mood-altering meds or just getting over a bad breakup.

Later, when I apologized to him, he always said, pleasantly, not to worry about it. Some of that was CJ being CJ, so mellow that one friend of his joked that his adrenal glands secreted some kind of cannabinoid substance instead of adrenaline. But I think CJ chalked most of it up to my washing out of West Point. It's amazing the shit people will let you get away with if they think it's coming from a place of anger and low self-respect.

Nonetheless, I always told him I was sorry—often too abjectly, because I was usually still drunk or high or stoned and therefore able to access my feelings in a way I couldn't when sober. "I love you," I'd tell him. "I'd kill anyone who'd try to hurt you."

"Those are lovely sentiments; go sleep them off," he'd say.

But underneath the fevered language, I meant it. The way I thought of it was, I had been born an only child, but in time, the gods took pity and gave me a brother and a sister.

three

The sister was Serena Delgadillo.

Technically, Serena and I went back to the seventh grade together. We'd both been chosen for an academic-achievement program called ReachUP, which singled out promising students in rural or disadvantaged schools in hopes of helping them compete with middle-class students at college admissions time. We'd also both played on the girls' soccer team that year, alongside each other as forwards. No question, she was better than me. The daughter of migrant workers, she had learned soccer on the hard brown fields of California's inland valleys from her four older brothers and other immigrant kids, all *futbol* fanatics.

We weren't friends, but we were friendly. That had been a big step for both of us at the time. Like me, Serena was skinny then, with Kmart clothes and hair her mother cut in harsh black bangs directly across Serena's forehead. It made her self-conscious except on the soccer field, where she lost her inhibitions, becoming speedy and fluid and exuberant.

Then, in eighth grade, something changed. Serena dropped out of ReachUP and grew distant. She began styling her hair in the high, lofty wall of bangs that hadn't quite gone out of style among Latina girls back then, and I only saw her with other Mexicans in the hallways. We sat next to each other in study hall, but she only spoke to me once, to poke me in the shoulder and say, "What's that?" She'd been looking at the Latin flashcards I was reviewing instead of doing my schoolwork.

"It's Latin," I'd said.

She'd flipped through a few cards. "Weird," she'd said, shrugging, and had gone back to her homework.

The next year, Serena was gone. That was a common thing. Farm-worker families are nomadic; the population of our school was always in flux.

I forgot her pretty quickly.

In my early days in L.A., after moving down from CJ's place, I was broke. The one luxury I allowed myself was food from cheap ethnic places. That month, I'd discovered pho, the Vietnamese noodle soup made with ox-tail and rare beef. Late one Saturday afternoon, I was waiting in line to get my fix, when I saw that I was being watched by a tall young Latina.

She was good-looking and slender, her cargo pants hanging off sharp hip bones, braless under a strappy tank shirt, her hoop earrings so large you could have worn them as bracelets. She had straight hair, not quite black, pulled back off her face, and almond-shaped eyes. When I caught her looking at me, she didn't smile or say "Sorry" like a lot of people would have.

"I think I know you," she said thoughtfully.

"Okay," I said. She wasn't familiar to me, but I've learned not to argue with people about that. When you've got a birthmark on your face, people can recognize you long after they've changed beyond identifiability for you.

"We played soccer together in junior high," she said. "Remember?"

"Holy shit," I said. "Serena?"

"Yeah," she said, laughing. Then: "You're at the front of the line."

I bought my pho; she bought hers, and we moved off to the side to talk. She remembered that I used to hang out with "that Southern boy," and that I'd been studying Latin. I asked her where her family had gone after eighth grade. She explained that her father had hurt his back and couldn't do farm work anymore, so their family had come to L.A. looking for industrial work for her mother and aunt.

Then she said, "Did you ever get to West Point?"

I'd felt my mouth drop open slightly and couldn't answer right away. First, because she must have heard that secondhand; I knew I hadn't told her about what had been, back then, an unlikely dream. Second, because it brought up the fresh pain of saying, *Yes, I was there; no, I didn't finish.*

"Yeah," I said. "I was at West Point for a while."

She said, "So what happened?"

"Didn't make it all four years," I said. "That's a story for another time."

Sometime after midnight we were in her car, or what I thought was her car. I was driving and she was in the passenger seat, leaning forward laughing, a bottle of Jack Daniel's wedged between her thighs. I forget what story I'd been telling or she'd been telling, just that we were both laughing and laughing and then she'd said, "Slow down, okay, *esa*? You're speeding. We can't afford to get pulled over."

And I'd joked, "Why, is this car stolen?"

And she'd said, "Yeah, it is."

That was when I sobered up and really looked at her, and I realized that what I'd been registering as a birthmark high on her cheekbone wasn't; it was three tiny dots, the tattoo that symbolized *la vida loca,* the gang life.

At that point I had a choice: I could have drawn on the battered last of my West Point ideals, said, *This isn't cool,* and then found a place to pull over and walk away.

Instead, I said, "For how long?"

Serena knew I meant how long had she been in the life. She said, "Since I was fourteen."

I said: "I'll slow down."

That was how I learned what happened to her in the eighth grade.

Gang life is popularly associated with the cities, but it's been in

33

the rural areas a long time. In our small school, Serena had drawn the attention of Lita, a leader in a girls' gang. She recruited Serena, who'd said no, she couldn't, her parents wouldn't understand.

The next day, Serena heard that Lita had called her out. Serena's refusal to join had been a loss of face for Lita, a slur on her pride. From now until Serena gave in and let herself be initiated, no day would pass without the prospect of a fight with Lita or one of Lita's girls.

Serena wasn't stupid. She chose to have sisters instead of enemies.

"Looking back," Serena told me, "it was the best thing that could have happened. I wouldn't have wanted to come to L.A. a total virgin. When I got here, I knew the life. Well, sort of. Nothing can prepare you for what it's like in L.A."

What most people don't realize about urban gangs is how small their individual territories actually are. Many people have the vague idea that Gang A is on the East Side and Gang B on the West Side. In truth, the part of L.A. that Serena and her family moved to was like a checkerboard: Various Latino gangs—or rather, small splinters of the gangs, called sets or cliques—were spread out in small pockets throughout. A gang member could walk for only a few blocks, be in enemy territory, then a few more blocks and be safe again. Bitter, fatal rivals lived right on top of each other. It was impossible to ever feel truly secure.

It also made the question of gang allegiance an open one. Regardless of who controlled your particular stretch of your particular street, there was always a chance you could claim a different clique or an entirely different gang.

But virtually every young person claimed. Everyone needed protection, *familia*. Those who had no gang affiliation were in the worst of all worlds: considered untrustworthy by everyone, always at risk of being attacked, with no one backing them up.

Serena's older brothers immediately claimed the 13th Street clique, or El Trece. Serena wasn't unwilling to follow in their path, but this time her qualms were different from the ones she'd cited to Lita. She looked at the neighborhood girls who had affiliations to Trece and didn't like what she saw.

"They weren't really down," she told me. "They were just hoochies who slept with the guys. They didn't even get jumped in. They said they didn't have to, they were 'already down,' whatever that means." Her voice had filled with scorn.

It wasn't anything you could have made a high-school counselor see, but Serena Delgadillo was an overachiever. One short year after she tried to refuse Lita's initiation, Serena shaved her head, borrowed her older brother's flannel shirt and chinos, and went to Payaso, the leader of El Trece, and asked to be jumped in. Her brothers vouched for her toughness, and Serena, bloody and bruised, became a member of the gang.

Serena had to prove herself over and over again, backing up her guys, stealing cars, driving getaway, lying to the cops, and doing a six-month stretch in the California Youth Authority camp. It was the ironically familiar refrain of a woman in a man's job: She had to do twice as much as the guys to get equal standing with them. Through it all, she kept her head shaved and her clothes masculine. Sometimes the cops mistook her for a boy.

"I have a picture," she told me that night, "but it's at my house." She looked up at me, slyly. "Unless you're afraid to come to the hood to see it."

"Let's go," I'd said.

She lived in a one-story house of pale yellow stucco, with an orange tree in the yard and bars on the windows. A motion-sensor light flashed on as we walked up the driveway. Not surprisingly, the dead bolt on the front door was probably the newest and most expensive thing about Serena's home.

It wasn't dark inside, though it was dim. We came into the kitchen, and Serena peered over a cracked Formica counter into her living room and then raised a finger to her lips. I followed her gaze and saw a rumpled sleeping bag. It rustled, and a girl stuck her tousled head out and looked at us.

"*Quien es la rubia?*" she said. *Who's the blond girl?*

"*Nadie,*" said Serena. *No one.*

The girl withdrew back into her nest.

"Thanks a lot," I said.

"You know what I mean," Serena said mildly. "Are you hungry?"

We didn't talk much while she cooked, out of consideration for the girl sleeping in the dining room. As she heated water to boiling and poured in some short-grain white rice from a ten-pound sack, I looked around the kitchen. There were photographs on the refrigerator, and the subjects were all male—some school pictures, others obviously taken to establish gang cred, as the boys posed with guns and cars. All, though, were bordered with colored paper. On the margins were roses and *virgenes* and the initials *q.d.e.p.*

"What's q.d.e.p?" I asked Serena.

"*Que descansa en paz,*" she said quietly.

"These guys are all . . ."

"Dead," she confirmed.

"No girls?"

She said, "I've got the roll call for my *hermanas* on my leg."

"Your leg?" I echoed, not understanding.

She hiked her right foot onto the counter and pulled up the cuff of her pants so I could easily see the tattooed letters *qdep* high on her calf, and underneath that, two names: Tania and Dreamer.

I asked, "How did you decide whether to use the given name or their gang name?"

"Well, Tania didn't have a moniker," she said. "She wasn't in the life, she was just kicking it with some homeboys who were on their porch and got blasted in a walk-up shooting." She put her leg down.

Noting the way the names would descend to her ankle, I said, "What happens when you run out of room?"

She said, "Maybe I'll get out of the life."

. . .

When she was done cooking, Serena and I carried our late-night meal into her bedroom. Just before I followed her in, though, I heard the sleeping bag in the dining room stir, looked back, and did a slight double take.

Serena switched on a lamp and shut the bedroom door.

I said, "Either the girl out there has three legs, or there were two girls under that sleeping bag."

"Yeah, there were."

"Are you that low on blankets and sleeping space?"

"Well, the spare bedroom's taken, and so is the living-room couch," she said. "But the girls just like to be close. They're not gay, it's just that they like to feel . . ." She trailed off. "It's safety in numbers. It's just something you have to understand."

"Sure," I said. "I didn't mean anything by it."

We sat on her bed and ate, and then Serena reached under the bed for an old wooden box. She rummaged inside and found a Polaroid of a group of teenage boys, all with heads shaved, in voluminous shirts buttoned only at the top, and creased khakis. Serena tapped her finger on one of them, sitting on "his" heels in front. "That's me," she said, "at sixteen, when I was banging hardest."

I held the photo by the edges and marveled at it, half in amazement that I would never have recognized her, but also because the picture reminded me strongly of something else.

I had a photo from my West Point days that looked remarkably similar. It was me in full camo, posing with my Sandhurst team. Sandhurst is the war-games competition West Point holds every year against the British and the Canadians. All of West Point's companies field teams, who compete against one another as well as the foreigners. Every team has one female member, and I was chosen from my company.

Of course, the Brits kicked our asses—they do almost every year—but our company had a pretty good showing, and that day I was glowing with the pleasure of just being part of it. And then we'd posed for the photo in which I, like Serena, had to point out to people which cadet among the guys was me.

When I told Serena this, she looked at me in shared fascination. That was probably the main reason we didn't hug each other around the neck at the end of the night and go our separate ways. The outside world would have said we were nothing alike, but we were. Those parallels cemented our friendship, and that friendship would set a lot of other things in motion.

In time, Serena told me about her dreams of Vietnam.

They had started in early childhood, around five or six. They weren't frequent, but they were vivid and remarkably consistent. Serena dreamed of explosions and bloody chaos in the jungle. She dreamed of white and black men in olive drab. She dreamed of snake-silver rivers and huge machines that hovered in the air, the wind they generated beating the grass flat.

"It was Vietnam," she told me. "I know what you're thinking, that it's Mexico, right? But I've never been to Mexico, and even if I had, my parents are from the north; it's dry as Arizona. There's no jungle there."

Serena believed that not only had she served in Vietnam as an American GI, but that she had died there.

I must have looked skeptical, because she'd gone on. "I saw white men and black men in my dreams back when I'd only ever been around Mexicans," she said. "Come on, where would I see a helicopter at that age? Five years old?"

"There are helicopters all over California," I pointed out. "They're in the sky all the time."

"*Way* up in the sky," she corrected me. "Not down low where the sound of the blades feels like your own heart beating." She placed her fist on her sternum. "I swear, Hailey. The first time I saw a helicopter up close, on TV, I *knew* that sound. I had this feeling like someone walked over the place my grave is going to be."

The dreams had stopped around the age of fifteen, when she'd been jumped into El Trece. "When *mi guerra nueva* started, I stopped dreaming about the old one," was how she put it.

I don't think Serena told many people this story. At least she said she didn't. But she wore a pair of dog tags as jewelry, dangling low under her shirt. And somehow her gang brothers had sensed something of her beliefs, because among the cheery, innocuous gang monikers they gave one another—Droopy and Smiley and Shorty— they'd given Serena the name Warchild.

Two years after her juvenile conviction, Serena did a second stretch, this time in jail. It was there that she finally began to let her hair grow. Jail was a clarifying time for her. She was eighteen now. By middle-class America's standards, that was barely out of childhood, but gang-bangers aged differently. For them, twenty was virtually middle-aged. Serena, having survived to eighteen, was a *veterana*. She had some thinking to do about the future.

The movies spread an old, common misperception about gang life: the "blood in, blood out" thing. It was a saying that meant that your gang jumped you in with a bloody beating and you stayed in until you were cut down in a bloody premature death . . . or, if you tried to leave the life, that your own gang assassinated you.

The less exciting truth was that gang members left the life all the time, especially girls. It was *por vida* in name, but age and mother-hood often slowed girls down, sidelined them from the life. Others went straight after doing jail time. A few were even "jumped out," meaning they failed to be tough enough or ruthless enough for gang life, and were beaten by their gang as a contemptuous dismissal.

Serena was not married, nor was she tied down to a baby. And modesty aside, she was more than *veterana,* she was *leyenda,* a legend, because of her exploits with El Trece. There were plenty of Serena stories in the neighborhood, not all of them true. Serena had jacked a pharmacy not just for prescription drugs, but carried away boxes and boxes of contraceptives that she'd distributed for free among the girls of her neighborhood. Serena had gone into Crip territory, Grape Street, and robbed a crack dealer there. In the sexy clothes of an aspiring actress, Serena had trolled Westwood and Burbank, stealing Mercedeses and Jaguars right from under the noses of the Beautiful People.

A reputation is capital, and in jail, Serena began to think about how she wanted to spend that capital.

She realized that she wanted to lead a girls' clique, a satellite to Trece, the kind she hadn't found when she moved to the neighborhood. And when it came time to name her *cliqua,* Serena knew one thing: It wasn't going to be the "Lady" anythings, an innocent naming convention some gangs borrowed from high-school athletics.

Serena named her girls the Trece Sucias. It didn't translate directly to English. To call them the 13th Street Dirty Girls just didn't say it. The name *sucias* could evoke different things, the nasty girls or the sexy girls, but it also suggested dirty hands, with blood and guilt on them.

For all the fearsomeness of the name, though, Serena had higher standards for her sucias than a lot of leaders would have set. She wouldn't take girls under fifteen, the *quinceanera* year being symbolic of womanhood in Hispanic culture. That might sound painfully young to the rest of America, but in gang life, it was a high standard—it wasn't uncommon for children to start banging at ten or eleven years old. And the two crimes that the Trece Sucias specialized in—car theft and pharmacy burglaries—were both nonviolent, if done with enough caution.

And Serena was careful. Her crew only knocked over a few pharmacies a year, at quiet suburban locations Serena carefully scouted, and while she and a trusted second raided the back for lucrative prescription drugs that Serena resold around her neighborhood, younger girls swept the shelves of Pampers, baby food, cough syrup, and OTC meds—all things desperately needed among the young mothers of the barrio.

It would be nice to imagine Serena as a kind of urban feminist Robin Hood, but I knew better than to indulge in that kind of fantasy. Violence was inextricable from gang life: grudges and retaliations, attacks and counterattacks, beatings and shootings. I heard the stories Serena's girls told, thinking I didn't know enough Spanish to understand. And they routinely went around strapped, meaning carrying a gun.

But this lifestyle of retaliation and revenge was the price of having *familia*. In its perverse way, it was a virtue, the dark side of loyalty. Serena encouraged the same kind of loyalty among them that the guys had for one another. Unlike male gang members, though, girls affiliated with the same clique often fought viciously with one another, sometimes over gossip, more often over a boy. Serena said she'd never let her clique be divided over a man: "The sucias are for the sucias," she told them. "We represent like the guys."

I didn't learn all of this at once, of course. But after that first night, Serena was surprisingly open with me, given that we'd hardly known each other back in school, and that I'd once been the straightest of straight arrows, Cadet Hailey Cain.

I think that Serena had been waiting for someone she could talk to. She had to front around the guys, with whom sharing her feelings would have been a liability. And she cared for her sucias, but they were little more than children, with short attention spans and narrow worldviews. There wasn't anyone else like Serena in Serena's world. The person who came closest, skin color notwithstanding, was me.

Maybe she understood, too, that I'd honored her when, in time, I told her the full truth about why I had to leave West Point.

I'd like to say that I was wracked with guilt over telling her something I hadn't even shared with CJ, but it wasn't true. I didn't tell CJ because I knew he'd lie awake at night thinking about it. Serena wouldn't. She understood about bad luck.

The day after I told her, we went to the Beverly Center, L.A.'s cathedral of capitalism, and did something the rest of the world wouldn't understand but that made sense to us.

Perhaps it was inevitable that Serena started to kid me about getting initiated into her clique. She said I could become her second. I took it as gentle condescension. But she kept on it, asking me when I was going to take my beating, get jumped in for real. Slowly I began to realize that she wasn't entirely kidding, and I began to understand. The things that set me apart from her sucias were, in fact, assets—chief among them my white skin and blond hair. Those alone would make me the ideal driver on a pharmacy job. I was the anti-profile; any LAPD officer would think twice before pulling me over.

"Look at the way you live now," she said one evening, watching me gingerly put makeup on a bruise I'd gotten in a bar fight. "Getting beat on, partying, sleeping until noon, no plans for the future—how is that any different from *la vida*?" She'd put an arm around me and looked at us in the mirror. "Come and be *mi gladia*."

"*Gladius meus*," I said. *My sword*. Serena had learned all the words that went with her warlike life—*milites, hostes, bellum, mors*—but she tended to hybridize them with Spanish. "And no thanks. I've seen the beatings that your girls give each other jumping them in, and those are bad enough. I don't want to go through the beatdown they'd give a white girl to make her prove herself."

"Scared?" she said.

"You know better. But what's the point? I'd never be one of you. What would my street name be? Blondie?"

"The girls will accept you if they see I accept you. And they can learn from you. Nobody ever taught them anything about fighting, about protecting themselves."

"Think about what you're asking me. To teach young gangbangers to be better shots, better at beating someone up? I really need *that* on my conscience."

"You can teach them honor. Teach them when *not* to throw down, when to walk away."

"Honor?" I'd said. "Been there, done that, didn't get the gold bars. Listen, Serena, I don't make moral judgments about what you're doing. I'm happy you've got something that means something to you. But it's not for me."

She'd shrugged. "You'll come around," she said. That was how we left things. The last time Serena came by my place, I was waiting for my ride up to San Francisco, my old Army duffel at my feet. Serena had pressed the five-shot Airweight into my hands, told me to watch out for myself, and then kissed me on both cheeks, like an old-style gangster.

We hadn't kept in contact. Ours wasn't the kind of friendship that would survive long-distance. Which is why it surprised me to learn that she was trying to get in touch with me.

four

My living situation in San Francisco was pretty simple: I rented a room over the base of Aries Courier, in Japantown.

To get to my room, as I did when I came back from what had become a day's worth of pickups and drops, I had to walk through Aries's ground-floor space, which resembled a garage more than an office: bike frames and parts, freestanding filing cabinets, posters advertising bike races and rallies, a big, circa-1950s refrigerator full of Red Bull and Tupperware containers it was best not to open. When I came in, Motobecane over my shoulder, the owner, Shay Clements, was on the phone with his back to me.

Shay was a hard guy to figure out. Rather, he was the sort of person whom people assumed they understood immediately upon meeting him: bike messenger turned slightly bohemian entrepreneur. He was about thirty-five, six-foot-four with a straight, ice-blond ponytail and blue eyes and good facial bones. He still had the build of a cyclist. He wasn't married, and I didn't think he ever had been, but he would never lack for dates as long as there were coffeehouses and the kind of women who frequented them, looking for guys who were sexy in a left-wing way. You just looked at Shay and thought, *pesco-pollo-vegetarian, knows some yoga asanas, votes Democrat.*

In truth, like all blue-state small-business owners, Shay was remarkably Republican when it came to his own bottom line, full of complaints about regulations and taxes, and nearly as resentful of his own employees. Aries was all-1099, as riders put it, meaning everyone was an independent contractor, without job security or health insurance. This didn't do much to foster loyalty. Riders regularly quit Aries without notice. This led Shay to look on his riders as irresponsible flakes. It was a vicious circle.

My relationship with him was a little better than that, largely because I was reliable. I didn't kiss his ass, but I didn't have to. As I'd told Jack, I was usually his top-earning rider. I got hurt sometimes, true, but I also rode hurt, so it didn't cost Shay any downtime. Beyond that, if Shay wasn't the warmest guy in the world, well, he probably thought the same about me.

Seeing me out of the corner of his eye, Shay waved me over, not interrupting his conversation on the phone. I came over without speaking, and he handed off a pink slip of paper, a phone message. *Please call Serena Delgadillo.*

Only then did I remember the call I hadn't answered on the bridge. I took out my cell and brought up the call log, and sure enough, there they were, Serena's familiar digits. I raised my eyebrows, but Shay had already turned back to what he was doing and didn't notice my surprise. I slipped the message into my bag, lifted my bike to my shoulders, and went up the stairs.

Once in my room, I hung the Motobecane on its hooks on the wall, then went over to my little half-height refrigerator. I took out a pint bottle of vodka, drank, then kicked off my shoes and lay down with my bare feet up on the wall.

I'd lived over Aries for nearly as long as I'd been in San Francisco—not quite a year—and I still didn't have enough possessions even to make this small room look lived in. There was the bed and a dresser and a mirror. The bathroom was down the hall, and the kitchen was the little refrigerator and a single-coil burner, with my few cooking supplies on a pair of high, plain shelves.

Had I been religious, a cross on the wall or a Buddhist altar would have given the room's bareness a kind of monastic sense. But I wasn't. Nor could I bring myself to care about personalizing the place. The things that made me who I was weren't on display, but under the bed, out of sight: My *Wheelock's Latin,* with my birth certificate and my only photo of my father tucked inside. A scarlet dress, never worn and still in the box. My class ring, set with real West Point granite, and my cadet sword.

Feeling the vodka filtering into my bloodstream, feeling relaxed, I dialed Serena's number.

"*Hailecita,*" she said. "It's been a while, eh?"

"Yeah."

"How's life up there?"

"It's all right," I said. "Kind of dull."

"I figured," she said, and the conversation lagged.

I tipped the bottle again, drinking. "This isn't just a call to catch up, is it?" I said. "You want something."

"Yeah," she said. "It's not a big thing, honest."

"What?"

"There's a girl up in your part of California who needs to go back to Mexico, to the village where her mother grew up and her grandmother still lives. The *abuela*'s sick, and this girl, Nidia, is going to take care of her."

"Okay," I said, meaning, *Go on.*

"This girl needs a, what do you call it, an escort. There's no one who can take her, and I thought of you."

"Me?" I said, surprised. "What, on my bicycle? I don't even have a car. And what do you mean, there's no one who can take her? I don't want to be racial here, but don't Mexicans do everything together? Go places eight to a car, sleep four to a bed?"

Serena laughed, unoffended. "Her family is undocumented, and so are a lot of the people they know. They're scared to cross the border and try to come back."

"They can't put her on a bus?"

"She's not just crossing the border into Tijuana," Serena said. "*Abuelita* lives up in the mountains of Chihuahua state, the northern end of the Sierra Madre. It's a long way, and off the main roads. And the family doesn't want this girl to have to travel alone. She's not a tough Americanized girl who knows what time it is. She's different."

"Oh, yeah? How'd that happen?"

"She's really religious," Serena said. "She used to want to be a nun, until she was thirteen years old."

"Let me guess," I said. "Then she discovered boys."

"She discovered a boy," Serena said. "Johnny Cedillo, his name was. He was Dominican and part black, and her parents were kinda worked up about that until they saw how serious he was about her. He was talking about marrying her from high school on, gave her a ring, like, what do they call it? Not a real engagement ring, but—"

"A promise ring." Some of the more sincere kids in my high-school class had done that.

"Yeah, a promise ring. They were real serious about each other. Nobody doubted they were really gonna get married and have beautiful little kids."

"So what went wrong?" I said. "Where's Johnny now? Did he go to Vegas, get a little on the side, and Nidia found out about it?"

"No," she said. "He was totally into her, and since she was making him wait for their wedding night, as far as anyone knows, Johnny Cedillo died a virgin."

"He's dead?"

"Johnny didn't go to Vegas. He went to Iraq."

"Ah, shit."

We were quiet a second, then Serena said, "The other problem with her traveling alone is that apparently this girl's beautiful, a real knockout. In her neighborhood, even after Johnny went away to war, no one bothered her. It got around that she was saving herself for her wedding night with him, and even the *vatos* respected that. But strange men, on a cross-country trip? They'd hassle this girl no end."

"Wait, back up," I interrupted. "You're talking about this girl like you know her, but you said 'apparently' she's beautiful. What's up?"

"I don't know her personally," she said. "But you remember Teaser?"

"Sure." Teaser was Serena's lieutenant, her most trusted among the sucias.

"She's dead," Serena said.

"Sorry," I said. I didn't have to ask how. Another name for Serena's roll call in tattoo ink.

She went on: "Teaser was her cousin. They didn't live in my neighborhood, Nidia and Johnny, so I never met either of them," Serena explained. "But I guess they were pretty well known around their neighborhood. People looked up to Johnny; he was an athlete in high school and never got ganged-up, but he was a stand-up guy with his friends, not a squeaky-clean teacher's pet type. That whole trip. Teaser would ask me why guys like that don't go for girls like us, and I'd tell her, Because we're girls like us, that's why. She also said that people liked Nidia a little more because of him."

"Liked her more than what?"

"Well, she's pretty religious, didn't go out or party. Not the sort of girl you'd expect people like us to like," Serena said.

Then she realized she was getting off point. "Anyway, I got a phone call from Teaser's sister, Lara Cortez, about Nidia needing to get to Mexico and asked if I could help. So I called Nidia's family to talk about it, and I mentioned you. I told them that you could handle yourself and look out for Nidia."

"You can handle yourself, too," I pointed out, "and you're someone they'd trust, a Mexican. Why not you?"

"I don't have a passport," Serena said. "They changed the rules about the border, remember? It takes weeks to get one, and the family doesn't want to wait that long." Then, in a lighter tone, she said, "Besides, you know what *la vida* is like. I gotta TCB"—take care of business, she meant—"here, in my neighborhood."

"Yeah," I agreed, "those cars won't steal themselves."

"I don't do that small-time shit anymore, you know that," she said.

"Yeah, I know," I said.

"And, I should've said right up front, you'd get paid. Her family's sending some money to cover the expenses, but if it's not enough, I'll make up the rest. And I'll match whatever you'd make per day up there."

"You don't know what you're offering," I said. "A good bike messenger pulls down a lot of money."

It was a little-known truth about the job: If you were committed to it—steady and reliable in reporting for work but fast and heedless on the street—you could outearn some of the young suits you sped past on the street.

I stood up and walked over to the window, looking down at the traffic. "You're doing all this for Teaser's memory?"

"Yeah," she said. "I know it may not seem like there's much of a connection to you, but *la raza* can be a small community. And Teaser was one of mine. The sucias are for the sucias. You know how it works."

"I know," I said.

"No you don't, not really," Serena said. "You ought to get you some *familia,* someone who'll never not back you up."

I'd never told her about CJ. The two of them had been the bright and dark of my old life. They didn't mix.

"But don't worry about the money," she said. "Times are good right now."

I didn't believe her. I'd seen the truth of Serena's glamorous gangster life in the faded brown shag rug of her rented house and the twenty-year-old sedan under her carport.

But then she added, "You know, your pay wouldn't have to be all in cash. I could open up the drugstore for you."

Her gang brothers in Trece dealt coke; Serena had her pharmacy heists. Cocaine meant speed for the street, and Xanax and Ambien were peace for the evenings, when memories of West Point and Wilshire Boulevard troubled me most. Serena was smart. She once told me that drugs were money in places money couldn't go. Clearly she hadn't forgotten that. I hadn't used since I'd left L.A., but now the prospect was tempting to me where mere cash wouldn't have been.

I ran my hand through my hair. "I'm not saying yes right away, but let me think about it," I said. "I'll have to look at a map and figure out how many days this'll take, then I'll give you an estimate on what it'll cost. I'd want to be sure the expenses were really covered."

"They will be," she said. "Whatever you need."

"I just mean this trip is going to take the time it takes," I said. "I'm not going to drive way over the speed limit, or push myself until I could get tired and make an error in judgment. I can't be reckless on the road. You know why."

"Yeah," Serena said. "I know."

What we were both remembering was the reason I left L.A.

five

If you keep up with the entertainment news at all, you've probably heard of a man named Lucius "Luke" Marsellus. He ran maybe the second-biggest gangsta rap label in America. Or, if you were an LAPD cop doing gang suppression in South Central about fifteen years ago, you knew him for different reasons. I could say that people who knew Marsellus when he was a teenager knew him "before he was famous," but that wasn't quite accurate. He just had a different kind of notoriety back then. There are different words for it—*made guy, OG, veterano*—but most gang members reach that status young. When you're liable to be dead by twenty-one, you have to. Luke Marsellus was ganged-up by the time he was ten and a hood celebrity by fifteen.

At that age, Marsellus had become the right-hand man to a dealer named J. G. Deauville, a man who'd climbed the distribution chain from street-corner dealer to having two dozen guys working for him. And Marsellus was constantly by his side, his protection and enforcer. His shadow: tall, silent, feared. The extent of his crimes in Deauville's service still isn't known: The gang unit never made anything stick to him.

His boss wasn't so fortunate. Deauville taught Marsellus a lot, but perhaps the most important lesson was this: Luck always runs out. He taught his lieutenant that the hard way: After years of luck, in which the DEA and the LAPD failed to touch him, the IRS nailed Deauville, like Al Capone before him, on tax evasion, and he went to prison.

Marsellus was the obvious heir to Deauville's enterprise, but he didn't do the expected thing. To the eyes of those who'd long been watching him—the police, the feds, gang rivals—he seemed to drop off the radar. Several smaller, warring gang sets carved up Deauville's territory, and life went on.

Maybe a year after Deauville's arrest, Marsellus resurfaced in an entirely new role. Using money he'd apparently saved from his gang-land years, and completely unknown talent from the streets, Marsellus founded a rap label. He was twenty-two years old.

But he quickly proved to have a natural business acumen rivaling that of his old boss. Marsellus signed the coldest and angriest of the gangsta rappers; their live-fast-die-young words were echoed by white kids in the leafiest of suburbs. The usual suspects boycotted his music—parents' groups, law enforcement—but that only sold more CDs.

So Marsellus became a legit businessman, but it'd be going too far to say that he'd entirely left his old ways of doing things behind. He made no apologies for the fact that his private security men were all ganged-up. And while nothing stuck to him, disturbing incidents followed the Marsellus name. A troublesome ex-girlfriend, report-edly about to sign a contract for a tell-all book, was beaten so se-verely she lost the hearing in one ear. A young white talent agent who'd lured several artists away from the Marsellus fold found a new line of work after a gunman put two rounds through the win-dow of his house. Federal agents subpoenaed boxes and boxes of documents from Marsellus's downtown L.A. offices, but no charges ever followed. The local cops hadn't been able to nail Marsellus on anything in his dealing days, and in his newer, bigger life, the feds couldn't, either.

This was how Marsellus ultimately defied them: He became re-spectable. When a South Central African Baptist church was burned down in what was assumed to be a hate crime, Marsellus paid to have it rebuilt from the ground up, not as the humble shag-carpeted refuge it had been before, but as a graceful edifice with high clerestory windows and slate floors. He bought a home in Beverly Hills. He was generous with his siblings, and threw storied birthday parties for his nieces and nephews. And when he married, the ceremony was attended by not only his large extended family and his music-industry peers but by a former congressman, and several well-known actors and pro athletes.

And about seven years after their marriage, Luke Marsellus and his wife became parents. They'd been trying in vain for some time to conceive, so when their son was born, it was cause for greater celebration than their marriage. In a ceremony even better attended than the Marsellus wedding, the infant Trey was baptized at the church his father had had rebuilt, wearing a christening gown from Neiman Marcus.

I learned everything I knew about Marsellus in my last days in Los Angeles. Before that, I wouldn't even have recognized his face. Even CJ didn't know him, not beyond shaking his hand at a fund-raiser.

I did remember liking some of the music Marsellus's artists put out. Angry, unapologetic, fatalistic, unafraid—the music had fit with my life-after-West-Point frame of mind. In those days I hadn't thought any further ahead than sundown. Those had been my *omnia gaudia vitae* days, and to be honest, I'd been partying a lot, whether it was beer and grass with Serena, or kaffir lime vodka shots in the Westside clubs I went to with CJ.

But on what I consider my last real day in L.A., I was sober. It was important to me that people knew that, or it would have been if I ever told anyone this story, which I didn't. But I was sober and driving the speed limit that day on Wilshire Boulevard; it's just that the late-afternoon sun was in my eyes, and when six-year-old Trey Marsellus ran out in front of my car, I hit and killed him.

six

I never saw Marsellus, not once. Trey hadn't been with his father, nor any of his family. He'd been out with his young Haitian au pair. It had been her shrill screams that made me realize I hadn't hit a large dog, which was what I'd thought at first.

The family, once notified, went directly to the hospital. I was taken to the precinct "while we straighten this out," in the words of the traffic-division sergeant. Once there, I called CJ, but he didn't answer.

I was at the precinct for several hours. The police hadn't been sure at first what really happened. They couldn't get anything out of the grief-stricken nanny. I kept saying that Trey had run right out in front of me—which was true, though what else would you have expected someone who'd hit a child to say?

Fortunately, there had been pedestrians who'd seen the accident— not the usual "I heard squealing brakes and shattering glass and turned to look," but people who'd actually seen Trey Marsellus run from his nanny and dart from between two parallel-parked cars.

As the traffic sergeant said to me, "We're not going to hold you, but don't leave town, okay? Not until we've closed the official investigation."

I agreed, walked stiffly out the front door, and went to the hospital. I had an immediate and all-consuming need to apologize to the family.

I hadn't succeeded. Two very large young black men, with tattoos and exquisitely tailored suits, blocked my way. "The family's not seeing anyone right now," one of them said.

At the time, the question *Who are these guys?* didn't occur to me. I was mentally numb, except for being fixated on making this right. "I need to talk to them," I said. "I'm the one who—"

"The family's not seeing anyone," he said again, and I broke off, finally realizing they were serious.

CJ, who'd gone to the precinct too late, found me as I was walking back to visitor parking. He was pale and shaken, almost as if he'd been the one to hit a child, but he was immediately supportive. He took me back to his place, where I paced, angry and guilty, saying over and over that the kid had run right in front of me, that the sun was in my eyes, that I couldn't have stopped.

"I know, baby," CJ said. Then he asked me to repeat the boy's name.

"Trey Marsellus," I said.

"Mmm," he said.

"What?"

"Nothing."

"What?" I persisted.

"I think you might've hit Luke Marsellus's kid," he said, pensive.

"Who?" I'd said.

An hour later it was on the news: Rap mogul's son killed in Wilshire Boulevard accident. I still didn't get it. The news reports cast him only as a respected music-world figure, not as Marsellus the South Central OG.

I should have known something was really wrong when CJ picked up a pack of cigarettes a friend had left on the coffee table and tapped one out. CJ almost never smoked, so this meant he needed something to do with his hands, which meant he was nervous. Which was bad, because CJ was almost never nervous.

"Are you okay?" I asked. Stupid question, considering.

"Yeah," he said. He lit the cigarette, exhaled smoke, and said, "Listen, give the family a couple of days, all right? Marsellus is . . ."

"Is what?"

"He's kind of heavy."

"I can't turn my back on this," I said.

"I know," he said, "but I need to think about how best you should approach him."

As it turned out, CJ never did hit on the right way for me to talk to Marsellus. Something else happened first that changed everything.

Two days later, I was awakened by my phone ringing at ten-fifteen in the morning. I picked up the receiver and found myself talking to the traffic sergeant who'd taken my statement and then kicked me loose. His question was direct and to the point: Had Miss Beauvais, Trey's au pair, been in touch with me?

No, I said, why would she have been?

I'm just checking in with you, he'd said.

Not seeing any significance, I tried to go back to sleep—I hadn't been sleeping well at night—but an hour later, CJ was pounding on my door.

"Take it easy, would you," I said, pushing hair out of my eyes and letting him in.

"Pack up your things," he said as soon as I'd closed the door behind him. "Not everything, just what you really want."

"What?" I thought it was a joke, though he seemed genuinely on edge.

"Trey's nanny is missing. The cops are looking for her. Nobody's seen her. Pack up just what you need, I'm getting you out of L.A."

I pulled back. "What are you trying to say?"

CJ ran his hands through his hair. "Just listen to me, Hailey. I didn't want to scare you the other night, but as soon as you told me Trey Marsellus's name, I was thinking of something like this. I hoped I was overreacting."

"Something like what?"

"This happened in New York," he said. "A mobster's son was hit by a car, by accident, and not long after that, the neighbor who did it just disappeared."

I said, "You of all people know that 'gangsta' is just a figure of speech. Marsellus isn't really a gangster."

"Yes, he is, Hailey." He paused. "I hear things, and maybe I don't know for sure what's rumor and what's fact, but I meant what I said the other day, when I called Marsellus 'heavy.' He's not a 'no harm, no foul' kind of guy. And he and his wife tried for years to conceive before finally having Trey. She hasn't been pregnant again since. What does that tell you?" He answered his own question: "You took from him the one thing that can't be replaced."

My face felt hot. "Don't you think I feel bad enough—"

"You're not *listening*," he said. I'd never heard CJ sound so frustrated. "Goddammit, what's it going to take to get through to you? You can feel as bad as humanly possible; it won't help. You killed this guy's only son. 'Sorry' isn't going to fix it."

I said, "But if he's really the kind of man you say, I think not apologizing and then running away is only going to make it worse."

"There isn't a way to make it better."

"But—"

"No," he said, taking both my hands in his. "I know what you're thinking of, all that honor-and-duty bullshit you never really left behind, but that doesn't apply out here, and it's going to get you killed. West Point is over, and now L.A. is over for you, too. Pack your things."

What convinced me that he was right was this: His hands were very slightly shaking. It had been a long time since I'd felt those kind of nerves, so his anxiety served as a kind of external gauge for me, of what I should be feeling but wasn't.

"Are you sure about this?" I'd said.

"I don't like it, either, baby," he'd said quietly. "But this is how it's gotta be."

To this day I don't know if there were any ramifications, criminally, for my leaving town before the traffic division's investigation was officially closed. It had just been a formality, but the cops took a dim view of people skating when they'd been told to stick around. It was possible that if I was ever picked up on something minor in San Francisco, I'd be shipped back to Los Angeles and charged with some kind of obstruction. It wasn't the charge that would be problematic, but jail would actually be the easiest place for Marsellus to get at me. Anyone gang-connected could.

CJ would have stayed longer with me in San Francisco, but I hadn't let him. When we parted, we'd both acted with exaggerated casualness. He'd said, "Look, I'll come up and visit you soon. I'll be around so much you'll be sick of me," and I'd said, "Sure, I know," and we'd hugged and then he'd driven away, toward the 101 back home.

In those first weeks, I'd lived with a drab, hollow feeling not unlike how addicts describe their first day without alcohol or a cigarette: *Is this what my life's going to be, from here on out?* I'd alternated between that sense of lonely tedium and a stomach-clenching guilt. I'm not sure those feelings ever went away, but they did lessen. In time, I found an adrenaline-junkie job and threw myself into it. I made more money than I needed and stashed it carelessly in a coffee can. I made a few friends and drank with them. Drank without them, too. I met Jack Foreman.

But I still felt restless at times, particularly in early summer, when business at Aries was slowest and San Francisco was shrouded in the kind of weather coastal Californians called June gloom. That was probably why, in the end, I called Serena back and told her I'd take a girl I'd never met to the mountains of inland Mexico.

seven

Several days later, sometime after nine in the evening, I was parked in front of a house in a working-class section of Oakland. It was an inexpensively well-kept place, with a small trimmed lawn, and no weeds between the stepping-stones that led to the house. There was a geranium by the front door, blooming red. This was where Nidia Hernandez was staying with friends.

Shay had looked pretty sour when I told him I was taking nearly two weeks off, but there was nothing he could do. I was an independent contractor; I worked, or not, at both my will and his. He could have fired me just as easily.

That afternoon, packing had been quick and easy. Hot-weather clothes, one heavy jacket for the evenings. A recently purchased guidebook to Mexico. A bottle of Bacardi and several minis of Finlandia, tucked protectively between layers of clothing. The little care package Serena had sent to me—a sheaf of twenties and fifties, the promised expense money, and a handful of Benzedrines wrapped in foil, to help me stay alert on the road. The rest of my pay would wait until I was on my way back up north; Serena and I had arranged that I'd stop at her place and we'd settle up then.

Finally I'd cleaned and oiled the Airweight, which was now taped under the front seat of the car I'd rented. I didn't expect any trouble in Mexico. I was just being careful.

A young man with a peach-fuzz mustache answered the door when I knocked. "Are you Hailey?" he said.

"I'm in the right place, then."

"Yeah, hello, yeah," he said, and moved aside. I stepped into a narrow entryway of brown-checked linoleum, and the boy called to someone farther back in the house in Spanish so rapid I didn't catch much of it, except for Nidia's name.

A middle-aged woman came around the corner into the entryway. She was thin, with red-tinted hair pinned up on her head.

"Is it her?" she said in a gently accented voice. "Oh, please come in. My name is Herlinda."

"Hailey," I said.

"Come into the kitchen."

I followed her. The floorboards felt slightly warped under my feet, and the house smelled of many, many meals cooked there. We rounded a corner, and I got my first look at Nidia Hernandez.

She was sitting in a chair slightly pushed back from the kitchen table, two scuffed suitcases at her feet. I could see where she'd draw unwanted masculine attention. Her hair was cinnamon-colored, in curls weighed down into near-straightness by their length. Her eyes were green-brown, and she had a heart-shaped face. She wasn't very tall—maybe five-two—and slender except for the little potbelly a lot of girls had nowadays, the obsession for flat abs being over. She looked from Herlinda to me.

"Hey," I said. "I'm Hailey."

"Thank you for coming," she said.

"I was sorry to hear about your boyfriend. Serena told me," I said.

She nodded and said something that I thought was "Thank you" but couldn't be sure: She was that quiet. We both looked to Herlinda to take over.

Herlinda did, fixing hot chocolate and offering pan dulce, both of which I accepted, although I wasn't hungry. Then she spread a map of Mexico on the table and began the debriefing I'd been promised. "Have you ever been to Mexico?" she asked.

"To Baja California, yes," I said.

"Did you drive?"

I nodded. It had been CJ's idea, a road trip to a seaside town he'd heard about.

"Good," Herlinda said. "So you know a little about driving on Mexican roads." Even so, she went on to tell me things I'd already heard: that in isolated areas, drivers tended to go down the center of the road until they saw oncoming traffic, and that it was common for both parties to be jailed in case of a traffic accident. If I were in one, she said, I should be exceedingly polite to the police and keep my ears open for the subtle implication that a bribe would clear the whole thing up. I nodded assent. Her son leaned against the refrigerator and listened.

Then Herlinda turned her attention to the map. I saw a star, hand-drawn in ink, in the northern Sierra Madre region.

"That's where we're going?" I said.

"It's the nearest town to the village," Herlinda said.

My confusion must have shown on my face—I didn't understand the distinction she was making—so Herlinda said, "You won't take Nidia all the way; the road isn't passable by car. You'll take her to this town, and you'll see the post office there. It has a Mexican flag over it. Take Nidia inside, and the postman will take her up to the village when he goes with the mail. They do it all the time, her mother says."

"If the road's not passable by car, how does the postman go up? Horseback?"

Herlinda smiled. "He has four-wheel-drive."

I was embarrassed at my assumption. "If I'd known," I said, "I could've got something with four-wheel."

Herlinda shook her head. "It's not just that," she said. "The road's narrow and it's steep, and I guess city Mexicans don't do well with it." She left the obvious unsaid: *Not to mention gringos.*

Then she looked up at the kitchen doorway. I followed her gaze and saw a thin girl of maybe twelve or thirteen there, wearing a long pink nightshirt.

"You're supposed to be in bed," Herlinda told her.

"I wanted to say good-bye to Nidia."

I moved from the kitchen counter and told Nidia, "I'll take your bags out to the car," thinking they'd want privacy for their good-byes.

Outside, I sat behind the wheel of the car I'd rented, a powerful V6 Impala. When I'd first driven it that afternoon, I felt a small rush of elation and power. Then, just as quickly, I'd been stabbed by a memory: Wilshire Boulevard and a hard thump from the front end of my car.

He darted out of nowhere; it was an accident; there was nothing you could have done. It had become my mantra in moments like these. But I wondered, if I ever owned a vehicle again, how long it would take before I could drive without thinking of Trey Marsellus.

eight

It was in northern Arizona that I first tried to have a substantial conversation with Nidia.

We had been traveling by night. That was my plan until we got to the border. Nocturnal travel was cooler in the Southwestern heat, and it would lower our chances of setting off a speed trap, because despite what I'd told Serena about being cautious on the road, I was pushing my luck just a little on speed. I wanted the trip to be done in about seven or eight days. It would have helped if Nidia knew how to drive, but she didn't.

So, mostly, she'd been dozing as we drove through the night, or sometimes working on a knitting project in her lap. We didn't talk much.

I couldn't decide whether I liked Nidia or not. She was polite to me. Very polite, in fact, as though I were an authority figure just by virtue of being chosen to take her to Mexico. If she disapproved of my occasional bad language, or the liquor I drank neat over ice when the driving was done, she didn't say anything about it. But my occasional attempts at small talk had all died pretty quickly. I just couldn't seem to make any connection with her.

Tonight I didn't mess around with small talk at all: I turned down the radio and asked her something serious.

"So what's wrong with your grandmother?"

She looked up at me. "What?"

"Your sick grandmother," I repeated, "what's wrong?"

"She's very old," Nidia said slowly.

"It's just old age?" Her answer surprised me; it seemed like a flimsy reason for a girl of Nidia's age, just starting out in life, to be dispatched to a remote village indefinitely.

Nidia added, "She hurt her leg. Her hip, I mean."

"A fall?"

She nodded.

"So how'd you"—I didn't want to say the first thing that came to mind, which was, *draw the short straw*—"become the one who goes south to take care of her?"

Nidia said, "It's something I'm good at. That was my job for a long time, taking care of a man who was sick."

Serena hadn't mentioned that. "Sick with what?" I asked.

"Cancer," she said.

"What happened to him?"

"He died," Nidia said. "It was . . . it was very sad, he was—" She turned her face toward the window, and I knew she was fighting back tears. I focused back on the road, averting my eyes. She wasn't really thinking of the cancer guy, of course. She was thinking of Johnny Cedillo, whom I deliberately hadn't brought up, thinking it still too raw a wound.

Then she spoke again. She said, "Adriano was smarter than anyone I'd ever known. He studied math for a living, but not math like people usually think of it. Adriano's work was the kind of math you can't even really use. I asked him why he was interested in stuff like that, and he said it was like being an explorer in the desert, places no one had gone yet. He liked being out putting his footprints in sand no one had ever walked in before."

Nidia wasn't crying, but she was speaking quickly, as if she was distracting herself from her grief with trivia about the cancer patient.

"You guys talked a bit, then, it sounds like," I said.

"Yes," she said. "I was working for him for a little more than a year. At first I just came over to make some meals, clean up his apartment. But then he got sicker and needed someone living there, so I moved in."

"Where was his family?" I asked. "There wasn't anyone to help take care of him?"

"No," she said. "He had a brother who died, and his mother was already dead, too. His father was still alive, but they didn't . . ."

"Get along?" I supplied.

"Maybe," she said. "And he never got married. Adriano didn't have a life like most people had. His mind was different. He just wanted to be a—what's the word? Like a student, but even more serious about it . . ."

"A scholar?"

"A scholar," she said. "He wanted to understand the universe, everything about it. I think God knew that. God took him early so he could finally have all the answers he wanted."

God apparently had a protracted, painful way of curing intellectual curiosity, but I didn't say that.

nine

The following night took us through New Mexico, and then, aided by a short roadside nap, I pushed on until we crossed the little handkerchief-corner of westernmost Texas. Maybe my desire to get us over the state line before quitting for the day was symbolic. I was Texan by birth, though I couldn't remember my early days there. So, around five, Nidia and I were rolling into El Paso.

I decided to spend a little more money on a hotel, checking us in at a place with a pool and some restaurants nearby. We needed somewhere nice. It would be Nidia's last night in the States, and I was so tired from driving that my eyes felt gritty. I intended to get a long, long sleep tonight. Starting tomorrow, we were going to drive days instead of nights, and I was going to slow our speed way down. Herlinda had warned me about getting into a dustup with Mexico's police, and I'd taken her words to heart.

Nidia and I brought our things in from the car, into a room where the air conditioner was already working hard, exhaling frigid air to keep the Texas heat at bay. I bought a Diet Coke from the vending machine, poured it over ice, and laced it heavily with Bacardi. I drank while sifting through my clothes, looking for something to wear in the pool. I hadn't brought a suit, but right now, even though it was still about ninety degrees outside, the thought of a long soak appealed to me.

"Want to come?" I asked Nidia, but she shook her head quickly no.

I slipped my feet into a pair of rubber flip-flops. "Be thinking about what you want for dinner," I said. "It's your last night in America. There must be something you'll miss."

She nodded seriously, as if I'd posed her a study question for an exam later. I drained the last of the rum and Diet Coke and left.

There were too many little kids in the pool for me to swim laps, but I dived into the deep end, then opened my eyes and navigated around them until I came up for air in the shallow end. Then I sat on the steps, body half in and half out of the water, tipped my head back, and closed my eyes. Though it was nearly six, it felt like midafternoon. We were only a few weeks past the summer solstice, and the sun was fairly high in the Texas sky, the heat maintaining its midday levels.

When I opened my eyes again, I saw a guy looking my way. He was sitting on one of the lounge chairs, but he hadn't come here to swim or sunbathe. He was dressed in business casual, dark trousers and white shirt, no jacket or tie. He was around thirty years old, with an athletic build and close-cropped dark hair that looked like it would curl if allowed to grow any longer.

"How's the water?" he asked, unashamed to be caught watching me.

"Come in and find out," I said, and raised my hand to rub my birthmark lightly, a gesture I thought I'd outgrown.

"Can't," he said. "I didn't bring anything to swim in."

But he got up from his seat and walked to the water's edge, and sat on his heels to test the water temperature with one hand. I tried to decide how I'd describe his face to someone else: It was clean-shaven and soft, but not in a way that suggested flab or weakness, more like the slight jowliness of a mastiff or a Great Dane, that actually connotes strength. His eyes were Mediterranean, deep-set and heavy-lidded in the way that looks like world-weariness to a casual observer.

"You from Texas?" he asked me.

"California," I said.

"I'm heading across the border into Mexico tomorrow," he said. "Just into Juarez City, on business. It's my first time. I hear there's no real good time to cross; the traffic's always backed up at the border. Have you heard anything about that?"

I shook my head. "I have to cross tomorrow, too, but I haven't really thought about traffic. It'll take the time it takes, I guess."

We spoke a minute or two longer. I said I was on a "summer road trip" with a friend and left it at that. It was pleasant, after Nidia's alternating politeness and silences, to be talking easily with another American. I wondered if his friendliness was just that, or if it was the beginnings of a pickup.

"Well," he said, "drive safely tomorrow."

Just friendliness, then. "You, too," I said, and watched as he walked back to the pool gate and disappeared from my view.

"There's a storm coming, and the people of this sleepy town . . ."

The TV was flickering with the sound low. I'd tuned it to the Weather Channel, waiting for the local forecast, but at present, the screen was filled with images of tornadoes wreaking havoc in the Plains States. Nidia was sitting cross-legged on the bed in her nightgown, her hair wet from the bath, watching the TV. I was rearranging the things in my backpack, putting what I needed in easy reach. Earlier, we'd had dinner in the hotel's restaurant. I was ravenous, though I'd done nothing more strenuous than driving, and ordered a barbecued half-chicken and a baked potato and salad. I persuaded Nidia to have a real American meal on her last night here: a hamburger, fries, and a milkshake, the kind that came with extra in a tin cup on the side.

Still half listening for a change to the forecast for Texas and northern Mexico, I dug my passport out of the duffel bag and transferred it to my messenger bag, where it'd be more convenient in the morning. Nidia, of course, not being a U.S. citizen, only needed her Mexican birth certificate and a photo ID, not a—

That thought gave me pause. Nidia wasn't a citizen. Unlike me, once she crossed the border, she had no legal way of getting back.

Though she'd need to be in Mexico awhile, maybe even until her grandmother's death, it seemed to me that Nidia's family was abandoning her to indefinite life in Mexico.

Was that so bad? Maybe I was being an American chauvinist. Except there was a reason so many Mexicans, including Nidia's parents, had come to El Norte. I wondered why Nidia's mother hadn't taken it on herself to go back and take care of her ailing mother, instead of sacrificing the hopes and plans of a daughter just on the cusp of adulthood.

"Nidia," I said, picking up my cell phone, "I'll be back in a minute, okay?"

She nodded, undisturbed.

I went out to the pool area—it was deserted now, though the water glowed an inviting warm turquoise—and made a call.

Serena picked up on the third ring. "Hailey, what's up?" she said. "Where are you? Mexico?"

"We're still in Texas," I said. "Listen, I'm getting a funny feeling about this."

"What's wrong?"

"What do you really know about this family?" I said. "Did you know any of them except Teaser?"

"Why? What's wrong?" she repeated.

I sat down on a chaise, still looking at the calm water of the pool. "Well, Nidia's only nineteen," I said. "Once she crosses the border, who knows if she'll ever get back? Most Mexican parents who bring their families across do so at great risk, so their kids can have better lives. It just doesn't make a lot of sense that they're forcing her to go back."

"Maybe it makes sense because their grandma is sick and needs help," she said. "Mexicans are very family-oriented, and—"

"No. No way," I said. "Don't even start with that you're-white-you-wouldn't-understand rap. This girl's fiancé died in Iraq, and then the cancer patient she was taking care of died, and now she's going off to live in the middle of nowhere with an invalid? I think she's had enough death and dying. I don't think it's right."

There was a second or two of silence before Serena spoke. "Has she said she doesn't want to go?"

A beat passed before I admitted, "I haven't asked."

"Well, she packed her stuff and got in the car, *prima*. Doesn't that tell you something?"

"I'm going to ask her straight out."

"I don't think you should interfere," she said. "This is about family. If this were your father, if he were sick, how far would be too far for you to go to take care of him?"

I closed my eyes. Nowhere, of course. I would have gone to the other side of the planet.

"Hailey?" she prompted.

"If I ask Nidia directly and she says she doesn't want to go to Mexico, I'm not taking her," I said.

"Fine," Serena said, her tone short. "Go ahead. I can tell you what she's gonna say, though."

"I'll call you later."

I disconnected the call and walked back to the room. "Nidia," I said as soon as I'd closed the door behind me, "are you absolutely sure you want to do this?"

"Como?" she said, confused.

I set my cell phone down on the dresser and said, "You're undocumented. Once you cross the border, you can't come back. Not easily. The U.S. is allocating more money to border security all the time."

She seemed on the verge of speaking, but I needed to finish. "My hand to God, no one can make me muscle you off to Mexico if you don't want to go. Just say the word, and I'll turn around and take you back. If you can't go to your family, Serena would take you in. I'm sure she would, for Teaser's sake."

It seemed like an odd thing to say, given the testy exchange we'd just had on the phone, but I knew Serena. If push came to shove, she'd help this girl.

"No," Nidia said, straightening, and there was a sharp tone to her voice I hadn't heard before. "I want to go. No one's making me. You aren't going to change your mind about driving me, are you?"

I licked my lower lip, surprised at how adamant she seemed. "Nidia," I began. Then I turned and walked over to the window. The sheer inner curtains were drawn, but I could see the parking lot outside, the peach glow of the lights. I wasn't looking for anything or at anything: I was about to say something delicate.

"I don't want to offend you by talking about something that's personal, but Serena told me about Johnny, your fiancé," I said slowly. "He obviously cared about you a great deal. What do you think he'd advise you to do here?"

There was no hesitation before I heard her say, "Johnny would want me to go."

I turned around to face her. There wasn't any doubt in her green-hazel eyes. "Okay," I said. "Then I'll take you."

She relaxed. "Good," she said. Then she added, "My *abuela* needs me. That's why."

I picked up my cell phone from the dresser. "Listen, I'm going to go out and get a drink," I said, scooping up my hoodie off the back of a chair. "Don't wait on me. Get some sleep."

I called Serena as soon as I was far enough away from the motel room not to be overheard through the walls. She obviously recognized my number on caller ID and answered with, "So?"

"She wants to go," I said, turning my face up against a light breeze. "I'm taking her."

"Told you."

"Yeah, I know," I said, watching the white lights of the freeway in the distance. "Serena, you know I love you, right?"

"Wow, you get over being mad quick," she said, amused.

"That's not what I'm saying," I told her. "What I'm saying is, I love you, but don't ever throw my dead father into a conversation to score points off me again."

I'd hoped that the world-weary-but-nice-looking guy from poolside would be in the bar, but he didn't show in the time it took me to nurse two margaritas, so finally I just paid and left.

ten

Mexico.

Crossing the border wasn't a big deal. The traffic was the worst of it, inching up to the low brown structure of the border checkpoint, where forbidding signs advised that bringing a firearm into Mexico was punishable by Mexican law. But after showing our various forms of ID—my driver's license and passport, Nidia's Mexican birth certificate—we were told to drive on. They didn't even ask about a gun. I smiled and finger-waved like an excited tourist as Nidia and I pulled away, the Airweight taped under my seat.

Then we were into the crush and color of Juarez, American logos competing with old Colonial architecture. Most of it I'd expected from pictures. Little things surprised me, though, like passing a storefront church advertising meetings of *Alcoholicos Anonimos.* You didn't expect things like that in Mexico.

After that, we drove on the main highways in broad, bright daylight, jockeying among big semi-trailers. It was hot, and I worried about the air-conditioning straining the Impala's engine, no matter how new and well-maintained the car, so I cycled the a/c on and off, alternating with the whipping wind of two rolled-down windows.

Our second day, we started out early, because this was the day I believed I'd get Nidia to her destination. I wanted to leave us plenty of time to navigate the smaller, secondary roads we'd take once we got off Highway 16. We'd be climbing up into the mountains, and I had visions of the Impala inching along behind a flock of sheep being driven by a sheepherder on foot, or following a lumbering farm truck at twenty-eight miles an hour.

And I was worried about Nidia, who'd shown a minor tendency toward car sickness even on the straighter roads. She never complained, but several times when I stopped for gas, she'd asked me for ginger ale, to settle her stomach.

Now we were beginning to climb up into the mountains. The sun had just gone down, and the traffic had thinned out as the trees and brush on the roadside got thicker. The surrounding landscape re- minded me of the mountains of eastern Nevada, but more extreme: steeper, lusher, more remote.

Nidia had taken out her knitting again. When I asked her what she was working on, she told me it was to be a sweater: It got cold in the mountains at night, regardless of the season. I had to take her word for it—not about the weather, but that the knitting project would someday be a sweater. It was shapeless now, though I liked the yarn she was using, a dun brown variegated with pale pink.

We didn't talk much, and I cruised the radio dial for any kind of American music. Like Herlinda had suggested, I'd taken to driving down the center of the road—there was no dividing line, anyway, and no traffic going the opposite direction. Once or twice, I thought I spot- ted a car about a half-mile behind us; I saw it on lower switchbacks in the highway, when I glanced in the rearview or out the window.

Ahead, in a steep mountain face, the dark opening of a tunnel yawned before the Impala. I slowed down and edged the car to the right side of the road in case of oncoming traffic, and as we drove into the narrow dimness of the tunnel, the radio cut out as though turned off. I reached down to flick on the headlights, and they flashed off what looked like a low wall of dark metal in front of us, a wall that resolved itself into a stalled car, sideways, blocking the road.

"Jesus!" I hit the brakes so hard that Nidia's body snapped against the restraint of her seat belt and the shapeless knitting project bounced off the glove box and onto the floor. We skidded to a stop about six feet from the dark, stalled sedan.

"Sorry," I said to Nidia, touching her shoulder. "Are you okay?"

Then I noticed headlights behind us. It was the car I'd caught glimpses of in the rearview. Unlike us, they didn't have to brake hard or skid to a stop. They rolled up behind us to a smooth stop. It looked a lot like planning.

There was also a strong similarity in the make and color of the two cars, front and back. The driver of the car behind us had stopped in a diagonal position, so that we were effectively hemmed in. I did not like this.

"*Que pasa?*" Nidia said, frightened into her native language.

"I don't know," I said. I reached down and hit the electronic controls, locking all four doors at once.

Now, in front of us and behind, men were emerging from the cars. White men, well-built, with guns.

"*Que pasa?*" Nidia said again. "*Que pasa?*"

"*Calmate,*" I said, although I wasn't at all sure that calming down was appropriate.

The men spread out around us in a circle. Seven white men in rural Mexico. This didn't make any sense.

Nidia had her hands to her face. "*El padre,*" she whispered.

I reached under the seat and wrenched the Airweight free of its tape, but for the moment, I kept it out of the men's line of sight. I didn't want to start the shooting. I was far too outgunned.

Sure, five rounds is all most civilians will ever need. If you can't shoot your way out of something with five rounds, you can't shoot your way out of it at all. It had sounded good at the time.

"Nidia," I said calmly, "take off your seat belt and get on the floor, as low as you can."

She was staring at the gun in my hands. She didn't move.

I reached over and unclicked her seat belt. "Down!" I said. "*Ahora!*"

She slid down, whispering what I assumed were prayers.

My mind was working pretty well in that cool, empty space where fear should have been and wasn't. This had to be a case of mistaken identity. They thought we were carrying drugs, or drug money.

One of the men approached. Even from a distance, he was familiar, and up close he became the Young Nice Guy Businessman from the pool of the El Paso hotel. He gestured for me to roll down my window.

Carefully, still keeping the gun out of sight, I rolled down my window to a gap of about two inches and said, "We're not carrying anything of value. No drugs, and no money."

He stepped closer, close enough now to see the gun in my hands, but it didn't seem to worry him. He said, "We want her."

Nidia? "Why?" I said.

He said, "Not your problem."

He was surveying me with what almost looked like friendly curiosity. He said, "Please just put the gun down and unlock the doors. My friend over there will take Miss Hernandez gently out of the car and your role in this will all be over."

I understood that I was not going to shoot our way out of this, not with five rounds, probably not with three times that, had I been better armed. But the Impala was still in drive. If I hit the gas and smashed straight into the back end of the sedan in front of us, maybe I could just bull our way out.

Three problems: One, they could start shooting. Two, even if they didn't, Nidia was on the floor without a seat belt and could get banged up pretty badly. Three, two of them were standing right in front of the car.

Of course, it was better for Nidia to get banged up than shot. As for the guys in front of the car, could I live with myself if they died of their injuries? Yes, I could, if it was Nidia's life and mine against theirs.

I inhaled as though steadying my nerves and said to the guy outside the car, "Okay, just let me explain to her. Her English isn't very good."

Turning to Nidia, I spoke in Spanish, telling her, *Brace yourself.*

Then, crouching low behind the steering wheel, I stepped hard on the gas pedal. The Impala's engine roared in response. The last thing I heard was gunfire.

Part II

eleven

The first thought that came to mind, when I woke some time later, was that I was in the barracks, that I had overslept and was going to be late for morning formation. When I opened my eyes and looked around, I realized that wasn't it.

"How are you feeling?" an accented voice nearby asked.

The speaker was a tall, heavyset man with a broad, kind, copper-brown face and the sort of brushy, full mustache that only Hispanic men look good wearing. He was also wearing a white lab coat. He was a doctor. I was in a hospital. At my side, I saw an IV needle taped to my wrist.

"Are you having difficulty understanding me?" the doctor asked.

I cleared my throat to speak. "No, I understand you," I said. "You're speaking English."

He smiled indulgently. "So I am."

I realized that wasn't what he'd meant.

He shone a small light in my eyes. I blinked, but tolerated it.

He pulled up a rolling stool. "Do you remember your name?"

"Hailey," I said. "Hailey Cain." My voice was thin and dry.

"Well," he said, "it's a pleasure to finally know your name. We didn't know. I've been calling you Miss America."

"That's flattering."

"Do you know where you are?"

"Mexico," I said.

I knew that automatically, but less clear was why. I hadn't been on vacation. I hadn't flown down; I had been driving. And something had gone wrong.

Suddenly I stiffened. "Was I shot?" An impossible idea, yet as soon as I said it, I knew it was true. "Doc?"

"Yes," he said. "You were shot, twice. You also had some blunt-force trauma to your face."

From when the Impala hit the tunnel wall. Now I remembered.

"Nidia," I said. "Where is she? Is she all right?"

The doctor looked thoughtful. "You mentioned that name before," he said.

"Before?"

"Do you remember being awake earlier?"

"Vaguely," I said. "What do you mean, I mentioned her? Isn't she here? Haven't you guys treated her?"

He drew in a deep breath. "About most of this," he said, "you'll need to speak with the police. It's out of my area of expertise."

"How long was I asleep?"

"You weren't asleep; you were in a coma. For eight weeks."

Jesus. Then something occurred to me. "How did you know I was going to wake up when I did?" I asked. "You were right there."

"I woke you up," he said. "The coma you were in wasn't natural."

"I don't understand."

"It was medically induced," he said. "You needed time to recuperate from internal damage from the gunshots and from loss of blood. The best thing for your body was a short-term coma."

That was a hard thing to wrap the mind around. How screwed up did your body have to be for it to need a coma to get better?

"Plus," the doctor added, "during the brief periods when you were awake, you were agitated. You were interfering with the tubes and your IV."

He talked to me a little bit about my injuries, the two gunshot wounds to the chest and the damage they'd done. Then paused, frowning slightly. "Do you remember saying, 'They were white'?" he asked.

I shook my head.

"Do you know the significance of that?"

"I'm not sure."

"You said it twice. It seemed to be very important to you."

I shook my head again, and the doctor got up from his stool. "Try to rest."

"Wait," I said. "You already know something about Nidia, don't you? Is she dead? You can tell me. I'm strong, I won't go into shock."

He said, "You were traveling alone, Miss Cain."

The rest of it I learned from an officer of the state judicial police. His name was Juarez. He was taller and thinner than the doctor, though with that same mustache. He took down some basic introductory details first, my full name, where I lived.

Juarez went on to tell me that I was found just outside the tunnel, alone on the edge of the road, bleeding profusely, without ID, money, or a car. The farmworkers who found me had believed that I was in a bizarre hit-and-run in which I had been walking on a remote highway. No one had realized I'd been shot until I was examined at the hospital.

"I wasn't traveling alone," I told him. "I was traveling with a girl, Nidia Hernandez. Even if she wasn't at the scene, her things were in the car."

He said, "There was no car. No luggage, and no girl. Just you."

"That doesn't make any sense."

"Why don't you tell me your story from the beginning."

I did, leaving out only the fact that the friend who had gotten me involved in Nidia's situation was a semi-notorious girl gangster in L.A. Serena became, loosely, "a friend of Nidia's." The rest was the unvarnished truth, from Oakland to the border to the tunnel.

"They were white," I said, "and armed. These guys were pros. I don't know why they wanted Nidia, but they did."

When I was done, Juarez didn't ask the questions I would have expected. He didn't ask for details about the ambush, or for a more thorough description of Nidia, which would have helped the police find her. Instead, he asked about my life in America: in particular, what I did for work.

"A bike messenger," he said, "that's a young person's job, I understand. Not very lucrative, no?"

"I don't need much money."

"Really," he said. "I've heard that life in America is quite expensive, particularly California. People have high standards for what their lifestyle should be. Everyone reaching for the golden apple."

I had a sinking feeling about what was motivating this line of questioning. I said, "Can I ask why you're so interested in my lifestyle and income?"

He looked thoughtfully at nothing in particular. Then he turned his attention back to me.

"Miss Cain," he said, "let me be blunt. When an American meets with violence in Mexico, far from tourist areas, and without frantic American family members demanding information—"

"I'm not a drug mule," I said.

He looked out the window, hesitated, and began to speak more slowly and deliberately. "In my experience," he said, "when women become involved in the drug trade, it is rarely because of their own vice. Usually they become involved at the insistence of corrupt men who hold too much influence in their lives and do not have their best interests at heart. The law is commonly gentle with such women."

"That's nice to know, but I'm not in the drug trade," I said.

I'd wanted to say it since he was about five words in, but it had been obvious that nothing was going to proceed until he'd finished his little speech inviting me to fall into the sympathetic arms of the Mexican law.

I said, "You're skeptical about my story, okay, I can understand that. But Nidia is out there somewhere and needs help. I don't want your suspicions about me to keep people from looking for her."

"To be honest," he said, "it occurs to me that if you needed an explanation for why a group of armed men would ambush you on the road, and you couldn't tell us they were in search of money or drugs, a young woman would make a sympathetic substitute."

"You don't even believe that Nidia *exists*?"

"We have only your word on that," he said. "Look at this from my perspective: You've described your traveling companion as a Mexican-born teenager without money or connections. Why would she be of interest to men like that?"

"I don't know what kind of men they were," I said, "so it's hard to speculate."

"Speculate," he repeated, leaning back a little. "You have a certain level of education."

"I did nearly four years at West Point. I didn't finish."

"That's the American military academy?"

"One of them," I said.

"Why didn't you finish there?"

"I was discharged. Not for using drugs, if that's what you're thinking," I told him. "Listen, whatever you think of me, Nidia needs your help. She's only nineteen. You owe it to her to have people looking for her."

Juarez hesitated, then said, "I must admit, you are convincing in your zeal." He raised pen to notepad. "Tell me as much as you can about her and I'll get her description out."

"To the U.S. authorities, too?" I said. "In case these men took her back over the border?"

He nodded.

When we were done, I had one last question for him. I said, "The doctor told me that no one here knew my name."

Juarez waited for the rest.

"Didn't you identify me from missing-persons reports?"

"I'm sorry, Miss Cain," he said, "but no one matching your description was reported missing."

twelve

Sometimes one offhand comment can bring a truth about your life home to you. Until Juarez's statement, I hadn't realized how isolated I'd let myself get from other people. CJ, Serena, my mother in Truckee—there was no one who wasn't accustomed to not hearing from me for weeks on end. My disappearance had not registered with anyone in my life.

Except for this: I'd promised to see Serena on my way back north. I'd never shown up, yet she hadn't reported me missing. Serena, who was the only person in my life who'd known where I was going. Wasn't that an odd thing?

It was she who had asked me to do this in the first place. She'd called me out of the blue, after we hadn't spoken in nearly a year, wanting me to take a girl I'd never met to central Mexico. Conveniently, none of Nidia's family, nor Serena nor her sucias, could do the job. Only a white stranger in the Bay Area seemed to be able to do it.

A stranger to Nidia, that was. I was no stranger to Serena; we were friends, and now I couldn't help pulling at the threads of that friendship, wondering how much they'd weakened in the time we'd been apart. Enough to allow her to set me up to be killed?

Some time later, a nurse came in and gave me a pill. I didn't ask what it was. Maybe it was a sleeper, because sleep came on fast.

The next day, Juarez returned. I couldn't tell from his long, sober face what he'd concluded about my story, but he blandly told me that when I was well enough to leave the hospital, I would be taken to the U.S. Consulate and would become their problem.

thirteen

Seventy-two hours later, I was riding high in the cab of a Peterbilt truck, rolling across the dry, severe Arizona terrain, heading back toward California.

I was exceedingly grateful for my military service, because having my fingerprints in the system had streamlined the process of proving who I was—and therefore my citizenship—to consular authorities. Of course, they'd wanted to hear the whole story, and I'd told it to them. I stressed the part about Nidia's disappearance as I had with Juarez, but it didn't make much of an impression. Nidia was not an American citizen, therefore not their problem.

I, on the other hand, penniless and stranded, was their problem. They arranged for me to get on a bus to the U.S. border, where I'd stuck out my thumb and eventually found what I was looking for: a truck driver headed to Los Angeles. That was Ed. Ed had rusty, curly hair and seemed decent; he kept his hands to himself and, as evening fell, had given me his jacket. At the hospital, they'd found me some civilian clothes to replace the ones that had been ruined in the attack. They gave me jeans and running shoes, and a T-shirt with the word NAVY on it in block letters, which I'd taken with a small inward smile. A little joke on the part of the universe.

"You're young to have been on your own in Mexico," Ed said. "You're what, nineteen, I'd guess?"

People always lowballed my age, because of the open, guileless features I'd inherited from my father.

"Twenty-three," I said. Then: "No, wait, twenty-four. I just had a birthday."

July five, the day after I'd been shot. I'd turned twenty-four in my sleep.

"You got someone you can call when we get to L.A.?" Ed asked.

"Several people," I told him. "There's one friend in particular I'm dying to get caught up with."

I was thinking, of course, of Serena. I still didn't want to believe that my old friend had set me up, but it was the theory that best fit the facts.

Serena used to call me *prima*, meaning cousin. Yet I'd heard her call other girls *hermana*, or sister. I had never been sure if this was because they were sucias or because they were Mexican like her. It would have been uncool to ask. But the very fact that she made that distinction troubled me now. I was white, and since I'd moved north, I was no longer an everyday friend. Had those things made me expendable?

It was painful to consider that possibility. But if it was true, what had been her motivation for setting Nidia up? Money? Serena knew a lot of people, and she saw and heard a lot. Maybe she'd known that someone wanted Nidia, and had exacted a price for helping them to get her. Maybe that was why, when I'd called her from El Paso having second thoughts, she'd said, *I don't think you should interfere*. Of course not, not if her big payday depended on me getting Nidia to the abduction point.

But if Serena's incentive had been money, what was the motive of whoever had hired the seven men in the tunnel? Juarez's skepticism on that point was entirely understandable. Seven armed men had braced us in a tunnel in a sophisticated maneuver, and shot me, and they had done all this, apparently, to abduct or kill a nineteen-year-old daughter of Mexican illegal immigrants. How to explain that? To have a plausible theory, didn't you need to start with a plausible event?

I bit my thumbnail and shifted in my seat.

"You okay?" Ed asked.

"I'm cool," I said.

It wasn't necessary to think so far ahead. The theory I had

now—that Serena set me up—was enough. It was credible and I could act on it.

That was why Los Angeles was my destination, instead of San Francisco. I was going to ambush Serena, and then she'd have to tell me what was going on.

Either that or I would screw up my ambush and she, being Warchild, would kill me.

fourteen

So, for the second time in my life, I washed up in Los Angeles, broke and without a plan. I'd had to ask Ed for ten dollars to buy a meal. This made him skeptical all over again that I really had friends in L.A. I could call. I assured him several times I'd be fine before he left me in the vast parking lot of a shopping center and drove away.

I wasn't lying, strictly speaking, about having someone I could call. CJ could have provided most of what I needed: a safe place, a meal, a bed, and money. But I wasn't going to call him, because I was into some heavy shit right now, worse than the Marsellus thing, and I was not going to get my cousin involved. This was my private, post–West Point honor code: You might have to lie, cheat, or steal, but you do not endanger Cletus Jeffrey Mooney.

Instead, I started walking.

If San Francisco was bigger than it looked for a person on foot, Los Angeles was huge. East L.A., where I was headed, wasn't even in L.A. proper. I wasn't sure how many miles lay ahead of me. I did know that in the oppressively bright, hot weather, I was going to have a wicked sunburn.

It's just another road march, *I told myself. At West Point we had done them* all the time, with our rifles and heavy rucks on our backs.

A lot of what I'd learned at West Point was going to be useful here. The officers who'd taught us had foreseen the day when we might be dropped into a hostile landscape without resources and would need to survive by our wits. We'd learned to ignore hunger and other physical privations. We'd been taught to be resourceful, to find what we needed to survive in the territory around us.

You can do this, I told myself. *You're made outta this.*

I had a basic plan. I was going to find a fast-food place where I could get a meal for less than ten dollars, and then I was going to keep walking until I saw my destination: the donation center for one of the nation's largest charities.

Sometime before midnight, I was breaking into Serena's car.

This hadn't been Plan A, which had been to wait outside until she came home from some late-night mission or errand, and then brace her from out of the shadows. It had seemed like a pretty good idea at the time. It was rare for gangbangers to go places unaccompanied—they had an innate understanding of the fire-team concept—but Serena did it more than most, a combination of her bravado and her need for privacy. So I had a better-than-average chance of catching her alone.

Unfortunately, I'd arrived too late. She was inside the house, probably for the night. Staging a raid on the home base of the Trece Sucias was out of the question. Too many guns and trigger-happy girls inside.

So, Plan B: the car. I knew it didn't have an alarm. In Serena's neighborhood, the only kind of car you could park outside was an old and inexpensive one from which the sound system had already been stolen. That described Serena's car, a pale blue Chevy Caprice with no radio.

Fortunately, I'd thought ahead and supplied myself for a break-in.

When I'd gotten to the donation center, I'd wandered casually to the back and slipped unseen into a supply closet. Then I'd made a small barricade of boxes in case someone opened the door and looked inside. I spent three hours sitting with my legs tucked up against me, behind those boxes, until I'd heard the volunteer workers close up and leave.

When I came out, I was alone in an acre-sized warehouse of used goods. One-stop shopping. By the time I left, I was wearing a heavy flannel shirt over my Navy T-shirt, and thicker socks under my work boots. I had a canvas backpack strapped to my back, into which I'd tucked a sharp boning knife from the housewares section, a long, tough screwdriver I'd found on a table laden with assorted tools, and a wire coat hanger. I was also pushing a ten-speed bicycle. That had carried me to Serena's place.

Now I crouched against the passenger door of the Caprice, working quietly and feverishly. Unlike Serena and her girls, I had no experience breaking into cars. I'd only seen it done, under innocent circumstances—several times I'd seen my uncle Porter come to the aid of people who'd locked their keys inside their own cars. This was a very different situation, and not the brightest idea, not in a barrio neighborhood where anyone who saw me wasn't going to call the cops. They'd grab a gun and TCB themselves.

But the door gave way to the force I applied with the long screwdriver, just enough that I could get the wire coat hanger in and trip the lock. I was in.

I lay in the backseat for an hour, staying alert until I was pretty sure that Serena wasn't coming out on some late-night whim, like a trip to the 7-Eleven. Then, finally, I curled up and closed my eyes and gave in to my exhaustion.

fifteen

Everyone gets sloppy. Even someone like Serena. If she walked out of her house every day scoping for assassins, she'd have cracked up long ago. She didn't look through the windows at the interior of her car before getting in. She just unlocked the door and slid behind the wheel.

I rose up from my crouched position, grabbed her hair from behind the headrest, and laid the boning knife to her throat. She jumped, startled, but she also grabbed my wrist, ready to fight faster than most people would have been.

"Don't," I said. "Stay still."

"*Hailey?*" she said, incredulous, her eyes going to mine in the rearview mirror.

"Don't touch the wheel," I said. "If you lay on the horn and get your sucias out here, they'll shoot me, but not in time to save you."

"Where the hell did you come from?" she asked.

I ignored that. "Put your hands on the wheel."

"You said not to—"

"I am *not* in a joking mood, Warchild. Put your goddamn hands in the eleven-and-one position on the steering wheel and don't take them off."

She did it.

"Are you strapped?" I asked her.

"Of course."

"Where?"

"Right side pocket."

She was wearing loose olive-green cargo pants, the kind with generous pockets for carrying a weapon. I couldn't take my right hand off her throat, nor could I reach her right leg with my left hand. Stalemate. "Okay," I said. "We'll let that be for a minute. You know better than to reach for it."

"What are we doing, Hailey?" she said.

"A little Q and A. Did you set me up, down in Mexico?"

"What?"

"I said, did you set up that little girl, Nidia, and me to get jacked?"

"I don't know what you're talking about," she said. She'd recovered from her initial shock and didn't sound all that scared. I'd known she wouldn't be.

I said, "We got ambushed. I nearly died, and she's missing. You were the one who set the whole thing up. And you knew I was down there and when I was supposed to be back, but you didn't report me missing. That looks pretty bad, Warchild."

She said, "When you didn't come back from Mexico, I assumed you were dead."

"Maybe you didn't assume. Maybe you knew how and why."

"No," she said, shaking her head very gently, in order not to increase the pressure of the knife on her throat. "I called Teaser's sister, Lara. She said that no one knew where Nidia was, either. I knew something went wrong. I can prove it."

"But why didn't you report it?" I pressed her.

"*Hailecita,* use your head! Have you ever known me to call the fucking cops about anything? We all know the fucking *jura* doesn't care about illegal Mexicans! What were they going to do?"

I said, grudgingly, "What did you mean when you said you could prove it?"

"I added you to my roll call," she said. Her tattoos on her calf, she meant. She added, "Can I show you?"

It meant reaching down and pulling up the hem of her pants. "Are you fucking kidding me?" I said. "You think I've never heard of an ankle holster before?"

She drew in a steadying breath. "Okay, listen. I'm going to, real slow, pull my leg up where you can reach. You can get the nine I'm carrying in my pocket, okay? And then you can hold that while you reach over and look for yourself. Okay? Will that work?"

"Keep your hands on the wheel," I warned.

Carefully, I let go of the hair I'd been gripping in my left hand, leaned back just a little, and slid my left arm diagonally past the headrest, crossing over my right arm, which was still holding the knife. Then I couldn't get my arm down to her leg, because my elbow was locked in the wrong direction. I lifted my weight up slightly from the backseat, putting myself in position to turn my arm downward.

Serena flinched. "Hey!"

The shift in my weight had caused me to increase the pressure of the knife on her throat. "Sorry," I said, glancing at her neck in the mirror. The knife hadn't broken the skin.

I said, "I can't reach. Lift up your leg a little farther."

She did. I felt her body shake a little; she was laughing nervously. "This is some crazy shit, *prima*," she said.

I angled my arm down toward her thigh and managed to slide my hand into her pocket, feeling the cool metal of her nine-millimeter. Gently, I extricated it, drew back my arm, and set it down on the seat next to me.

"Feel better?" she said.

"Yeah, but I still don't want you going for your ankle. Pull your leg up where I can reach."

Serena was five-nine, and it wasn't an easy task for her to keep her hands on the wheel and slowly draw up her right leg, ease it past the automatic gearshift, and prop it on the dashboard. When she did, her knee was almost to her shoulder. I leaned forward and slid my arm along her leg, toward her ankle.

"Ghetto yoga," Serena said, a shimmer of near-laughter in her voice.

"Shut up and let me do this," I said, and with effort, I reached the cuff of her pant leg and slid it up, revealing the tattoo I remembered.

Two names had been added since I'd last seen it. The third from the bottom read, *Teaser*. And just below that, I saw the newest and freshest name, *Hailey*. It was like looking at my own obituary.

"Jesus, Serena."

"I told you," she said. "You went down to Mexico and didn't come back. I figured you were dead, *prima*."

It wasn't logic that they'd understand in the suburbs. But gang-bangers lost people all the time. In Serena's world, it made sense.

I eased the knife away from her throat. "You really just assumed I was dead, with no body, no news report, nothing? Next time, try to be a little more *aspirational*, will you?"

"You been expanding your word power, eh?" she said, amused.

"Yeah," I said, starting to laugh. "I did a sleep-learning program while I was in my coma."

Her laughter dried up. "You were in a fucking coma?"

"For two months," I said, unable to stop laughing, like it was the funniest thing I'd ever told anyone. "I fucked up, Serena. That little girl, I let them get her. I didn't know how serious it was. If someone had told me, maybe I could've protected her. God, I fucked every-thing up."

I was crying now, my arms crossed on the back of the driver's seat, my face tipped down, forehead touching my wrists. The knife was still in my hand. Serena got out of the car, opened the back door, and gently took the knife away from me.

"Come in the house," she said.

"Not like this. I don't want your girls to see me like this."

She nodded like she understood, although it didn't make much sense; I'd never had any standing with the sucias to lose. Serena walked away, plucked an orange from her tree, and peeled it, standing in the late-morning sunshine in her driveway.

I pulled myself together, got out of the car, and walked over to the spigot at the side of her house. I turned on the water and splashed my face clean.

"Weren't you on your way somewhere?" I asked, straightening up.

"It can wait," Serena said. "Believe me, *prima*, you've rearranged my day."

. . .

*Her house was like I remembered. Same homeboy memorials on the refrig-*erator, same subtle pulse of music from the sound system. One of her girls, heavyset with brown-red hair crinkly with a perm and then mousse, looked up from the television as we entered.

Serena was rummaging through her kitchen shelves. "What would you like?" she asked. "Chorizo and eggs?"

"Not right now."

"Coffee?"

"No, thanks."

"A beer?"

I shook my head.

"Mmm. Some Vicodin?"

"Oh God yes."

sixteen

A half hour later I was in Serena's bathtub, floating in a cloud of strawberry- scented bubbles and Vicodin peace. I was listening to my own voice telling Serena, who was sitting cross-legged on the closed toilet seat, about Mexico, about the tunnel rats, as I'd started to think of the seven armed men, and their leader, whom I thought of as Babyface for his soft features.

"You're sure it was about her?" Serena said. "They wanted her?"

"That's what the guy said."

"So none of this was about a sick *abuelita* up in the mountains."

I shook my head. "Nidia made that up."

"She lied? I thought she was really religious," Serena said.

"I think she was. Is, I mean," I said. "But scared. When push comes to shove, people lie." I paused. "She was so quiet on the drive up, and I thought it was just that the two of us didn't have anything in common. But now I wonder if she wasn't feeling guilty. She knew there was heavier shit going on that she wasn't telling me about."

"You said she 'was' religious, then you changed it to 'is,'" Serena said. "You think she's still alive?"

"I don't know," I said slowly, "but it seems like if they wanted to kill her, they would have done it and dumped her right next to me. They took her with them, which means they wanted her alive."

"Just because they needed her alive for the moment doesn't mean they needed her alive for very long," Serena pointed out.

I must have looked disturbed, because Serena said, "We've got to be realistic about this."

I didn't answer, tipping my head back and letting the warm water crawl through my scalp.

Serena said, "Come on, get out before you fall asleep in there."

When I stepped out of the tub, before I could get the towel around me, I felt her eyes on my body, the healed wounds that couldn't yet be called simply scars.

"They don't hurt anymore," I said, "if that's what you're thinking."

A few minutes later I was wearing one of Serena's T-shirts and a pair of boxers, pulling back the covers of her bed. She was still standing in the doorway.

"Thanks for letting me crash here," I said.

"That's what Casa Serena's always been about, *prima,* a place where my homegirls can go to ground. You're not the first."

"But how many of the girls you've taken in were holding a knife on you just minutes earlier?"

Serena shrugged. "Around here, shit like that happens." She looked at me thoughtfully. "Out there, if I'd said, 'Yeah, bitch, I set you up,' would you have cut my throat?"

Her words gave me a chill, even through the Vicodin calm. I said, "I don't know. You had a gun. That would have made it very dangerous for me to back down." But then I shook my head. "I don't think it would have mattered. I couldn't have cut you."

"That would've got you killed, then."

"You mean, if you'd admitted to setting me up, and I let you go, you'd have shot me, anyway?"

"Of course."

I couldn't pretend her answer didn't hurt. She saw it in my face. "Come on, Hailey. If you had a legitimate grudge, what else could I do? That's the number-one thing that gets people killed in *la vida.* It's always retaliation. If you had a grudge against me, if I'd done something to make you my *enemiga,* and I let you walk away, that's like"—she searched for a comparison—"like leaving rat poison around in the kitchen. It's something you just don't do. It doesn't matter that I started it." She saw my disapproval. "It's the same reason I don't hold it against you that you braced me with the knife. You had a legit reason. I respect that."

I shook my head. "Thanks, I guess."

"De nada."

"One other thing? That tattoo, my name on your roll call?" I gestured to her leg. "Can you do something about that? It's going to give me the creeps, seeing it all the time."

She winked and said coolly, "Might as well keep it. You know?"

I said, "That's cold, Warchild."

She turned sober: "Sorry."

seventeen

The Trece Sucias, who were almost exclusively Mexican-American, would have surprised an outsider with the diversity of their features and coloring. At first glance, they all conformed to gang style, with cheap tattoos and hard masks of eyeliner and dark lipstick, long nails painted fuchsia or black. Some sharpened those nails to points for an unexpected weapon in a fight.

Up close, though, you saw the differences. Their hair was reddish, golden, black, or brown; skin creamy pale or tawny gold. In Juicy Couture and Skechers, for example, Heartbreaker would have blended in with the UCLA girls on Melrose Avenue. She was five-ten, with a lean, flat volleyball player's stomach, golden-brown hair, and wide-set greenish eyes. Her cousin and closest friend, Risky, was a small, fine-boned girl who could have been taken for Italian, with straight brown hair, brown eyes, and pale skin. Trippy, Serena's lieutenant since Teaser died, was tall and strong, with chestnut hair in sharp bangs across her forehead and long down her back. Teardrop had classic Hispanic looks, straight black hair and rich brown skin.

The four of them, who made up less than half the sucias' number, were in Serena's living room when I came out a little after ten. I'd slept all day, and I still didn't feel too hot. The girls were playing with Teardrop's baby daughter and talking in Spanglish. I fixed myself a bowl of cereal and sat at the table to eat. They ignored me, except when Teardrop said in Spanish, *Look, she's all red,* meaning badly sunburned, and the rest giggled. I told myself it wasn't a slur I needed to answer and pretended I didn't hear.

I'd told myself more than once that it was stupid to seek validation from a tribunal of gang girls. Underneath the hard shell of gang identity, they were just teenagers, emotional and naive, sentimental about babies and their *abuelitas,* desperate for the slightest affection from a homeboy. Most of them knew little of the world outside East Los Angeles. I, on the other hand, had jumped out of planes in Airborne School and boxed on my company's team back east, sparring with guys my height and weight in the ring. But none of that mattered to the sucias. To them I was less than, just because I was white and unaffiliated.

They weren't hostile to me. The name they called me, *la rubia,* meant only *the blond girl.* That wasn't an epithet, yet I read a tinge of contempt in it: Blondie. And although Serena had told them I spoke Spanish, they never seemed to believe it: Whenever they spoke it in front of me, it was rapidly and with the clear implication that they were talking among themselves. She'd also told them I had been at West Point, but they seemed to have only a vague idea of what that signified. If Serena had said I'd gone to the South Hudson Institute of Technology, that would have gotten about the same response.

Tonight, though, I had a credential that even the most jaded gang-banger couldn't brush aside. When Serena came in from an errand, she looked at me and said, "Show them your scars."

"Why?" I said.

Trippy said to Serena, "What scars?"

"Hailey got shot," Serena told them. "Twice."

"For real?" Risky said with disbelief.

I stood from the couch, listing slightly before getting my balance. I lifted up my shirt, revealing the angry, corrugated reddish marks. There was an appreciative murmur as they drew near to get a closer look.

"Can we touch them?" Risky asked. "Will it hurt?"

I nodded—*Go ahead*—and felt their gentle fingers on my wounds. "That doesn't hurt?" Heartbreaker said.

"I'd tell you," I said.

Their fascination was gratifying, but I knew they weren't impressed by me, personally. I was like the nerdy kid who'd brought an awesome toy to show-and-tell.

Trippy didn't even direct her questions to me, looking instead at Serena: "Why would somebody shoot her? She doesn't even claim." She meant that I was unaffiliated with any gang.

Serena said, "Tell them, Hailey."

"Why?" I said. "I'm pretty sure that whatever Nidia was running from, it's not related to anything that happened around here."

I just didn't feel like giving a speech. For all that I'd slept, I was still tired, and vaguely dehydrated.

But Serena said, "You never know what people are talking about, what the girls might have overheard."

So I sat down on the arm of the couch and told the story from the beginning, Serena listening as patiently as she had the first time. When I was done, Serena said, "I've got some bad news. I called Teaser's sister Lara."

For a moment the name was unfamiliar, then I remembered the cousin of Nidia's who'd acted as a go-between, enlisting Serena's help in getting Nidia down to Mexico.

"And?" I prompted.

"Her mother said that the two of them had this crazy screaming fight and Lara split. Her mother doesn't know when she's coming back."

"Great," I said.

Serena turned to her girls. "Keep your ears open about where Lara Cortez is, Teaser's sister. Hailey'd like to talk to her. Which is the same as me saying I'd like to talk to her. Okay?"

I'd been rubbing my aching temple, but I stopped to look up at her. " 'Hailey'd like to talk to her'?" I echoed. "What am I going to talk to her about?"

Serena looked at me quizzically. "Where else would you start, to sort all this out?"

"You think I'm going to find out what happened to Nidia?"

"None of the rest of us would know how."

"And I would?" I said. "I went to West Point, not Scotland Yard.

Besides, you told me earlier today you don't even think Nidia's still aboveground. Your words were something to the effect of, 'They might not have needed her alive for very long.' So what's the point?"

"Retaliation is the point," Serena said. "That's what *la vida* is about. If those guys killed Nidia, they got something coming."

"I thought retaliation was by homegirls for homegirls. Nidia wasn't even one of you. And neither am I."

Serena said, "I thought—"

"You thought wrong," I said, getting to my feet. "Thanks for the ghetto hospitality, but this is your problem now. *Me vale madre.*" Loosely translated, *I don't give a shit*.

"Wait!" she said.

I didn't. I got to her entryway before she caught up.

"Hailey, stop! You don't have a car. It's not safe for you to be walking out there at night."

"Safe?" I repeated. "You mean, *safe* like I was down in Mexico? Serena, did you even listen to a word I told you this morning?"

She backed up a step, startled.

"Look," I said, "I'm sorry I screwed up the mission I didn't even fucking know was a mission! But you put me in an impossible position, Warchild! You know what happened on Wilshire Boulevard, what I did, and you put me in a situation where I had to run down two guys or get killed myself! Do you have any idea how that feels?"

"Hailey—"

Maybe I raised my hand to her. I must have done something that looked threatening, because suddenly I felt an impact. My back hit the wall, and there was an arm pressed hard against my throat. Also, a cold ring against the underside of my jaw that I recognized as the muzzle of a gun.

It wasn't Serena. It was Trippy. On the periphery of my vision I could see the other sucias, riveted.

"Thank you, Luisita," Serena said calmly. "Hailey will settle down in a moment. She's just not herself right now." To me: "Right?"

"Serena," I said stiffly, trying not to cough against the pressure

Trippy was putting on my larynx, "you need to get her off me before she gets hurt."

"Like you could, bitch," Trippy said.

Serena, though, was watching my eyes. "If I do call her off, are we all going to make nice?" she asked me.

"Yeah. Sure. Whatever."

Serena said, "Trippy, it's okay. Take the gun off her."

"Are you kidding? She just went fucking crazy."

Serena said mildly, "No, Hailey's been a little crazy for a while now." Then, more authoritatively: "Really. Let her go."

Trippy gave her a hard sideways glance, then, angrily, she stepped back. "This is bullshit," she said, the all-purpose face-saving line. She walked away, not back to the living room, but out the front door. It banged shut hard behind her.

Serena watched her go, then looked at me with concern. "Feeling okay?"

"A little light-headed," I said. It was coming on fast, along with a weakness in my limbs.

Serena's face was worried. "You haven't been out of the hospital for very long, right?" Her voice was kind. "Come on, lie down again."

eighteen

I spent the next few days mostly sleeping, whether from a fever or just sun and dehydration and overexertion, I don't know. Serena tended me. She'd clearly looked after sick people before, probably gangbangers too broke or too hot to go to the ER. She made me drink water and more water, fed me chicken broth and applesauce, and yelled at her homegirls to keep the music and the television turned down. I had a dreamlike memory of waking in the small hours of the night to see her dressed in dark clothing, with the cool smell of night air still rising faintly from her clothes and hair, counting money on the bedroom floor. She'd moved the lamp down from the night table and was counting cash by its small ring of yellowy light. Then she took down her framed print of Vietnam's Halong Bay, unclipped the cardboard backing, laid a single layer of bills between the poster and the cardboard, and then replaced the whole thing on the wall.

Seeing me watching, she said, "Go back to sleep," like a mother who'd come into a child's bedroom to put away folded laundry.

After two days and three nights of rest, I woke up at half past five in the morning, feeling better, alert and clearheaded. I kicked the covers aside and stood.

I did some stretches, then got down to the floor and tried some military-style push-ups, hands close enough together to make a diamond of my thumbs and forefingers. It wasn't as hard as I'd expected. I'd lost muscle in my chest and shoulders from lack of use, but at the same time, I'd lost weight, so it evened out. I did ten push-ups and then sat on my heels, feeling my heart subside into normal rhythm.

When I was fully dressed, I quietly opened the door and came out. Serena's living room, always messy, was bathed in the cool gray light of morning. On the couch, Serena slept in a pile of blankets.

I wasn't sure I'd ever understand her. Three days ago she'd told me that if she'd felt it necessary, she could have shot me to death in her driveway and not felt guilty afterward. Yet here she was, sleeping on her couch so I could have her room.

I was quiet going into the kitchen, but when I pulled my head back out of the refrigerator after surveying the contents, Serena was at the terminator of the hallway carpet and the kitchen linoleum, hair disheveled, eyes violet-shadowed underneath from inadequate sleep.

"Hey," I said. "Why don't you go get in your bed, get some more sleep? I'm up."

She shook her head. "I'm all right," she said. "A lot of nights I don't get eight hours." She moved into the kitchen, stood behind me at the refrigerator. "You hungry?"

"Let me fix something," I said. "You've cooked for me enough."

Not long after, we were at her table, having Diet Coke and omelets.

"I was thinking," Serena said, slicing into the center of her omelet, releasing steam, "that I was wrong the other night, to push you about finding out what happened to Nidia. It's not your problem."

"I know it's not," I said, "but I'm going to try, anyway." I paused. "Because the thing is, what if she's still alive somewhere?"

"You think she is?"

I hesitated. "If I had to guess, I'd say no. It's probably been too long. If they took her alive intending to let her go later, she'd probably have turned up somewhere by now."

"Unless they're still holding her."

"Unlikely," I said. "Back east, we learned a little about terrorism and overseas kidnappings and hostage situations. As a rule of thumb, shorter is always better for kidnappers. The longer you have people, the greater the chance of an escape, or a rescue, or a hostage finding a way to stick something sharp in you, or to despair and commit suicide. And then there's the logistics of feeding and guarding a hostage. It's a labor- and planning-intensive mission."

Serena considered this. "But maybe they're capable of it. You said these guys acted like pros."

"They did," I admitted. "They were following us for a while. Baby-face, the lead guy, he walked right up to me in El Paso and exchanged pleasantries. The scary thing is, he didn't ask me any questions about where I was headed; he wasn't fishing for information. He didn't have to. He already knew."

Serena looked curious. "So what was he doing?"

I shrugged. "Nothing," I said. "As far as I know, he was amusing himself at my expense. These guys are beyond my league."

"Yet you want to take them on."

"Well, if I get killed," I told her, "at least you won't have wasted money on that tattoo on your leg."

"There is that," she agreed.

nineteen

Several days later, I got off a Greyhound bus in San Francisco. Compared to the way I'd arrived back in L.A., I was generously outfitted for my expedition: a pay-as-you-go cell phone with two hundred minutes on it, a pint of Finlandia, a SIG Sauer P228, and two thousand dollars from Serena. Most of that was my per diem for taking Nidia to Mexico. I hadn't gotten the job done, but no one could say I hadn't earned the pay. Serena had thrown in a little extra for my expenses going forward, a gesture that said this wasn't just a private vendetta of mine, but that I had *la veterana* Warchild at my back.

The SIG was also a loan from Serena. It was chambered for fifteen rounds and was heavier than the Airweight, about two pounds, which was entirely worth it. Since the tunnel, I'd lost interest in guns with five-shot capacities.

I'd already programmed Serena's number into my cell phone and made sure that she had my new number. Maybe I needed to feel like I had a home base. Like if I disappeared this time, someone would report me missing.

I got off the city bus in Japantown and walked to Aries's offices. When I got there, Shay was sitting behind his desk, and when he looked up from the phone conversation he was having, his brows rose toward his hairline, like my old guidance counselor. When he hung up, he said, "Where the hell have you been?"

"I was in an accident."

Serena and her girls could take the news of a shooting in stride; for them, it was just a bad day at work. But when I was dealing with other people, *accident* was going to be my euphemism for the ambush.

Shay said, "An accident? I thought you were going out of town on personal business."

"It started out that way," I said. "The accident was accidental. Hence the name."

A new girl, olive-complected with springy black hair and a nose ring, was watching us now, alert to the prospect of drama.

"Why didn't you call in and let me know what was going on?"

My tone sharpened. "I couldn't, Shay. I nearly died; I was in the hospital a long time."

"Oh," he said. "I'm sorry."

"Listen," I said, quickly moving on, "I lost all my personal stuff, too. I'm going to need a new key to the room."

"The room?"

"My stuff's still up there, isn't it?"

My *Wheelock's,* my birth certificate, the picture of my father, my class ring, and cadet sword. Irreplaceable things. I didn't have any rental contract with Shay. If he'd assumed I wasn't coming back, and had pitched my things into the trash, I probably didn't have any legal recourse.

Shay let me wonder a long moment. Then he said, "Yeah, it is. I didn't think you were coming back, and I kept meaning to look into the law about how long I had to keep your stuff, but I never got around to it, and it seemed easier to store it up there than anywhere else."

"Thanks."

He said, "What about the rent, by the way?" He kicked his legs up on his desk. He was wearing shorts with sandals, revealing the impressive undiminished muscles of his legs. "I'm full up on riders, so I can't let you pay it off that way," he said.

"No problem," I said. I pulled out the two thousand dollars I had from Serena, kept in a rubber-banded roll. "I'm two months behind, right?" I began counting it out, enjoying the slight ripple of disbelief on Shay's face. For all he knew, I'd been laid up and not working for two months. He hadn't expected me to be flush; in fact, he'd probably wanted me to grovel for the chance to work.

When he brought the spare key, he said, "Look, if you're around a lot, maybe there'll be some work I can throw your way. You know how it is."

I understood why he was hedging. Shay always had new people walking in the door wanting to ride, but often they lost interest when they learned what demanding work messengering really was. Shay always needed riders he knew were reliable.

The truth was, I didn't know how much time the search for Nidia would leave me. And after two months of immobility, I wasn't sure I was in any shape for the street. But there was no point in antagonizing Shay. The most likely scenario in my search for Nidia was that I'd never find out who shot me or why, the money would run out, and then I'd be nothing but an unemployed bike messenger.

"Sure," I said, and took the key.

twenty

Herlinda Lopez's house in Oakland was already dark at half past eight at night, which was when I got there on foot, walking from the nearest BART station. At first glance, I thought maybe she and her kids had gone to bed quite early. Then I noticed that the geranium on the front step had turned brown, and the little strip of lawn was like straw.

The garage door had a row of narrow windows in it, just at sight level for an average man. I walked up the driveway, trying to amble casually as if I belonged there, then I stood on tiptoe to look in.

There was no car inside.

Maybe they were out. Maybe they'd never owned a car. It wasn't as if I'd looked in the garage when—

"Can I help you with something?"

I turned. The woman watching me at the end of the Lopez driveway was short and dark-skinned, but not Hispanic. Her accent was East Indian, or something close to it.

"Hi," I said. "I'm looking for the Lopezes."

"You're looking for them in their garage?" she said skeptically.

"Uh, not really," I said, walking back down the driveway. "I'm not so much looking for them as for a friend of mine, Nidia Hernandez. Did you meet her while she was staying here?"

The neighbor shook her head.

"I thought the Lopezes might know where she's living now," I said.

"They don't live here anymore. You're not from this neighborhood, are you?"

"No, I'm not."

"Mrs. Lopez went missing," she said.

"Missing? When?"

"About two months ago."

Two months.

She continued: "The kids went to live with someone else. The house has been empty awhile."

I said, "Has anyone but me been around here, asking for Nidia?"

She said, "I didn't even know there was somebody by that name living here. Even the police didn't mention her." Her lips thinned slightly in suspicion. "Who did you say you were?"

"Just a friend of Nidia's. My name is Hailey Cain."

"I have to go in now," she said, nodding toward the house next door. "Be careful out here. It's late to be walking."

MacArthur Station was probably my favorite place in the Bay Area. It was BART's main transfer station, a raised platform right in the middle of a tangle of freeways. From the platform, you could see the campanile of UC Berkeley, the Oakland hills, the towers that surrounded Jack London Square. You could do a lot worse with your evening than to spend a little of it at MacArthur Station, taking a breath and letting the world roll off your back.

Except I kept thinking about one thing: I sincerely hoped that all the shit that was gonna go down in the Lopezes' neighborhood had gone down already, because if any of the guys from the tunnel came around doing cleanup work, and they talked to the neighbor lady, I'd laid it right out there: *Hailey Cain, looking for Nidia Hernandez.* Without that, the would-be assassins would have no reason to think I was still alive.

Sometimes I didn't really think things through.

At home, I took the Finlandia out of my little refrigerator, cracked the seal, and drank. Then I called Serena and told her what I'd learned.

"I'm pretty sure Mrs. Lopez is dead," I said. I was standing near the window, looking down at the street. "If she realized she was in danger and left town, she wouldn't have left her kids in danger. I think the guys from the tunnel picked her up, found out what she knew, and killed her so she couldn't warn anyone."

"God," Serena said. "This is getting serious, Hailey." Like me nearly dying in Mexico and then later jumping her with a boning knife was all light sparring.

"What do you think she knew?"

"Well, where Nidia and I were going, for one thing," I said. "I'd wondered how, if they were just tailing Nidia and me, they knew to get ahead of us and set up that trap in the tunnel. This answers that. Herlinda Lopez knew about the village." I played with the drawstring of the blinds. "If Nidia told her something else, like what all of this is about, I still don't know what that was. That's the same guessing game we've been playing for days."

I tipped my head back and drank again, the vodka cool and antiseptic on my tongue.

"You still there?"

"Yeah," I said. "I was just thinking, this doesn't make me feel good about cousin Lara being unaccounted for. Maybe she really did fight with her mother, but she knows the stuff Mrs. Lopez knew, maybe more, and recent events are proving that's not a safe position to be in."

Serena said, "Be careful, okay?"

"I don't know how to do that and still find anything out," I told her. "Being careful would be forgetting all about this. Either I'm going to do this or I'm not. In fact . . ."

"In fact, what?"

I drank again, then leaned on the window frame and looked down at the street. Cars shuttled back and forth, red brake lights flaring and fading. I said, "Maybe it's best they know I'm out there looking for her."

"Are you kidding me?"

"I have no idea who these guys are," I said. "I could look for them the rest of my life and not find them, but if they come looking for me, that'll streamline things, if nothing else."

"Don't streamline yourself into an unmarked grave, *prima*."

twenty-one

What little there was to know about Herlinda Lopez's disappearance, I learned from the *San Francisco Chronicle.*

She was apparently taken from her own garage, in her own car. The garage had a back door that opened directly onto the Lopezes' small yard, and then another into the house. The investigating officers found that the door leading into the yard had been pried open, its cheap lock broken. A short time after that, Herlinda's old crimson Toyota was found in a parking lot in a quiet, light-industrial area. The implication was that whoever had taken her had broken into the garage in the small hours of the morning via the yard door and simply waited for her to come through the house door to her car, which she'd done at five that morning, on her way to her bakery job. She had raised no cry when confronted, probably intimidated by a gun and aware that her children were still sleeping in the house. She apparently let her attackers drive her away in her car, then they transferred her to a second car in the parking lot, where the trail stopped.

There had been an unfortunately long lead time on the case, because her coworkers at the bakery had been patient with her failure to show up, assuming that responsible Herlinda must have had a good reason to be tardy. They didn't call her home until ten, long after her kids had left for school through the house's front door, never going into the garage or seeing the broken door there. No one knew she was missing until her daughter played the answering machine message at four that afternoon.

The accounts of Herlinda's disappearance shed new light on the men who'd taken Nidia. My theory had been that they had waited to

take Nidia in Mexico because it was too risky to try to kidnap someone from a dense urban area with lots of potential witnesses. That
was true enough; the neighbor lady who caught me looking through
the garage windows was proof of that. But with Herlinda, these guys
had proven themselves capable of an urban kidnapping. That suggested that they hadn't known where Nidia was until just before I
came to get her. If they'd had time, they would have done the same
job on Nidia that they'd done later on Herlinda.

So they'd tracked Nidia down, but before they could move, I'd
come and gotten her. That had forced their hand. Almost on the fly,
they'd put together their plan to kidnap Herlinda and find out where
Nidia and I were going.

That worried me more than anything else. These guys could think
on their feet. The way they'd extracted Herlinda from her house had
been almost surgical, and that had been their Night at the Improv.

This was where I should have been saying, *Imagine what they
could do with a little lead time,* but I didn't have to imagine. I'd seen
it, in the tunnel.

I didn't learn anything else useful that day.

Serena called me and told me that no one had a line on Nidia's
cousin Lara Cortez, and that Nidia's family was somewhere in
California's vast agricultural-worker community. That could have
meant picking strawberries near Santa Maria or garlic in Gilroy.
Though I would have liked to talk to them, when I thought about
what had happened to Herlinda Lopez, I was glad Nidia's family
weren't anywhere they could easily be found.

twenty-two

*West Point prides itself on being a four-year university with a broad, well-*rounded curriculum. But it's also very much an Army post, and from your first day there, you're a soldier.

That was why, when I surfaced from BART and walked up onto the campus of UC Berkeley the next day, I stopped for a moment to look around at the student body all around me. I'd gone to college in a sea of cadet gray, and after all this time, the sight of a civilian student body gave me culture shock. Some wore jeans and Cal-logo T-shirts or caps, like the model students in a course catalog, but many more wore clothing as diverse as costumes: motorcycle boots, skater motley, Buddy Holly glasses, Afros, Birkenstocks, minidresses. Some wore tank tops and cutoffs that showed amazing amounts of skin; others were swathed almost head to foot in flowing ethnic prints. They drank lattes on the steps of Dwinelle Hall and Web-surfed on their phones. I'd nearly forgotten that students lived this way.

I wondered what they would do if they knew the student with the blond ponytail and the birthmark on her face had a loaded SIG Sauer in her backpack.

I was here to look for an obituary, that of the mathematician whom Nidia had cared for until his death. I didn't have a name, except Adriano, which Nidia might have Spanicized from Adrian. That would have made searching the *Chronicle*'s obits difficult. And if this guy hadn't done anything of real note, his death might not have made the *Chronicle* at all. I was fairly certain, though, that the university paper would have covered it.

So that was how I ended up outside the offices of the mathematics department, looking at a glass case on the wall where news and events were posted. There it was, an obituary for Adrian Skouras. Both the *Daily Californian* and the *Chronicle* story were posted. When I saw the accompanying photo, I had a dawning sense of understanding.

All along, I'd made a sloppy assumption: that a professor dying of cancer would have been a white-haired old man. But cancer is indiscriminate. Adrian Skouras had died at thirty-three. The photo both papers used had probably been taken years before that. The young man the camera had captured had almost sensual features—he was obviously olive-complected, though the photo was black-and-white, and he had dark curly hair and deep-set eyes. The effect, though, was offset by the thin sharpness of his face and his wire-rim eyeglasses, and like many people unused to attention, his smile for the camera was almost a wince.

I read both obituaries. They didn't disagree on any points. Adrian Skouras had been born and raised in San Francisco and had been fascinated with math and science at a young age. He'd graduated high school at fifteen and gone back east to study at Princeton. In his second year, he'd become a star in the world of mathematics by discovering a rare subspecies of prime number, now called a "Skouras prime," the definition of which went over my head. After that, he'd gone overseas to Oxford for graduate work, then come home to settle at Berkeley, working among some of the leading lights in the field.

He had never married and left no children behind. Associates said that Skouras had been "married to his work, in the best possible way," in the words of one. "When he was working on something that fascinated him, which was almost all the time, he'd forget to eat, much less to get out and have a social life. But if you knew him, you wouldn't have any doubt that he was completely fulfilled."

The best work of his career was undoubtedly ahead of him, they said, if only cancer had not stolen a fine mind from the world.

His father, Anton Skouras, was a San Francisco businessman and philanthropist; one brother, Milos, had preceded Adrian in death five years earlier. In lieu of flowers, donations could be made to the American Cancer Society.

I looked at his photo again. Adrian Skouras appeared shy, gentle, unsettled by the photographer's attention, and impatient to step back into academic anonymity. This was no cliché—the graybeard professor. This was a real person. Looking at him, I thought I knew what happened between this man and Nidia Hernandez.

According to his colleagues, Adrian had been totally satisfied as a bachelor, living his life on the higher plane of numbers and ideas. Of course, that was what anyone would want to think about a newly dead colleague. Between the lines, Adrian had likely been one of those geniuses who would have been able to converse easily with Newton and Sagan—and hard-pressed to make small talk with real people at a cocktail party or a university mixer. Adrian had probably spent his weekend nights in the company of ideas, not women. Maybe, as his colleagues wanted to think, he had been satisfied with that. And then he got cancer, and his whole life became about the survival rate.

But Adrian had had just a little time, time he'd spent with a very lovely nineteen-year-old living in his house, a girl who had the same otherworldliness about her. He'd denied himself simple human warmth and pleasure for too long; she was recovering from a terrible loss. Put two people like that in close proximity alone for too long, and anyone could tell you the result.

What if that little potbelly she'd had, the one I'd assumed was puppy fat, wasn't? What if it had been a baby, and Nidia had been going to Mexico to have her child away from the eyes of anyone who knew her?

It was a theory that made sense until the entrance of the seven armed men. That changed things. It said that Nidia hadn't run to Mexico to escape gossip and character assassination. She'd foreseen the approach of the men in the tunnel, whoever they were. And she'd warned her family, who'd effectively disappeared into the migrant worker community, for once using poverty and anonymity to their benefit. Nidia could have gone with them, except that if these guys were determined to find her, that wouldn't have been enough. A beautiful green-eyed redhead, and, if my theory was correct, increasingly pregnant? Anywhere she went, people would have remembered her.

So Nidia had 911'd cousin Lara, and Lara had called Serena, playing the card of loyal dead soldier Teaser. And Serena had called me, and that was how the only person without a stake in the matter nearly bled out in the mountains of Mexico.

I walked out into the midday sunlight. It wasn't going to help me to talk to people who'd known Adrian in the math department. Whatever there had been in Adrian's life that had involved him with men like the guys in the tunnel, his colleagues weren't going to know about it. I needed the story behind the obituary, the whispers that had never made it to print.

I sat down on the steps like a student, minus the latte. I dug my cell from my backpack and made a phone call.

"AP, Foreman."

"Jack? It's Hailey."

"Hailey?" he said, mildly surprised. "I thought I'd said something to piss you off. I called you and you never returned my message."

"My phone was stolen," I said.

"Really? That's too bad."

"Yeah," I said. "Listen, I need a favor and I don't have a lot to exchange for it. Maybe I could buy you a lunch or something."

"Depends what the favor is," he said.

"For you, it shouldn't be a problem," I said. "I need some background information, the kind of things reporters talk about but can't or don't print."

"About what?"

"A man named Adrian Skouras. He was a mathematician at UC Berkeley and died of cancer three months ago. His obit was glowing, but I need to know if there were things about him that were, I don't know, unsavory."

"Mmmm," Jack said thoughtfully. "Right off, can I ask you if this guy grew up locally?"

"Yeah, he did."

"Do you remember if he's related to a guy named Anton Skouras?"

"That was his father. You've heard of him?"

"Sure, he's probably the biggest unindicted racketeer in San Francisco."

"He is?"

"Unofficially, yeah. Officially, he's a 'prominent businessman.' I haven't had the opportunity to write about him that often. Someone who writes for the business pages over at the *Chron* would know his story better than me, printable news and unprintable rumors both."

"Could you ask someone over there?"

"It depends: Where are we going to lunch?"

"Anywhere," I said, guessing that his innate decency wouldn't let him hold me up for anyplace expensive.

"You know where Lefty O'Doul's is?" he said.

"I know it," I told him. Dim and comfortable, with old-style cafeteria-line food.

Before we hung up, Jack said, "Why are you interested in Skouras, anyway?"

I said, "I think he stole my cell phone."

twenty-three

When I saw Jack Foreman waiting on the sidewalk outside Lefty's, he was smoking, of course. I noticed that he'd let his hair grow since I'd seen him last. He'd probably just been too busy to bother getting it cut. He wasn't the type to change styles out of vanity, or to care that the new length made his gray more noticeable.

When he saw me, he tossed the cigarette down on the sidewalk and stepped on it, looking at me appraisingly. "You've lost weight," he said. "Come inside, we need to get some calories into you."

We went in and moved through the cafeteria line, then settled in at a booth. Lefty's was never empty, but it wasn't packed, either, and quiet enough for us to talk. We sat under the photographs of Tinker and Evers and Chance, and I looked at Jack and said, "So tell me about this Skouras guy."

"Well," Jack began, "he came from a big family in Greece. Before World War Two, they had money and landholdings, all that. But then came the German occupation, then the civil war, and it all went away. Tony Skouras talks about this in interviews, how he came here as a teenager with nothing, determined to rebuild. It's his bootstraps story.

"What he doesn't talk about," Jack said, "is that his first business venture in his twenties was to buy a pair of X-rated movie houses. He built those into a chain, and added a line of adult DVD-rental stores. They were so profitable that he was able to sell by the age of thirty and buy a shipping line, which was, on the surface, a more respectable trade."

"Why 'on the surface'? That sounds a lot more respectable than pornography."

"Well, he's using the shipping line and his import business to bring stolen art and antiquities into the country," Jack said, "but that's not the big deal. The bigger problem is he's bringing in illegal immigrants from southern and eastern Europe. He's got contacts in the Balkan states, where a lot of people's lives have been ripped up by the civil wars there, and they'll do anything to get out. If it were just undocumented young men looking for work that Skouras was bringing in, that'd be one thing, but a big part of the trade is young women. Skouras supplies prostitution rings. Essentially, the guy's a human trafficker, and he's said to dip into the rings he supplies quite a bit, like a private dating pool."

I nodded.

"None of that's been proven. The feds have sniffed around him; the SEC has subpoenaed papers, but he's got good accounting and good lawyering and nothing's stuck. In the past few years he's branched out further into legitimate enterprises. He owns a minority stake in a film studio in L.A., and he opened a seafood restaurant on the Embarcadero, Rosemary's, named for his wife. As far as I've heard, there's nothing dirty about those operations."

I nodded.

"But then there's this. About ten years ago, Skouras got interested in horse racing. He went in big, bought a costly colt from Dubai and had it brought here and stabled at Golden Gate Fields. Then it didn't live up to its potential. After it finished out of the money in several races, its heart just exploded during a routine exercise gallop."

"Drugged?"

"That was never proven," Jack said. "Which probably wasn't much of a consolation to the exercise groom who suffered a compound pelvic fracture in the fall."

"Nice."

"Yeah. Let's see, what other Skouras rumors can I dazzle you with? Oh yes," he said. "There's a very faintly whispered story that Tony had a daughter on the other side of the sheets, but that's never been confirmed."

I said, "A lot of the shit that sticks to him seems to be sexual—the X-rated theaters and the prostitution and an affair, and yet he was a family man. He had this genius kid."

"He had two sons," Jack reminded me. "Milos was a chip off the block. Followed his father into the family businesses, until the day he died of 'food poisoning.'" He put finger quotes around the words.

"You think he was murdered?"

"Seems likely," Jack said. "The kid was a piece of work. I guess Adrian was different. If you read his obituary, you'd know more about him than I do. Adrian never comes up much in conversations about his father. He certainly didn't go into the family business. I think they were estranged."

Nidia had said as much in our one conversation about him.

"Is his wife still alive? No, she's not," I said, remembering Adrian's obit. "Not a very long-lived family, are they?"

Jack shook his head. "The funny thing is, though, Tony Skouras was never a good bet to outlive his wife, much less both sons. He had heart trouble and had undergone major bypass surgery four years ago. It wasn't supposed to be a real long-term fix," he said. "People keep expecting this guy to drop in his tracks, but it never happens. He's a survivor. He just goes on and on."

I couldn't think of anything else I needed to ask. So I said, "You want some coffee?"

We went back to the cafeteria line and bought some, Jack stirring his a little too much, with the random gestures of a smoker who'd rather be outside having a cigarette. Then he asked the question I'd been expecting: "So, what's your interest in Tony Skouras?"

"Sorry," I said, "I can't talk about it."

"Yeah, I knew you were going to say that," Jack said.

I'd expected him to dig, and said as much. "That's it? You're satisfied with that?"

"I don't think it's going to help me any to be dissatisfied."

"I thought all reporters refused to take no for an answer."

"Are you kidding? We hear no all the time," Jack said. "And you're thinking of the Hollywood version of journalism, where a reporter hears a hot tip one day and two days later there's a big story splashed across A1. Real investigative journalism takes time. It takes slow circling around your subject, Freedom of Information Act requests, compiling and synthesizing of information. It doesn't happen overnight."

I wasn't sure what he was telling me. "You're saying that after today you're going to look a bit harder at Skouras?"

"People are always looking at Skouras," he said. "But since you're feeling guilty, throw me a bone. Answer just one question, totally unrelated to the rest of this."

"No, you had your chance," I said. "You already traded your information for a free lunch. Too late to change the deal now."

"You sure that's all the information you're going to need? You don't have to stay in my good graces in case of follow-ups?" He cocked an eyebrow.

"Fine," I said, making my voice sound more impatient than I really felt. "One question."

"The school you went to back east, the one that didn't work out, was that Annapolis or West Point?"

"I . . . yes. How the hell did you know that?"

He'd turned serious. "I observe people, Hailey. I always knew you were something more than you let on. So it made sense that the school wasn't any State U. But at the same time, I didn't get Ivy League vibes. That left one of the military academies."

I nodded. "It was West Point."

"Why didn't you finish?"

"I almost did."

"Maybe you'll tell me about that someday."

"No. Sorry," I said. "I just don't talk about that. Don't take it personally."

That afternoon, I called Serena to tell her what I'd learned. When I was done, she said, "You're thinking that the guys in the tunnel were gangsters."

"It makes sense," I said. "They were obviously well-funded and disciplined."

"So it sounds like you shoulda searched Nidia's suitcase," said Serena. "She took something from that rich guy."

"Not exactly," I said. "Think about it: If they just wanted an object, they'd have taken it from the car, shot her, and left her where they left me." I smiled, though she couldn't see my face. "She had something, though."

"Stop giving me an IQ test over the phone and tell me what it was."

"Something that belonged to her and Adrian both," I added.

There was a brief silence on the line. Then Serena said, "No way, *prima*. She was still getting over her boyfriend dying."

"Grief in itself can make people do funny things," I said. "I'm not saying she fell in love with Adrian, but there was something between them. She got a little weepy talking about his death. I thought it was because it reminded her of her fiancé. And she was thin except for her belly, and she was nursing ginger ale a lot in the car, to settle her stomach. Pregnancy makes women more prone to nausea. Not just in the morning, but anytime. None of this registered with me then, because I was used to thinking of her in a certain light, as a virgin-slash-war-widow, since the first time I heard her name."

"Say you're right," Serena said. "How would the grandfather find out, if he and his son didn't talk?"

"Fathers and sons tend to talk over deathbeds," I said. "Probably Adrian asked his father to take care of Nidia and the baby financially. A guy like Tony Skouras would probably react in one of two ways to that kind of news. Either he'd be appalled at the thought of having a half-Mexican grandchild and refuse to acknowledge Nidia's baby at all, or he'd embrace the fact that this is the only grandchild he'd ever have, and want full control of its upbringing. He doesn't strike me as the type to write support checks and let his grandchild be raised Mexican in working-class Mexican neighborhoods."

"Damn," Serena said. "All that for a kid? Most of the guys I know run away from their responsibility to a baby."

"This is a lot different," I said. "Skouras isn't just trying to build a fortune, he's been trying to build up his family again, after the troubles in his homeland. Everything that Skouras has amassed, the money and influence—what's the point if it all just disperses into the hands of strangers?" I paused. "That explains why he took the full-control route. He must have told Nidia he wanted his grandkid, and she freaked and ran away. We know the rest. In a way, this is good news. Because if Skouras wants the kid, then Nidia is still alive. She's only about six months' pregnant by now."

"Oh, God, she's living like . . . he's got her . . ."

"Don't trip," I said. "It's in his best interest to take care of her not just medically but psychologically. Trauma is very bad for pregnant women. He'd know that."

"Until she gives birth," Serena said. "Then what happens to her?"

"Well, he might feel that he's too powerful and she's too insignificant for her ever to get the American law to listen to her," I said. "Maybe he'll let her go."

Serena was doubtful. "Wouldn't it be safer for him just to kill her?"

"Yeah," I said. "It would."

twenty-four

Was there anything in my West Point training that could help me with the problem at hand? A criminal like Skouras wouldn't operate like a conventional military enemy. He'd be more like a terrorist. But the times being what they were, we'd studied a bit about counterterrorism in school.

Terrorists lived among the general population. They didn't wear uniforms. Sometimes you knew who they were but couldn't prove it. You could watch them, but their actions looked innocent on the surface, and their communications were carefully coded. You couldn't be sure who around them was a disciple and who was an innocent acquaintance. They attacked in small-scale but sometimes very deadly operations. They always needed money, and if you could disrupt their flow of funds badly enough, you could cripple their operation.

I knew how the Army would deal with a high-level terrorist: It would watch his home and track the movements of his vehicles with spy satellites capable of reading numbers off license plates. That didn't help me. That was the difference between being the United States Army and a twenty-four-year-old with one gun. If anyone was going to be crippled by dwindling funds, it was me.

I could try to watch Skouras, but I doubted that would lead me to Nidia. Surely she wasn't in his own home. It seemed unwise, in the first-place-anyone-would-look sense. And I just didn't think he'd want her around, no matter how many rooms his place had. Home was where a guy like Skouras went to ground. It was where he locked out his complicated world and poured himself a Macallan. He wasn't going to want a frightened teenage hostage in the next room.

Start over. You're going at this wrong. Imagine you're them, kidnapping Nidia. Start from the tunnel and go from there.

They shoot me, I lose consciousness and probably crash the Impala at a slow speed into the tunnel wall. They drag me out of the car, strip me of my ID, and take me outside the tunnel and shoot me, far enough off the road that no one is supposed to find me. That had been the important part of the story to me, but in terms of the kidnapping, it wasn't relevant. I hadn't been their objective. Nidia had been.

She might have been injured in the crash, though not badly. I hadn't had enough time to work up any speed. So assume she was basically all right, maybe dazed. Either she got out and tried to run, or they reached in and got her. They put her in one of the cars and drove away. They also drove the Impala away and disposed of it, probably in a river or a lake. Again, not important to the story. Where was Nidia at that point?

Getting a Mexican without papers across the border would have been difficult. Illegal Mexicans crossed the border all the time, of course. They simply walked across at unguarded, unobserved areas or were smuggled across in trucks allegedly carrying consumer goods. But Nidia wouldn't have been cooperative, and handling her roughly or drugging her would have been too risky; she was pregnant, and a healthy Skouras grandchild had been the point of the whole operation.

But Skouras had something better than a truck: He owned a shipping line. What if the tunnel rats had taken Nidia to a port and onto one of the Skouras cargo ships? They could have sailed her right to San Francisco. That made a lot of sense.

Whatever the logistics of getting Nidia where she was going, Skouras would then have to have someplace fairly private to keep her. That was most likely a second home or a vacation home, which could be almost anywhere. Once they had her safely there, the rest would be easy. It wouldn't take more than one guard to keep her in line, maybe a second to relieve the first one from time to time, and to keep him company. Other than that, Nidia would require only healthy food, some fresh air, maybe some prenatal vitamins, and—

I sat up. I'd been thinking, an occasional checkup from a doctor, but how were they going to work that? They couldn't just take a kidnap victim into town to sit around in a doctor's waiting room. I drummed my fingers against my thigh, thinking.

Like everyone else, I'd heard casual references in movies to "Mob doctors," but those films were never quite clear on where those guys came from. They were just there, available at any hour of the night, corrupt and unconcerned about whom they worked for. Or they couldn't have a conventional practice, because they'd never finished med school or been barred from practicing.

I thought about that a moment longer. Maybe I'd just found a way in.

twenty-five

An hour later, I was waiting at a bus shelter for a MUNI bus over to UCSF medical school. It was a little before six in the evening, the going-home hour, and several other people waited with me. Others moved around us in a thin but steady stream.

I wasn't sure whether the medical library would be open to the general population, or exactly what data base or archives I needed to ask for, but if somehow I could find a listing of doctors who'd been barred from practicing medicine in San Francisco in the past several years, I might find doctors who would be open to an overture from Skouras.

My theory was that Skouras would feel most comfortable reaching out to a man. No matter how ruthless he was, I didn't believe he'd ask a woman to help him use a powerless teenager as an incubator. So if I was right about that, it would narrow the field of candidates some. There weren't as many men practicing obstetrics as there used to be; it was an area increasingly dominated by women. A male ob/gyn who'd been suspended or expelled from the profession: That just might be a narrow enough bottleneck that I could catch the right suspect there.

In addition, a doctor with a prescription-drug problem, once separated from his supply, might quickly need money. That'd be an extra incentive to get in bed with someone like Skouras.

I was theorizing wildly and I knew it. This kind of work was uncharted territory for me. Not to mention the fact that all of this depended on my initial premise being correct: that Nidia was pregnant with a Skouras baby. This bordered on pointless.

The bus was approaching, but now I was undecided. As the people around me began to move into boarding position, I stayed back and glanced away, then stepped directly into the path of a well-built, nicely dressed man, who happened to be the lead gunman from the tunnel, the one I'd called Babyface.

When he saw me, surprise rippled clearly across his face and his steps faltered. Then a mask of normalcy fell over his face. He was very good. All this took maybe two seconds.

The bus opened its doors with a pneumatic hiss, and a section of the *Chronicle* skated around my feet. As if nothing had happened, I turned my attention away from him and stepped up, onto the bus. I'd been distracted enough that I didn't have the fare ready, and it took me a moment of rummaging in my messenger bag to find the coins inside.

I paid and moved down the aisle. Behind me, I heard someone else dropping coins into the fare box. I didn't look back but kept going until I found a seat close to the back of the bus.

When I was seated and looked up, Babyface was standing over me.

"Hailey?" he said. "That's your name, right? We met in Texas, remember?" He was looking at me with that same half-benign curiosity in his heavy-lidded eyes that he'd shown in the tunnel.

"Yeah," I said. "Hailey Cain."

I wasn't telling him anything he didn't know. Clearly, he and his guys had looked through the personal items they'd taken off me down in the tunnel.

"You mind if I sit down?" Without waiting for an answer, he slid down into the seat, forcing me to move over.

He was wearing a leather bomber jacket over a cream-colored shirt, dark trousers, good shoes, but no tie, no briefcase or PDA. It would have been hard to say what his line of work was or where he was coming from.

He said, "I wasn't expecting to run into you here. I thought you lived, what, in Los Angeles?"

I understood where he'd gotten that idea: The driver's license he and his guys took off me in Mexico had my old L.A. address on it. But we both knew the truth: Babyface hadn't been expecting to run into me anywhere aboveground.

"I do," I said. "I'm just up here for a few days."

We were playing a game. I wasn't sure what it was. But he hadn't been shadowing me. I'd seen surprise clearly on his face, however briefly, when he first caught sight of me. Had he been shadowing me, intending to kill or even seriously question me, he would have waited to get me someplace private. I didn't think Babyface had any idea of what I was doing in San Francisco. He'd seen me on the street, his curiosity was provoked, he'd followed me to satisfy it. This was plainview reconnaissance, the kind you did with an enemy so inferior that you had no fear of it. That was how he saw me, as no threat.

That was how I wanted to keep it, then. Sometimes you have to swallow your pride and get away clean.

I spoke softly. "I don't know what happened to Nidia, and I don't care." I hunched my shoulders slightly, trying to project fear. "All I want is to forget about it. Every night I feel guilty, wondering why I came home alive and she didn't."

"You don't need to feel guilty about that," he said. "You're just a kid who got mixed up in something a lot bigger than you realized."

I nodded and stared straight ahead, at the grab bar on the seat in front of me.

Babyface's voice was almost kind as he said, "If you forget all about this, you're going to live a long and happy life, Hailey." He took my hand, squeezing it as if to comfort me.

I nodded again.

"Well, this is my stop."

It wasn't his stop. But now his curiosity was satisfied.

Babyface said, "One thing, though. One of my guys couldn't get out of the way of your car in time."

In my mind's eye I saw the Mexican tunnel, how two men had been almost directly in my path as I floored the Impala's gas pedal.

Babyface took my little finger between two of his and said, "He's never going to walk right again."

Then he did something quick and efficient with his hand, and I both heard and felt bone crack as he broke my little finger.

twenty-six

"I need to get out of the city," I told Serena. "It's gotten too hot up here."

It was around ten in the evening. I was sitting on the bed, holding the cell phone in my uninjured hand. My broken finger was splinted to its neighbor, the left ring finger.

The splint wasn't a doctor's handiwork; I hadn't gone to the ER. After Babyface had gotten up and walked to the exit door, I'd stayed where I was sitting, bent over with pain, feeling the aftershock ringing up the bones of my hand and past my wrist. If anyone around me understood what had just happened—and believe me, I'd made noise when the bone snapped, a sound between a yelp and a short scream—they were determinedly refusing to show it. Rule number one of city life: Don't Get Involved.

Then, as if nothing had happened, I spent an hour and a half fruitlessly looking through Medical Board of California newsletters for the thumbnail reports on disciplinary actions against doctors. Finally the pain got distracting enough that I went home, found Aries's first-aid kit, and splinted my finger the best I could. I would have liked something stronger than Advil for the pain but didn't have access to it.

Serena said, "You're coming back to L.A.?"

"I ran into one of Skouras's guys today," I said. "The head gunny. Now he knows I'm alive and in San Francisco."

"He recognized you?"

"More than. He broke my finger."

"Jesus, Hailey," Serena said.

Had Babyface guessed that what I said about being "up for a few days" was bullshit? Did he truly believe I was as frightened and harmless as I'd acted? If he didn't, I had a problem. San Francisco wasn't a big city. Forty-nine square miles wasn't a lot when you had to share it with someone who'd already tried to kill you once.

Serena said, "I thought you didn't like being in L.A. Because of you-know-who."

"I don't," I said, "but it's been a year, and besides, where you live is pretty far from Marsellus's L.A."

Even so, I thought grimly that, having exiled myself from L.A. a year ago, now I was making deadly enemies in the north, too. Not wise. There was always Oregon and Washington, but they weren't for girls like me. I could never learn to walk in Birkenstocks.

"Well, you know my place. There's always room for one more girl on the run," Serena said. "But what're you going to do once you get down here?"

"Research," I said. "I think that trying to find Nidia through Skouras's real-estate holdings is the best prospect. He's got to be hiding her somewhere."

"You'll figure it out," Serena said. "I don't know how you learned to do this shit, *prima*. I can't think of anyone else I know who could have done what you've done."

"The thing is . . ."

"What?"

"I can't do this alone," I said. "If I find Nidia, there's going to have to be a rescue mission. I can't go in single-handedly." I paused. "Skouras's men are like soldiers. Criminals, but soldiers. I need the same kind of guys on my side, guys who don't scare easy and can shoot."

"You want El Trece," Serena said.

"Nothing against your sucias, but this is out of their league," I said. "Yeah, I need your homeboys. I hate to ask, Serena. This will be dangerous."

"I know."

"And they won't do it for me, a white stranger. I need you to ask on my behalf."

She was silent so long that I thought she was going to say no. Then she said, "It is a big thing, and I'll ask it for you, but there's something I want from you in return."

"Anything I can do, I will."

"Take your beating. Get jumped in."

This was her old tease, about me becoming one of her *sucias*. Except this time her tone left no doubt that she was serious.

"Serena," I said. "We've had this conversation before. There's too many white people out there already trying to be something they're not. I won't join them."

"That's not what this is," she said. "It's symbolic. You want me to go to the guys and ask them to ride on a mission with you, first you gotta be blood."

"That's my point. I'll never really be one of you."

"You'll always be different," she said. "But I'm different, too. How many girls shave their heads, put in work like a guy? What made me different let me become a leader."

"But—"

"But nothing. You're always saying you'll never really be one of us, but you know how often white people tell people like me to act white, to assimilate? They know we'll never really be one of them, but if we want the good job, the big house, we're always getting asked to make the effort. Why is it different when I ask you to make the effort?"

I stretched out on the bed and didn't say anything.

"I won't ask that much of you, either, afterward," she said. "I know you're never gonna steal cars for me and then kick it in my living room with my girls. But you want my help, that's my price."

There was an interesting correlation in Latin. The noun for close relative or good friend was *necessarius*. The same word, as an adjective, meant *unavoidable*. Family and obligation had been inseparable in the Roman mind. That's what this was about: Serena was my *necessaria*.

In other words, home is the place where, when you have to go there, they have to beat you up.

"All right," I said. "Yeah, okay. I will."

Part III

twenty-seven

A Saturday night, after dark, Serena driving us east of the city, to a small ranch property where my initiation was to take place. The landscape around us was dry grass, pale almost to whiteness in the light of the full moon. The poles of power lines were dark silhouettes against the deep cornflower of the sky.

Gravel crunched as we pulled into a long driveway. Up ahead was a low, one-story house, and around us were split-rail fences, delineating paddocks, but I could see no livestock in them.

"Who lives here?" I asked.

"Risky's *tio*, Sergio. He's not here right now," Serena said. "So we can use it."

She pulled around back, parking in front of a small paddock with tubular metal railings instead of wood. The gate was held open by chain wrapped tightly to the nearest post. Inside, the dirt was hard and packed, dust stirring a little in the air displaced by the car's approach.

Serena cut the lights, but we didn't get out of the car yet. We were early.

She said, "They'll be here soon."

I nodded.

"You want a drink? I've got a bottle of vodka in my bag."

"No. Maybe after."

She'd offered me the choice: Fight one of the guys from Trece, or get jumped in the more popular way, by being beaten by her girls as a group. There was supposed to be a third option, fighting Serena herself, but we'd both known that wasn't going to happen. If I won in front of her girls, she'd lose too much face.

139

A few more moments of silence passed before we saw lights on the road, traveling toward us like a comet or a meteor. The car turned down the driveway and resolved into an old Buick.

More cars were pulling in now. Thug cars: an old Monte Carlo, an Oldsmobile, a Chevy Cavalier. Then an Econoline van. With a slamming of doors and a mixed chatter of Spanish and English, the sucias acknowledged Serena, throwing up their signs to her.

Then I noticed that there were guys from El Trece present as well. It wasn't typical for them to take interest in a girls' initiation, but this was different. This was Warchild's old friend La Rubia, the one who'd nearly become a soldier. This was, even for the guys, an event worth watching.

I shucked off my hooded jacket and began to walk in a circle the way I used to do before fights, rolling my shoulders, ignoring the guys who were watching me. I needed to loosen up. I wasn't just here to get beaten. I was expected to fight back, to prove my mettle. I would honor the gang by striking back at my sisters-to-be, our shared wounds creating a bond between us.

Blood makes the grass grow, drilling soldiers used to chant.

Hitting back was going to hurt my not-yet-healed little finger, of course. I'd wrapped it and the ring finger with extra tape, but that wouldn't help much. The impacts would do fresh damage. That's why they call it the *vida loca.* Once you've committed to it, lots of things you do don't make sense.

"You ready, Hailey?"

Serena's voice brought me back to myself. I looked over and saw that seven, no, eight girls had crowded into the paddock and were waiting in a rough semicircle. Several others had climbed up to sit on the railing and watch. The young men leaned against the fence like farmhands. The one closest to the gate was smoking a cigarette. Its red eye glowed as he dragged on it. He stared at me openly, without animosity, but without any sympathy, either.

I walked into the paddock. Had this been a true multiple-assailant attack, my instinct would have been to get the paddock railing against my back. But in an initiation, that could be interpreted as cowardice, so I walked right into the center. The girls moved around me as I advanced, making the semicircle into a circle.

I had technique on my side, but eight was too many. I was going to sustain damage.

They had stripped off unnecessary clothes, like I had. They wore sports bras and strappy tank shirts or loose V-neck undershirts. They had taken off their earrings, but a few had heavy, chunky metal rings. Those were going to hurt.

Trippy was among them, of course. But also Heartbreaker, who I'd thought might stay out of it to protect her good looks, and little Risky, too. Other girls I didn't recognize. All of them had faces like hard masks, appraising me from under heavy bluish eyeliner. Serena alone, outside the pen, was looking at me like she was on my side.

She nodded at me, and I nodded back. Ready.

Serena said to her girls, "Go."

There's no way to describe something like that unless you've been through it: bright stars exploding in the periphery of your vision, your vision itself shaking like an old filmstrip coming off the reel. You feel impact more than pain. The pain follows.

For a few seconds, I didn't know how long, I was all right, rolling with it, striking back as best I could. But I'd known eight was too many. One of the girls landed a blow on my nose. I felt the nasal passages swell instantly, then tasted blood in the back of my throat. I fell to one knee, hands up to protect my head. It was instinct.

That's the lie referees always have to say, in the ring: *Protect yourself at all times*. It's a lie because you can't. You came to fight. If you were really interested in protecting yourself, you'd get out of the ring and go home.

The sucias had closed in, raining blows.

Hailey, do not protect yourself. Get up. Fight back.

I shot for the legs of the nearest girl and successfully took her down. There was a mixed sound of surprise—you don't see a lot of wrestling moves in these kind of fights. It bought me enough space to get to my feet. I no longer cared that I was outnumbered. I wanted to do damage.

There was howling and yelling all around me as we engaged. From the girls who were fighting. From above, the spectators on the railing.

Then the gunshot echoed into the night, and we all went still.

"I said, That's *enough*." Serena's voice, calm. Her nine-millimeter was smoking. She'd fired into the air to make us stop.

It was as if we'd all been awakened from a dream. It seemed to take Heartbreaker a second to realize that she was holding on to a fistful of my hair and to let go.

I didn't remember dropping to my knees, but the girls were extending their hands to me, lifting me up. "Stand up, Rubia," one of them said, and there was no mockery in the old nickname.

Serena jumped off the fence and the girls parted to let her through. I fell onto her neck and we embraced.

"You did good, *prima,*" she whispered.

I'd hit one of the sucias, the fat girl with permed hair, hard enough to make her nose bleed, like mine was. She wiped it gingerly with the back of her hand. Then, sounding totally unconcerned, she said, "We need to party."

All in a day's work.

Fifteen minutes later, I was in Tio Sergio's living room, sitting on the couch with a beer in one hand and a cigarette in the other. Throbbing beats from the sound system filled the air. Some of the girls and guys were dancing. Others were in small knots, talking.

To my surprise, the girls who'd looked at me so coldly before the initiation now wanted to know if they'd hit hard enough. Maybe it really had sunk in when Serena had told them about West Point and my boxing there. Now they wanted reassurance that they measured up. I wasn't kidding when I reassured them that they did. I could already see the terra-cotta-colored marks where bruises would be by morning. Plus, I kept rubbing my collarbone where one of the girls, who obviously knew a thing or two about fights, had jammed her thumb down into the tender underside of the bone and squeezed. There's no fat there to protect you. It hurts like hell.

Serena came over, holding a forty-ounce, and leaned over me casually. "Come on, Sig's going to do your ink." She tipped her head toward a doorway. "In the bedroom."

"Are we going to give her her name?" Risky asked, sounding excited.

Whatever you called it—gang name, street name, moniker—you didn't pick it out yourself. It was chosen for you, based on some facet of your personality.

Serena smiled, indulgent. "It's already decided, thanks."

Risky settled back into the couch cushions with a small frown, like she'd been left out of naming a new pet. I picked up my beer and followed Serena into the bedroom, which was blessedly dimmer and quieter.

Sigmundo, or Sig, was familiar to me from Serena's neighborhood, a paraplegic with a racing-style chair with the wheels canted inward for stability. He was artistic before his shooting, a tagger as well as a banger. Afterward, graffiti wasn't much of an option; good wall art requires a certain amount of flexibility, as well as an ability to flee venues ahead of angry property owners and patrolling cops. Sig's days of sprinting down backstreets and jumping fences were over.

His work with the needle, though, was much in demand. I knew it was a gift to me that Serena had gotten him here.

"Thank you for coming," I said.

Sigmundo merely nodded. "You can lie down on the bed," he said, indicating the queen-size bed with a cheap chenille spread. "Where do you want it, anyway?"

"Um, lower back, I guess," I said. My lower back had remained unscathed in the initiation, and there the tattoo would remain mostly out of sight.

Serena hoisted herself to sit cross-legged on the bureau, then spooned partially frozen pineapple juice concentrate into a half-full pint bottle of vodka.

I lay down on the bed and pulled my T-shirt up to expose my back, listening to the sounds of Sig's prep work and the gurgle of Serena's vodka bottle. I felt very peaceful. Tomorrow I would be hurting, but for now, the post-battle endorphins were flowing, giving me the feeling that all was well.

"So?" Sig was saying, not to me but to Serena. "What am I doing?"

Serena got up and handed him a folded slip of paper. He opened the fold and looked at the word she'd written. "Okay," he said.

Serena smiled, dazzlingly, at me. "You trust me, right?"

"Right," I said.

The truth was more complicated. Who knew what Serena was thinking? It seemed likely that she'd chosen something Latin. She hadn't whispered it to Sig, she'd *shown* it to him, suggesting that he'd needed to see the spelling. What troubled me about that was the possibility Serena had chosen a name that defined me only in relation to her—*gladia*, for example, or *dextra*, which meant "right hand." I was just proud enough to have my own loss-of-face issues about that.

But it'd be another breach of etiquette to speak up now and make sure that she hadn't. So I was going to trust her.

Sig began to prep me, tracing the letters of the pattern with his pen. I half tried to pay attention and figure them out but couldn't.

The needle's buzzing filled the air, not loud but pervasive. I rested my head on my forearm, eyes closed, barely flinching at the first pinpricks of sensation. After a moment, I got used to it, the needle nibbling away at my old identity to make room for a new one.

When he was done, Serena got off her perch and walked over, looking down at Sig's handiwork. "Nice," she said. "I like it. You want to see, Hailey?" She tilted her head toward the bathroom.

I got to my feet and followed. The bathroom was small and narrow, and the mirror was a small one, high over the sink. Serena handed me a ladies' mirror, the round kind with a pearlized plastic handle, because only in the second reflection would the tattoo be in readable order, left to right. Holding the mirror, I turned and looked over my shoulder. No good. The mirror was still too high, and I was too close to it. I moved awkwardly forward, until I was standing over the toilet, legs wide. I said, "I guess it wouldn't have killed me to have this done someplace more readable, like on my arm."

"It's good where it is," Serena said. "Where it is, no one has to see it and hassle you about it, if you don't want that."

In the wall mirror, I could see the ash-gray Old English lettering, and so I held the hand mirror by my hip and tilted it until the letters came into view.

"Oh," I said.

I'd guessed it was Latin. I hadn't guessed this.

The new name Serena had chosen for me was Insula, Latin for *island*.

"Are you surprised?" She was looking closely at my face with an uncertain expression I'd rarely seen on her.

"A little," I said.

"I know it's funny, because this whole thing, getting jumped in, was about you becoming part of something," she said, "but *insula*, that's who you are. Even way back, when you were studying Latin while everyone else was doing Spanish and French, thinking about West Point—you were the only one of us who thought she was meant for something different, and that's a lonely thing." She paused, then smiled. "Did you think I was going to put something like 'Fearless' on you?"

I shook my head.

"So you like it?" she pressed.

"I do," I said.

In the bedroom again, Sig gave me a salve to rub on the tattoo for the next few days. Then Serena poured me some vodka and pineapple juice in a plastic cup, and I knew the toast she was going to make before she spoke.

"*Como vivimos?*" she asked me.

"*Ad limina fortunarum,*" I answered.

We'd invented that one, half Spanish and half Latin. *How do we live? To the limits of our fates.* It meant that we were going to push our luck, to live until fortune said it was time to die.

twenty-eight

We were going to see Payaso, the leader of El Trece.

He lived about six houses away from Serena. That surprised me at first, then I felt stupid for being surprised. Their name, Trece, meant 13th Street. It wasn't as if he'd live across town.

Serena was wearing a trench-length down coat in a shimmering gunmetal color, with fur trim on the hood. The weather outside wasn't cool enough to justify it, but she looked great, every inch the gangster. I'd borrowed a scuffed leather jacket, which, along with my boots, made me look like a young aspiring biker. I'd woken up this afternoon stiff from the beating, but I'd limbered up okay since, and I hadn't put any makeup on the bruises; they were part of my credentials.

It was a day after my initiation, a little before eight in the evening. The sky was overcast, the low ceiling limned with bright peach from the reflected streetlights. Serena and I crossed 13th Street, her strides long, her coat rippling around her calves. She began to coach me for the meeting.

"Payaso's interested in you," she told me. "Mostly because of West Point. I told him about that."

I nodded.

"If he offers you anything, a beer or a cigarette or a joint, accept it," she said. "That's hospitality around here. To refuse is rude."

"I know."

"When you talk to him, don't front and try to act real tough," she went on. "Don't be a shrinking violet, either. Act like you respect yourself, but that's all. And, this is important, if he plays with you"—she meant if he made a joke at my expense—"and you think of a comeback, don't say it. He's the man. Let him feel like the man. But don't flirt with him, either. You're here for business."

We were on the sidewalk in front of his house, where we'd stopped so she could finish her thoughts.

"He's not a bad guy, and I think he knows that you're more qualified to lead the mission than he is. What I'm saying is, when the time comes, Payaso will let you lead, if you act respectful of him. If you front, he's gonna have to front, and that's not gonna be good for anyone."

"I understand."

"Okay."

We went up the walk. There was a metal port in the door, like from a Prohibition speakeasy.

"Damn," I said, impressed.

"Yeah," Serena said. "Old Payaso read about these things somewhere and decided he had to have one."

She'd explained "Old Payaso" to me earlier. The Payaso we were coming to see wasn't the one who'd led Trece when Serena joined at fifteen. That had been the former Payaso, who'd shared his moniker with a promising fourteen-year-old. Sharing the name hadn't made Lil'Payaso first in line to take over, but when Payaso was shot to death by rivals, Lil'Payaso became just Payaso, and in time he fought to lead Trece and won.

A skinny, shaven-headed boy pulled back the port, saw Serena, and nodded. He closed the port, and a bolt slid back.

"Not a lot of protection from gunfire to the face, that thing," I said.

"Not for him," Serena agreed.

The inside of the house wasn't substantially different from Serena's. There was a low throb of music and a pervasive scent of cigarette smoke, and about six or seven homeboys lounging in the living room. A pit bull barked once, not really interested.

The only surprise was that I wasn't the only white person there. A red-haired teenager was on the couch, in the arms of one of the boys.

Her hair was braided in a complicated way up over her head, and her shirt was open nearly to the waist, revealing a lacy blue bra. It apparently served like a tank top or camisole; she seemed to feel no modesty about revealing it in front of a roomful of guys.

I didn't need to be told which one was Payaso. For one thing, the name was tattooed high on his pectoral muscle, which was laid bare by his wifebeater shirt. It was also implicit in the grouping of guys around him, the way they loosely surrounded and faced him. He didn't look tall, maybe five-nine, but he had good muscle, like a fighter. When he saw us walk into the living room, he nodded to the white girl on the couch. "Go kick it with Mel and Jaime for a while," he said to her. "We're gonna talk some business."

The girl got up without argument, though she looked at me with veiled curiosity before disappearing into one of the bedrooms. I wondered if it was my white skin or the bruises from my initiation that she found more curious. I wondered if she thought I let a man give them to me.

There was a small reshuffling as a place was made for Serena among the guys. I could already see where I was supposed to sit, in a straight-backed chair that had clearly been borrowed from a dining table and which faced Payaso directly, job-interview style. I took my place and let him look at me.

"*Trece eres?*" he asked. Loosely translated, *Are you one of us?*

"*Por vida,*" I said. *For life.*

Payaso pulled an exaggerated face of skepticism, his long, mobile mouth turning down, but with a trace of amusement. "Funny, I ain't seen you around the neighborhood," he said.

"I know."

His eyes flashed with humor. "I'm just playing with you," he said. "I know who you are. You're the famous Hailey."

"I doubt I'm famous."

"Warchild used to talk about you, not just recently, but a long time back. Talking about how you used to jump outta airplanes for the Army, shit like that, saying how tough you were."

This was news to me. I disciplined myself not to look back at her in surprise.

Payaso said, "You want something to drink?" He looked at the boy who'd answered the door. "Get her something. Warchild, too."

"I'm cool," Serena said. Apparently, her status with Payaso was such that it was acceptable for her to turn down hospitality.

When the boy came back with a Coors for me, Payaso said, "Warchild tells me they just initiated you last night."

I nodded.

"Yeah, you got some marks on you," he said, and smiled. "I bet you didn't know Latin girls were so tough, eh?"

I shook my head modestly. Actually, I had expected a good beat-down from Serena's sucias, but Payaso wanted to brag on his home-girls, and I wanted to let him.

He said, "So now you're In-*soo*-la," exaggerating the second syllable. "What kind of name is that?"

"Latin," I said.

"You really speak that?"

"Mostly," I said. "I couldn't get a job translating or anything."

"There's jobs translating Latin? I thought it was a dead language."

"It is," I said, "but scholars are still doing new translations of the classic poems."

"Why do people translate things that have already been translated? What's the point?" he said.

I said, "The same reason that bands cover songs that someone else has recorded, I guess. To put their own spin on it."

He nodded thoughtfully. His homeboys were all watching and listening. I wondered if they really found this interesting, or if it was their way of showing Payaso respect, pretending to be absorbed in everything he found interesting.

Payaso said, "So what's my name in Latin?"

"Fossor," I said, for *clown, jokester.*

"Fossor?" He frowned exaggeratedly again. It was easy to see where he got his moniker; he did have mobile, clownish features, with intelligence underneath them.

I said, "Sorry. It does sound better in Spanish. Latin isn't as pretty a language as a lot of people think. It can make a lot of things sound like an STD."

His guys laughed.

"You were at West Point, too," he said.

"Yes."

"What's that like?"

"Hard," I said, "but like a lot of things, if you work hard and respect the underlying ideals, people respect you. It's rigorous in a lot of ways: academically and physically and psychologically. A lot of people don't make it. Including me."

This was risky. If he wanted to know why I washed out, he'd ask now, and I didn't know if I could refuse him. And if I did tell him the answer, I didn't know how he'd feel about it.

But he just said, "They got a lot of girls there? Are the guys cool with that?"

"Most guys are," I said.

"What about guys like me? Does West Point take *vatos*?"

"I don't know if I'd call them *vatos*," I said. "They take Latinos, if they're as square as I used to be."

Payaso lit a cigarette, not offering me one. He took a drag, held it, and exhaled at length. Then his face changed, turning serious. I didn't have to be told it was time for business.

He said, "So tell me about the shit that went down in Mexico."

I told him the story. Fast through the part I knew Serena had told him already, about Lara and the arrangements to take Nidia to Mexico. More detailed on the things only I witnessed, like the ambush in the tunnel, and my run-in with Babyface up in San Francisco. Briefly, I talked about what lay ahead, getting Nidia back. In doing so, I salted the conversation with words from my military background, calling the information-gathering I was doing *intel* and a prospective mission against Skouras *asymmetric warfare*. I wasn't just playing to Payaso's earlier interest in West Point, but to every gangster's romantic conviction that his life was part of a war. It was no coincidence that most writing done on the Mafia, for example, referred to *lieutenants* and *foot soldiers*.

"These guys are serious," I said. "I told Serena and I'll tell you, this isn't going to be a walk in the park." Did that sound too authoritarian? I went on: "But I can't do it without the kind of backup that you can provide, guys who can shoot and don't scare easy."

"That's us," Payaso said, and his guys murmured agreement.

He stubbed out his cigarette. "All right, Insula, me and my homeboys are in. Whatever you need. Those guys are gonna learn they can't mess with a Mexican girl like that."

The guys around him nodded.

Payaso added, "But I'm gonna need to know what you're planning, though, the details of it."

I shrugged wryly. "As soon as I plan it," I said, "you'll be the first to know."

He stood up, and we shook hands, formally.

Then he looked at Serena. "Warchild," he said, "there's a car out in the driveway, a blue Volkswagen. Go drive it to Chato, to his shop."

*The car turned out to be a rather nice Passat with leather seats and a high-*end sound system. Somebody out there was missing this car in a way insurance didn't make up for.

"You don't have to go with me," Serena told me. "I can just take you home."

"It's okay," I said. "I'll go with you."

"You want to drive, then?" she asked, abruptly reversing position. "I'm getting a headache."

I'd worried about being dragged into sucia business, and here I was, volunteering for it. I didn't know exactly why, except that I'd felt bad for Serena, back in the house. I was used to seeing her among her sucias, the undisputed leader; I wasn't used to seeing her take orders. I'd known gang life was hierarchical, but I'd felt a twinge of distaste nonetheless.

I navigated her darkened neighborhood, then up onto the freeway. While I was merging into traffic, Serena flipped on the Passat's sound system. There was a CD in the drive, but I didn't notice the music until Serena said, "What the fuck are we listening to?" Alerted, I listened, and in a second recognized the song coming from the speakers: vintage Simon and Garfunkel, the lilting strains of "Feelin' Groovy."

Without waiting for an answer, Serena jabbed at the controls, replacing acoustic music with rap. "Who listens to that shit?" she said, lower-voiced but still irritable.

I didn't answer. It would be easy to dismiss Serena's outburst as ghetto monoculturalism, like a child rejecting a food she's never really tried, but I knew her better than that. What she was really saying about the song's easy, happy lyrics was not *Who listens to this?* but *Who lives like this? Who feels this way?* She didn't. Nobody she knew did.

After a moment, she spoke again. "You know what really bothers me?"

"What?"

"Payaso and his guys," she said. "I knew they weren't going to sign on to this for your sake, but they're not even doing it for me. They're doing it for her, Nidia, and they don't even know her. It's what she represents to them. The nice girl from the block, the sweet little *virgen*."

"But she isn't, not anymore," I pointed out. "She's pregnant, for God's sake."

"Yeah, now she's the madonna, or she might as well be," Serena said. I understood what she was saying. In the world Trece's guys lived in, there were nice girls, and then there were girls who let themselves be passed around. There really wasn't much in between. Someone like Nidia, who had slept with only one man, apparently for love—that was nearly as good as still being a virgin.

"It's messed up," Serena said. "I've done more for them than a girl like that ever will. I've lied to the cops and hidden their guns for them. And still, they wouldn't go to all this trouble for me. But they're doing it for *her*." She was just getting started. "Some little mousie, some little vic who thought that because she prays all the time that God was going to stop the traffic whenever she had to cross the street." She repeated, "It's messed up."

I said, "I wish you'd gotten in touch with this resentment a lot earlier. If you'd never asked me to take her to Mexico, I wouldn't have gotten shot."

Serena gave me such a sharp look that I nearly swerved the car.

"Kidding," I said hastily.

She shook her head. "That's why I'm doing this," she said. "I mean it, I'm doing this for *you*, Insula. Because you got shot, and that shit's got to get paid for. It's not about her."

"Okay," I said. "Relax, I believe you."

twenty-nine

Late that night, I was in bed with Serena, staring up into the dark, waiting to sleep.

A lot of people wouldn't have understood it, two adult women sharing a bed. But now I understood what Serena told me when I'd seen two of her sucias sleeping close together: Sleep was the most vulnerable time, and there was safety and comfort in numbers. My borrowed SIG was on the nightstand. Serena's Tec-9 was under the bed.

I knew she was straight, but I really couldn't have told you what Serena did for sex. During her adolescent years, when she'd shaved her head to run with Trece, she'd had to put away her sexuality for later, like female soldiers pack away dresses. Later, when she became the leader of the sucias, Serena had celebrated her new power by growing out her hair. But if she'd reclaimed her femininity, sex was still full of danger. An alliance with Payaso or any of the Trece homeboys, no matter how consensual, would have cost her dearly in respect. Gangbangers commonly referred to a girl "sexing" a guy. It was a term whose closest analog was *servicing*.

As for a boyfriend outside the gang culture, well, it wasn't like UCLA grad students in Chicano Studies were going to come by her house with flowers. Serena was a victim of the ways she'd exceeded the limitations around her. I thought of her as a *chola* in the truest sense of the word: someone who lived between two worlds.

"The girls were riding your bicycle a couple of days ago," Serena said. She meant the one I'd taken from the charity donations center, not the Motobecane, which was still in San Francisco.

"Risky tipped it over. They were all cracking up," she said. "It's funny to see them acting like kids."

"Kids," I repeated.

When we'd come in, I'd overheard Trippy talking to several of the homegirls. She'd seemed high—not pharmacologically, but on adrenaline—and I'd soon gotten the drift of what she was talking about. She was bragging about running into a girl from a rival *cliqua,* "some nothing hoodrat," and beating her until she'd cried and begged for it to stop. Trippy hadn't said that the girl's only crime had probably been being from the wrong neighborhood or flirting with the wrong guy, but that went without saying.

I rolled over onto my stomach and rested my head on my crossed arms. I didn't like Trippy and wouldn't have even if we hadn't had our dustup the last time I'd been staying here. I thought Serena had made a lousy choice in lieutenants, but that was an opinion I was going to keep to myself. I knew what Serena would tell me. She'd say that my kind of ethics were a luxury, that nice girls were eaten alive in her neighborhood, that Trippy and girls like her didn't get to go east to war school and learn the rules of engagement.

I changed the subject: "Listen, Serena, speaking of bikes and all, I can't keep doing what I'm doing on city buses and whatever. God knows, when we find Nidia, we're going to need a car to take her away in."

"You know Chato's always got a couple of cars," she said.

"Too dangerous," I said. "I'm not going to use this car for an hour or two and dump it. I'll need it long-term, and sooner or later, some patrolling cop or meter reader will run the plate. I can't afford to get arrested for driving a stolen car."

She said, "We've probably got a legit car around here you could use."

"True," I said, "but I'm thinking of something specific. I don't know if I can outrun Skouras's guys if it came to a chase, but I don't want to be in a four-banger, just in case. It's got to carry a couple of soldiers and, eventually, a pregnant girl, and reasonably comfortably.

It needs to be plain enough that I can do surveillance in it. And it can't be a speeding-ticket magnet for cops or a theft magnet for—"

"People like me?" Serena said archly. "So what you really need, then, is money."

"Yeah," I said. "This mission is gonna run up expenses that go beyond just the car."

"We can help; I told you that," she said. "Trece's got some *plata*."

"Not that much," I said. "You guys are living proof that crime barely pays."

"So what's your idea?" Serena said. "Gonna go to Bank of America? That's a loan program we could use around here. 'Whether you're starting a small business or starting a gang war, BofA is here to help.'"

I rolled over again, looking up speculatively at the ceiling. "That's not exactly what I have in mind."

thirty

LAX has a great energy: the constant flow of people whose lives are in motion, and, of course, the diversity. It's hard to think of anywhere else you see such a racial and economic mix of people. It's like a gigantic jury pool.

It was also a useful place for me to meet someone: accessible by public transportation and crowded enough for me to blend in. You'd think I'd chosen it as a place of meeting. I hadn't. Nonetheless, around four in the afternoon, I was sitting in a bar off a main concourse, people-watching, with an ice-choked Pepsi in front of me. I'd been there about fifteen minutes when I saw him: CJ, half a head taller than the people around him, wearing tight, wash-faded cords and a T-shirt with the classic picture of Che Guevara over the legend *I Have No Idea Who This Is*. He was carrying no bag, just his Dobro guitar in its case, and a small box wrapped in paper from the Sunday comics and a red self-adhesive bow, the artless way men wrap a birthday present. It had been CJ who chose our meeting place. His flight to New York left in fifty-five minutes.

"I like your shirt," I said, by way of greeting.

CJ said, "Funny, I was just about to say I liked yours. I think it's a healthy step in you moving on from your relationship with the Army."

Serena had loaned me a few things, but I was getting fond of the Navy T-shirt, which was why I was wearing it.

He set down his guitar. "I don't feel really great about you being in L.A. like this," he said, sliding onto the opposite stool.

"This isn't even L.A.," I said. "And I'm pretty sure someone like Marsellus travels by private plane."

"People think someone like me travels by private plane," CJ said, "yet here I am."

I said, "I doubt you're even going first class, dressed like that."

"First class is a waste of money," he said dismissively. "I just want to get there; I don't need my ass kissed."

"Maybe," I said, "though I'd expect you could use the extra legroom. Speaking of, isn't your guitar too long for a carry-on?"

"I always clear it with the airline in advance," he said. "If they lose my bag, that's no big deal. I wear the same thing two days running—people just assume I went home with a girl and never got back to my room to change. But I lose this"—he nodded at the guitar case—"then we have a problem. I promised some people I'd play for them."

At that moment, the cocktail waitress approached. "What can I get you to drink today?" she asked him.

CJ shook his head. "Nothing, thanks. I'm not staying."

She said, "Are you sure? It'd take me no time to bring out a Rolling Rock, or mix up something."

Women loved to get things for CJ. And because I didn't want to see him leave quickly, either, I said, "How did you know? He *loves* Rolling Rock."

She smiled at me as though we were co-conspirators and went back to the bar.

CJ said, "You want me to miss my flight?"

"I didn't notice you telling her that if you wanted your ass kissed, you'd go first class."

He gave me a look and said, "Someday I'll understand why asking favors and having them granted actually makes you meaner instead of nicer," putting the newspaper-wrapped, ribboned box on the table between us.

I glanced down, gently shamed by the sight of it. "CJ, I—"

Then the waitress, true to her word, came back with the Rolling Rock. She noticed the box. "Somebody got a present."

"Yeah," I said.

"Lucky you," she said, and walked away, CJ watching the swing of her hips as she went.

I tried again: "Listen, I don't know how to thank you for this. I'll probably be years repaying you." *If I'm alive to do it.* "You don't even want to know what it's for?"

"That isn't a lot of money for me," he said. "And I know things have been tough for you."

It was best to let him think I'd let debts pile up, so I didn't say anything to that.

He drank a little Rolling Rock and then said, "I'm sorry I haven't been up to see you."

I shrugged. "It's okay."

I saw it in his pale eyes, that he was weighing his next words. Then he said, "You should know . . . Marsellus's wife left him."

I raised my eyebrows.

"Or he asked her to move out, I don't know," CJ went on. "I just thought you'd want to know. I'm not saying it's anything to do with Trey. Marriages fail for a lot of reasons."

"I know," I said.

But my voice must have sounded leaden, because I saw the sympathy in his gaze as he spoke again. "Hailey, we've talked about this," he said. "That boy's death—"

"Is something I'm supposed to feel bad about, fault or no fault," I interrupted. "That's not being morbid, CJ. It's being human."

"You're right," he said after a moment. "I get it. I do." Then: "I just wish things were like they used to be."

I nodded.

"Hailey," he said, "the other thing is, it's not like I want you even farther away, but there are cities a good deal farther away from Marsellus. Places where you could live more out in the open."

"Like where? Wichita?"

"Well, probably not New York or Miami, those are places that Marsellus and his associates travel to. But I always figured someone like you would do great in Alaska. Or down on the Gulf Coast."

"Doing what?"

"I'd loan you a little money if you wanted to start a bar. Someplace on the water. You'd never have to pay me back, as long as I could drink there for free, and you learn to cook something Cajun for me when I come down."

It sounded like paradise, except it was two thousand miles from L.A. and my God-given brother and sister. In that regard, it was purgatory, just like everywhere else. I said, "I can't cook for shit."

"For crying out loud, you can learn. Hailey, you're twenty-four, you have all the time in the world."

I didn't mean to wince at that, but I guess I did, because he said, "What?"

"Nothing," I said. "That sounds nice. I'll think about it."

He took a last sip of his beer and said, "I gotta run, sugar." He got off his stool, picked up the guitar, and kissed me quickly on the lips.

I stayed at the table and watched until he was out of sight. Then I left money for the drinks and joined the crowd headed for the exits, just an average-looking girl in a T-shirt and jeans, carrying ten thousand dollars in cash in a newspaper-wrapped box.

thirty-one

*I was on the bus home when my cell rang. I checked the screen: Not surpris-*ingly, it was Serena.

"Prima," she said, "you gotta come home right away. There's some-one here you need to talk to."

"Who?"

"Wait and see."

"I've had enough surprises for a while, Warchild."

"Just come home."

Serena's coyness irritated me, but after I hung up I thought about it, and by the time I was getting off the bus, I was pretty sure who was at the house.

Cousin Lara Cortez didn't look much like Nidia. She had pale olive skin and brown eyes but straight hair chemically lightened almost to blondness. She was in the living room when I got there, on the couch, with a schoolgirl's bright yellow backpack sitting at her feet.

"Risky and Heartbreaker ran into her at the Pollo Loco," Serena told me when we briefly conferred in the kitchen. "No one's asked her anything yet; we were waiting for you."

I went into the living room, Serena at my heels.

"Are you Hailey?" Lara said as I entered. "You're the one who got shot."

"Yeah."

Her eyes were worried. "Did Nidia?"

"Get shot? I don't know," I said. "I don't know if she's still alive. I'm just trying to piece together what happened."

Lara pulled out a pack of chewing gum and unwrapped a piece.

"So," I said, slowing my speech as I reached the critical point, "this is the big thing I need to know from you." I moved to stand over her, close enough that I could smell her hairspray and the sugary watermelon scent of her gum. I said, "Was Nidia pregnant?"

Lara looked down at her cheap plastic sandals, and then she nodded. She looked up again and shot a nervous glance at Serena, behind me. "Am I in trouble, for not telling about that?" She didn't wait for an answer. "Nidia was scared, she didn't want to tell even me about the baby. She said she had to get to Mexico right away, because our grandmother was sick. But I knew that wasn't true; my mother has a letter from Grandma every couple of weeks, so I knew she was fine. I said to Nidia, 'What is it really?' and she started crying and told me about the baby. She said its grandfather would steal it from her and she'd never get it back, that the old man was already looking for her and she had to get to someplace safe. She knew I knew Warchild a little through Teaser, and she thought that Warchild would know how to make it happen. I said I'd ask for help, but then she begged me not to say the real reason. She wanted me to tell the story about our grandma."

She turned still-worried eyes to Serena. "I didn't want to lie, but she said it was too dangerous for people to know about this."

"More dangerous not to know," Serena corrected. "Hailey drove into an ambush blind because none of us knew what was really up."

"I know," Lara said, chewing her gum hard. "And I'm sorry. Really sorry."

"If you were one of my girls, you'd take a pretty good beatdown for lying to me, but lucky for you, you're not," Serena said.

Lara shifted as if to get up from the couch right away, but I held up my hand.

"One last thing, Lara," I said. "Stay alert. If the old man knew about you, he'd probably have sent someone much earlier. But be careful. You see anything, you even feel anything's not right, call Warchild."

She nodded.

Then I said, "Other than that, try and forget about this stuff.

You're supposed to be on your way out of this story, not deeper in. *Out* is the smart direction here."

Lara nodded seriously and got up off the couch and left, as if she'd been dismissed from class by a teacher.

Serena said, "Now what?" She and I were still headed deeper into this story, the wrong direction.

"Call Payaso," I said. "Have him bring over the guys he trusts. It's time for a war council."

thirty-two

Two hours later, I was sitting on the floor, cross-legged, notepad on my leg.
Serena was nearby, on the couch.

Lara had confirmed my theory, and yet I had mostly given up on
the idea of finding Nidia by finding a doctor fallen from grace; even
if I trolled extensively through Medical Board of California records,
there was no effective way to follow up a hunch about which ones
might have been receptive to a Skouras overture. My plans, for now,
were fixed on finding out where Skouras held property, particularly
individual properties in isolated areas.

Serena got up to answer a knock at the door, and came back with
Payaso and his 24-7's, his most trusted homeboys, Deacon and Smiley
and Iceman. A few minutes later, Trippy and Risky and Heartbreaker
came in. Not that the girls were going to be in on this mission, but Serena said they could listen.

"They might as well learn," she'd said. "Even if they'll never be
able to use this shit. Think about it, Insula. This is the kind of thing
people like us are part of maybe once in a lifetime. If that."

She'd sounded awestruck. I hoped she didn't think this was going
to be a harmless adventure, like the movies. She'd seen too much to
be thinking that way.

Maybe, though, she was being romantic precisely because what
we were doing was so different from the usual banging. Saving Nidia
and her child, it was honorable. So I didn't say anything to bring her
down.

Serena, Payaso, and the crew settled down in positions around the living room. Heartbreaker was adding rum to a half-full two-liter bottle of Coke, and passing ice and glasses around.

"Okay," I said. "We're not ready to plan the mission itself yet, because that can't get done until we've learned where Nidia is and checked out the layout and all that." I sipped a little of my rum and Coke and went on: "We need to figure out the smartest way to proceed. In other words, how to find out where Nidia is without drawing attention to ourselves in the process."

Payaso said, "What're you thinking?"

"There are two things I'm sure that Skouras needs right now: a corrupt doctor willing to take care of Nidia extralegally, and an out-of-the-way place to keep her. Getting a line on the doctor is going to be next to impossible, given that there'd be no paper trail. So right now I think we should concentrate on finding out where he owns property."

"And then we go get her," Payaso said, "Trece style."

"Yeah," I said. "But after that, we can't really stand down. When we have Nidia, we're going to be in essentially the same situation that Skouras's guys are in now. They're going to be looking for her, so we've got to keep her under wraps, safe, and healthy. And she'll need medical care during the last weeks of her term."

"And someone's gotta birth the baby," Payaso said.

"Yes," I said. "We have a couple of choices there, none of them ideal. The best choice is probably to take her to an ER. If we've lain low enough, and Skouras's men don't know where we are, he can't have every maternity ward in the state being watched."

"What about computers?" Heartbreaker said. "Could he have people in his organization who could hack into, you know, hospital computers?"

I hadn't thought of that. "Beats me. But I don't think it's going to help us to start thinking of this guy as the master of the universe. We'll get too paranoid to plan anything."

"But if we can't go to the ER," Payaso said, "maybe we could jack a doctor, get him to birth the baby. I heard about some *vatos* that did it for a gang member who got shot. They let the doc go afterward. They didn't hurt him."

I'd heard those stories, too. "That's one way," I said slowly, "but I'm not wild about sticking a gun in the face of someone who's spent his or her life trying to help sick people. It's a cliché, but I don't want to become like Skouras to defeat him."

I watched Payaso, to see how he took this rejection of not just his idea but his gangster ethics. He didn't look mutinous.

"Speaking of that, though, there's a middle way," Serena said. "You said there's got to be a doctor who's looking after Nidia. If he's there when we come in and grab Nidia, we could take him, too, keep him until her due date."

"One-stop shopping," I agreed. "Tempting, but the problem with that is controlling the doctor over a period of days or even weeks. I know some of you guys have jacked people before. What's the key to controlling a vic in that situation?"

"Fear," several voices said.

"Right. So the key to keeping the doctor in line would be keeping him—or her, I guess—pretty well psychologically traumatized, as well as never giving him any privacy in which to escape. You may think you're ready for that, but there's a difference between keeping a jacking victim under control for two minutes, and keeping someone intimidated for two weeks. You may not be as prepared as you think. You may not like who you have to become."

There was a moment of silence around the circle. Then Payaso said, "What about us delivering the baby? No doctor. Women have been having babies for centuries without help."

I exchanged glances with Serena. People loved to say that about childbirth, and they never seemed to apply it to other medical situations. No one ever says that people have been having infections for centuries before we had antibiotics. I only said, "That's something else to think about."

I didn't want to oppose Payaso too much in one meeting. There'd be time later to argue against that idea.

. . .

Another conversation in Serena's bed:

"So, *prima*, you gonna tell me where you got that ten K?"

"No."

"I thought we were *familia* now. No secrets between us."

"Everyone's got secrets," I said. "You have secrets from me, I'm sure."

"Like what? Ask me what you want to know."

I rolled onto one elbow. "When you were in high school, with your head shaved, dressed cholo, you did a lot to prove you were one of the guys. You told me that."

"Sure."

"When teenagers are banging hardest, that's usually when they do their killings. They walk into parties or up to porches and blast away. Often they get away with it."

"That's what you wanna know? If I did that?"

"I'm just making a point," I said. "That's something I've never asked you. So we do have secrets between us."

"You're assuming the answer is yes," she pointed out. "If I didn't, then I don't have a secret, do I?"

"That's true," I said, "but it's not an answer."

"So if I tell you straight out," she said, "are you gonna tell me where you got the money?"

"No."

"Stalemate," she said.

thirty-three

Right away, out of the money CJ gave me, I put another month's rent in the mail to Shay, who undoubtedly was pissed at me all over again for disappearing without word. I was sure he'd never offer me work again. I could live with that; I just didn't want him to pitch my things out in the street.

Then I spent the rest of that day at the library, looking up articles on Tony Skouras.

As Jack had told me, Skouras had been profiled several times in magazines, and he spoke passionately and articulately about his ancestry, his proud fallen family, and his need to grab with both hands at the life he'd come here to attain. But he scoffed at the rumors that he was some kind of gangster.

"In the twenty-first century, that's an outdated business model," Skouras said in one article. "Intimidating people you need on your side, always looking over your shoulder for law enforcement and the IRS—what businessman would possibly want to run his operations like that? There's just no need for it anymore."

I almost believed him, but I had two bullet holes in me that said otherwise. The times never really get any less rough; the masks just get more civilized.

Straighter, briefer news stories detailed how Tony Skouras sold off the South Asian arm of his imports line—"the profit just wasn't there"—and mounted a successful takeover bid for a rival shipping line. Nothing in these stories told me anything useful, except that one cited his lawyer, a Nicolas Costa.

At that point, I went outside and called San Francisco directory assistance, getting a number for Nicolas Costa, attorney at law. I programmed it into my cell. Just in case.

In addition to the business stories and the profiles, I found two short articles on Skouras's heart attack and subsequent quintuple bypass surgery several years ago, and some reviews of his seafood restaurant, Rosemary's. Skouras was quoted in one review as saying that he and his sons used to fish for their own suppers back when he owned a house in Bodega Bay. The quote made it sound very past tense, though, and I figured he'd probably sold the place long before.

But then, in one piece on Rosemary's, there was mention of a fund-raiser held there, a six-course black-tie dinner that Skouras had held. The proceeds were to go to the family of a firefighter up the coast in Gualala. The firefighter had been killed on the job and left three kids behind, and it had come to Skouras's attention because he was having a vacation house built in the steep, forested hills outside of town.

I felt something stir down in my stomach, and I wrote *Gualala* on my notepad.

"Time for a road trip," I said to Serena when I got back.

"Yeah? You find something?"

"He used to have a beach house in Bodega Bay, and to be thorough, I'm going to check property tax records there," I said. "But more recently, he was building a house in Gualala."

"Where?"

"Exactly," I said. "If it's as remote as it sounds, it'd be ideal."

thirty-four

Two days later, I was under a bush, watching a house I was pretty sure belonged to Tony Skouras.

As I'd predicted to Serena, I'd struck out in Bodega Bay. Property tax records had shown no housing in the area belonging to an Anton Skouras. It would have streamlined things greatly if Gualala and Bodega Bay had been in the same county. They almost were. But "Gualala" comes from an Indian word meaning "water-coming-down place," and that creek was also the boundary line between Sonoma and Mendocino counties. Which required a trip to a whole new county office to search through records. It had been ten minutes to closing time when I'd finally learned that Tony Skouras owned a house there, not far from the creek.

Gualala itself was a quiet town where steep hills of redwood and manzanita came down almost to the Pacific's edge. The town had grown up alongside Highway One, a strip of graceful motels and small shops. I'd guessed that the vehicles of choice up here would run to tough, working-class pickups and SUVs. That had influenced my choice when I'd gone car shopping the day before with about half the money CJ gave me.

He'd been generous, but I still couldn't afford to buy off the lot. I'd used up half a day looking through classifieds and auto-trader magazines before finding what I needed: a late-nineties Ford Bronco, a red-brown SUV with a swath of gray primer paint on the side passenger door, an automatic transmission, and four-wheel drive. It was the kind of car that would fit in on the north coast of California, and with a V6 engine, it wouldn't outrun everything on the road, but it'd get out of its own way. Serena had looked skeptically at the patch of gray primer and the hundred-thousand-mile-plus odometer, but I'd shrugged off her concerns. "If it weren't for those things," I'd said, "I'd never have been able to afford it in the first place. I know the gray paint makes it easy to identify, but when we actually go get Nidia"— by which I meant *if*—"we'll be in and out so fast, Skouras's guys won't have time to spot us again."

Now my new ride was parked about a mile behind me, alongside a fire road; I'd hiked from there. Already, the quiet was unnerving, and I knew the coming night would be blacker, and the stars more plentiful, than anything I'd seen in years of city living.

The night before, knowing what lay ahead, I'd dosed up on ghetto pleasures. Serena and I had walked to the liquor store for a bottle of inexpensive tequila, and then we drank and ate her homegirl cooking and played nearly two hours of Grand Theft Auto before crashing a little after midnight.

The next day, I'd driven my new SUV up into the real Northern California.

It wasn't an easy journey. The gatekeeping mechanism to this rural paradise was Highway One, a mostly single-lane road that devolved into twenty-five-mile-an-hour twists and turns that induced carsickness in nearly everyone but the driver of the car.

If you weren't distracted by nausea, though, you could enjoy some of California's most beautiful scenery. Fields of mustard flowers, glimpses of cobalt Pacific and white breakers, farm stands, silver-timbered barns, pumpkin patches, on and on. At intervals, you drove through towns where signs repeatedly invited you to stop for espresso, artisan chocolates, and bed-and-breakfast lodging.

The house below me was a classic mountain vacation place. It was built of what looked like natural redwood timber, with plate-glass windows, a broad deck with a gas grill and a hot tub, both covered for the autumn and winter ahead. I had very little doubt that it was the Skouras house, for two reasons. One, it was occupied; electric light glowed from several windows. At this time of year, most of the houses up here were likely unoccupied and closed up tight. Second, I was pretty confident in the orienteering skills I'd learned back east, despite the well-known NCO joke about GPS devices being "lost lieutenant finders."

I hadn't seen Nidia. I hadn't gotten a good look at anyone. I'd seen figures behind the windows that were clearly grown men, but that was all.

I was not long on patience. This was not a pleasant place to learn it. As I waited, I reviewed the things I was here to find out. Was Nidia here? That was the key question. If so, how many men were guarding her? Was there an alarm system in the house? Was it the kind that went off loudly and alerted the household to an intruder, or was it one that silently tipped off a security team elsewhere? What about the simplest of security systems, a dog?

The night grew darker, making the inside of the house ever more visible through what windows were unobscured by blinds. I trained my binoculars on the window and observed. There were two men inside. Both were white and in their twenties. One was lean and clean-shaven with gold-brown hair. The other was shorter, squat, with thinning brown hair and a chin beard. A television flickered in the room they were in. Occasionally one or the other got up, probably to go to the kitchen or the bathroom. I caught a glimpse of the shorter guy with a bottle of beer in his hand.

Except there was someone in the upstairs bedroom as well. There was light shining there, and a blue flicker as of a TV, but maddeningly, nothing was visible through the window except an expanse of beige wall and part of a sliding closet door. No one came to the window to look out. Dammit, weren't prisoners always supposed to be looking out the only windows available to them, gazing in great melancholy at the outside and freedom? *Nidia, come to your window.*

She did not. The night grew darker still.

Finally the lights in the house went out. I gave the inhabitants of the house about twenty minutes to fall asleep, then I came out from under the bush to do my close-up reconnoitering. My legs shook underneath me and my muscles groaned from being folded for so long. I took the SIG out of my backpack and slipped it into the waistband of my cargo pants, and carried my flashlight in my hands.

The temperature had already fallen under the dew point, and the natural grasses were wet under my feet as I crossed the yard. Quietly, I circled the house. There was no chance of my getting inside tonight, nor climbing up to that window to see who was in the guarded bedroom. This was just reconnaissance of the outside, the doors and windows.

I saw no telltale wires or window stickers that would have suggested a security system, and that made sense. Most security systems were wired into a central office that would send out an armed guard when the alarm was tripped. If Skouras's men were holding a hostage here, it wasn't like they were going to want some rent-a-cop charging up here. Skouras's men would TCB by themselves.

All the locks that I could see were standard, a dead bolt on the front door and a plain knob lock. Regular locks on the sliders. Nothing on the windows. A break-in would be child's play for Payaso or Serena, if only I could predict whether the guys ever left Nidia here by herself. They might never do so.

I walked the driveway. It was a good quarter-mile long, all dirt, and about half that length was visible from the front of the house. So we'd be able to get halfway up in the Bronco before the guys inside would even know strangers were coming. All the way, if they weren't looking out the windows and they had the TV or stereo on loud enough not to hear the engine.

The garage had a window. I looked inside and saw the looming shape of a black SUV, newer than the one I was driving. I raised the flashlight and aimed the beam down at the license plate, repeating the seven digits to myself several times until they were locked in my memory.

As I headed back up the hill to my bivouac, it occurred to me that everything about the house spoke of confidence. They didn't have special locks and security. There was no dog. It was clear that they knew—or rather, thought—that no one was looking for Nidia.

That was probably the only thing we had on our side.

It was midmorning the next day when I finally saw Nidia.

I was under my sheltering bush, stiff, tired, and still hungry after eating two energy bars. The bright light of day made it hard to see anything that was going on inside the house. I'd only caught glimpses of the same two guys, moving back and forth, typical morning stuff.

And then motion outside the house caught my eye. I grabbed the binoculars.

Two people were walking the rolling unfenced land. One was the tall young clean-shaven guy. The other was Nidia. She was not only recognizable, she was recognizably pregnant, her stomach full and round.

Her reddish hair had not been cut, so that it now hung well past her shoulder blades. I couldn't see her expression clearly through the glasses, and I was glad about that. Because this was an abomination. They looked like they could have been lovers, or a young husband and wife expecting their first child. He was close by her side, almost solicitous, in case she stumbled.

It sickened me. Three months of that. She'd lived in the hands of strange young men who pretended to be taking care of her, when I suspected they'd be ready and willing to kill her when the time came. Three months without contact with anyone who cared about her, her family, her friends. If I'd had a rifle, I might have shot him. I had been a good enough shooter at school to do it.

Taking a steadying breath, I lowered the binoculars and withdrew deeper into the bush.

thirty-five

"Tell me again, why you didn't stay up there another day?" Serena asked me.

"I could have," I said. "But even if I'd spent three or four days in research, there's no guarantee their schedule wouldn't change the day we go up there. I just want to go up and do this, soon."

We were in a narrow, windowless theatrical-supply store. I was watching what I said, not wanting the clerk to overhear anything suspicious.

Serena was looking at a lovely and fairly authentic-looking diamond choker. Paste, of course. All around us were romantic things: jewelry and feathers, yards of satin, glass slippers. It was dissonant in the extreme with everything else Serena and I had purchased today. That list would have given anyone pause: pepper spray, duct tape, gloves, ski masks, handheld radios, and another pair of binoculars.

"You and me always make the most interesting shopping trips together, *prima,*" Serena told me, raising her eyebrows. She was thinking, I knew, of the trip we'd made a year ago to the Beverly Center.

"I hope we live to make a few more," I told her.

I'd planned the raid on the drive home, and had quickly realized that I wouldn't need as much gang backup as I'd thought. Later, if we got Nidia out safely, we'd need more guys, to guard her in shifts. But for now, based on my reconnaissance, we were only going to be taking down two unsuspecting guys in an isolated house. What it would require was a fire team, not a squad. If Payaso, Serena, and I couldn't do this by ourselves, we probably couldn't do it at all.

The clerk ambled down the counter toward us. "What can I help you girls with?" he said.

"Stage blood," I told him.

thirty-six

Two days later, I was lying by the edge of the road in Gualala. It was the only road down to Highway One from the Skouras place, the only one the tunnel rats could take to get groceries and supplies. It was also very lightly traveled, which was why I could lie on the roadside, stage blood staining my cheap disposable jacket, as though I had been in a hit-and-run.

Serena had wanted to play the victim. Her argument had been convincing: It was likely that the guys guarding Nidia were part of the ambush team in Mexico, therefore they'd seen me before. They'd seen me in the exact same position, at roadside. She'd worried that it'd be a tip-off.

I'd considered it but argued her down. "I'll have my face turned away from him," I'd said. "He'll never make the connection to Mexico. It's way too bizarre. You're overthinking this."

The truth was, this part was dangerous. I'd wanted Serena safe on the hillside, watching the house. Payaso and I would be the first team.

There was a vehicle coming my way. Serena, in the same surveillance spot I'd taken above the house, had already radioed down to Payaso and me that one of the guys was coming, allowing us to take our positions. I'd gotten the idea from something one of my West Point instructors mentioned, offhandedly, about overseas security and diplomat-protection postings. He'd said that terrorists and kidnappers like to put empty baby carriages in the road to get Americans to stop and get out of their cars, and that drivers have to be trained to

177

ignore them. I'd used myself in lieu of the baby carriage—it would allow me to get into point-blank range automatically rather than trying to walk up behind the guy.

In our plans, we'd taken as a starting assumption that Skouras's guys never left Nidia alone. For that reason, a roadside ambush was useful. A single guy would be easy to take down. We'd get the car he was driving, his keys to the house, and an extra weapon. Then we could walk right through the front door of the house, no trickery or door-kicking necessary.

I was sure, I'd told Payaso and Serena, that no one could drive right past a girl lying on the roadside motionless. "Even if this guy's no Samaritan," I'd said, "morbid curiosity alone will make him stop."

If he didn't, our job would get a lot harder. We wouldn't have his keys to the front door. But we'd go through with the raid, anyway.

The engine sound grew stronger, louder. The air stirred around me as the SUV pulled up and stopped. A door opened and slammed. Athletic shoes made their squinching rubber-soled noise on the asphalt.

And then—what a fucking gentleman—he *nudged* me with his toe. "Hey," his voice said.

I waited for him to sit on his heels beside me before I rolled over and stuck my SIG in his face, cocking it so he'd know I was ready to fire. "Don't fucking reach for anything or I'll put a round in your face," I said. "Don't test me. I will."

He was the stocky guy I saw through the windows last week. Up close, he had almost innocent brown eyes, now wide with shock.

"It's you," he said. He was also one of the tunnel rats, it seemed.

"Yeah," I said. "Teach me about roadside ambushes, prick. See how good I learn."

Behind us, Payaso had come out of cover, holding his gun on the driver. I didn't have to tell him to search the guy. We'd discussed it all in advance. "Get his everything," I'd said. "Billfold, cell, gun if he has it. Who knows what'll come in handy?"

Payaso did this, and then walked him off the road to bind him in duct tape.

I called after him: "Put on your gloves. I think duct tape holds fingerprints."

Admittedly, it was unlikely that Skouras's men had access to any law-enforcement computers, but if they did, they could learn Payaso's real name from his prints. That was something even I didn't know. Much less did I want Skouras having it.

I walked down to where we'd parked the Bronco out of sight. Our handheld radio was in the passenger seat. I picked it up and radioed Serena. "Warchild, this is Insula, we've achieved our objective down here. Over."

"This is Warchild. You guys rock. What's your ETA? Over."

We should have stuck to cell phones. There was nothing like CB radio to inspire totally idiotic speech patterns.

I said, "ETA five minutes. Holler if you see anything funny, otherwise radio silence, okay? Over."

I didn't need to tell her any more. Her job now was to cover the house and driveway, to radio in if there were any unexpected visitors while Payaso and I were inside.

I drove the Bronco back up to the roadside. When I got there, Payaso was already behind the wheel of the SUV. I led him to the driveway of the Skouras place and tapped my brakes to make the brake lights flash, then pulled over. I shut off the engine, grabbed a brown paper grocery bag, and ran to the SUV. I climbed in the passenger side but didn't stay there, getting into the back instead. If the other soldier was looking out the front window when we drove up, it was probably too much to hope that he wouldn't notice that his partner had morphed into a Hispanic male, but if he did, well, there was no point pushing our luck by having a blond girl visible in the window, too.

I crouched on the floor. The grocery bag was mostly a prop, filled with crumpled newspaper to give it shape, but there were a few things we'd need at the bottom, and I dug them out. A ski mask. A canister of pepper spray. The duct tape.

When Payaso stopped the SUV in the driveway, near the house, I handed him his ski mask and the handcuffs.

"Anyone in the windows?" I asked, getting the pepper spray out of the bag.

"No, they're clear," he said. "Why don't you have a mask?"

"The guy in the bushes down there saw my face already."

I opened the side door, shook the pepper spray, and squirted a little into the gravel of the driveway. This would be a bad time for the nozzle to be clogged. It wasn't.

"Okay," I said. "Keys?"

Payaso pulled the keys from the ignition and handed them to me. I sorted through them, fast. One was a smallish mailbox key, one was a Honda key, probably to the guy's private car. Three were what looked like house keys. I chose one at random, isolating it from the others between my thumb and index finger. Then I jumped out and raised the grocery bag to obscure my face. I walked fast to the front steps and up them, stopped at the front door. I stuck in the key I'd chosen. It didn't go in. *Dammit.* I tried another. It slid in and the door swung open.

Inside, the entryway was empty. No one was in my line of sight. I leaned back out, signaling Payaso to come.

I stepped quietly into the entryway, onto a floor of linoleum marked to look like distressed gray tiles. I listened for noise and heard it from the kitchen. The other tunnel rat was in there.

Payaso appeared behind me, masked now, gun in hand.

"Jeff?" a male voice said, from the kitchen. "That was fast. You forget something, you dildo?"

His footsteps drew near. Up close, he had that all-over-golden-brown coloring that some southern Europeans have: golden-brown hair and eyes, a touch of warmth to his skin tone, his jawline stubbled in a lazy-fashionable way.

I didn't let him get all the way to the doorway. Instead, I walked through it, pepper spray in hand, and sprayed him directly in the face, and when he yelped and stumbled back, I threw my hardest straight right. He fell, and as he pitched forward, I grabbed him around the neck and rammed a knee into his liver. It's always tempting to aim for the testicles, but it's harder than many untrained fighters realize to hit that sweet spot that causes instant incapacitation. Liver, kidney, solar plexus—these were all more accessible and nearly as brutal.

I wrestled the soldier onto his stomach and began wrapping his wrists behind his back with duct tape. Out of the corner of my eye, I could see Payaso covering us, holding his gun two-handed like a cop.

"I got him," I said. "Watch behind us, too."

Serena's surveillance had suggested that there were still only two guys living in the house—now both accounted for—but you couldn't be too careful.

The soldier turned his head to the side, to where he could almost make eye contact. His nose was dripping blood from where I'd hit him.

"What the fuck?" he said. "Who the fuck are you guys?"

"Shut up," I said, winding more tape around his ankles. "Is there anyone else in the house besides Nidia?"

"Who?"

"Nice try," I said. "Is there?"

"Fuck you."

I sighed. "I'm gonna leave you for a minute while I go get Nidia from upstairs. Don't think my associate won't shoot you if you give him trouble. Tip your head back and breathe deep; your nose will stop bleeding in a minute."

Then, to Payaso: "Don't let him provoke you into conversation, okay? We're keeping this guy on a need-to-know basis, and what he needs to know is *nothing*."

Payaso nodded.

I searched the rest of the house. It was a nice place: could have been anybody's Lovely Vacation House with the sectional sofa and the flat-screen TV and the big, clean sliding glass door. You wouldn't think two organized-crime guys and an imprisoned mother-to-be had been living here.

Outside the door that I believed to be Nidia's, I tried the remaining two keys, the second of which slid easily into the lock. I took a deep breath and opened the door.

Nidia was in bed, her back to me, under the covers. The TV set was flashing, but without sound. In her position, I'd try to sleep most of it away, too.

But she wasn't asleep. She rolled over and saw me.

Her green eyes had deep purplish shadows underneath them, and when she saw me in the doorway, gun in hand, her expression was one of amazement but not of relief. She didn't seem to understand what she was seeing.

"You're safe now," I said. "We're leaving. Get dressed."

She stared.

"*Andale,*" I prompted. "*Tenemos prisa.*" *Come on, we're in a hurry.*

Finally getting it, she scrambled up from the bed.

When Nidia saw Payaso, ski-masked, armed, and standing over the tape-wrapped, bloody-faced form of the soldier, she jumped and nearly backed into me, frightened.

I said, "*Esta bien,* he's with me."

Payaso hastily ripped off the ski mask and echoed me: "*Esta bien, no tenga miedo.*"

So much for protecting Payaso's identity, I thought, seeing the soldier get a good look at his face. But it was clear that Payaso's main priority was reassuring Nidia. He was staring at her: beautiful despite the shadows under her eyes, and real to him for the first time. If he'd had a hat to tip, he would have.

I looked at Nidia, then nodded at the tunnel rat. "You want to kick him in the ribs?"

"*Como?*" she said, confused.

"Go on," I urged her, "it'll be cathartic."

She just stared at me. I realized I was pretty jazzed on adrenaline and success. I mean, little Nidia Hernandez was not going to kick this guy in the ribs, and it wasn't just because she didn't know what *cathartic* meant.

"Never mind. Let's go," I said.

The soldier's nose had stopped bleeding, and his eyes had stopped streaming from the pepper spray, and as we left, he found his voice and his bravado, calling after me.

"You've signed your own death warrant, bitch," he said coldly. "I recognize you now. We know who you are."

I stopped in the doorway, then looked at Payaso. "Go on out to the car with Nidia," I told him. "I'll be right there."

Payaso wasn't sure. "*Cuidado*," he said, but he took Nidia out.

When they were gone, I walked back to the tunnel rat and sat on my heels. It'd been a long time since I'd felt this way, high on adrenaline, sure of myself, full of purpose. It was making me overconfident. I knew it was pointless to engage with this guy any further, but I just couldn't help myself.

"You guys know who I am?" I said. "I know who I am, too. I'm Staff Sergeant Henry Cain's daughter. And to clarify, you're the *fuckup* who just let a one-hundred-thirty-five-pound bike messenger kick your ass and take Mr. Skouras's unborn grandkid away from you. You think there's a Christmas bonus in your future?"

He snarled, "You'll be dead by Christmas. You have no *idea* how badly you've fucked yourself up here."

I let him have the last word.

thirty-seven

*Skouras's SUV was the last thing we wanted to be driving with his men look-*ing for us, so we only took it to the end of the driveway. I was silent on the drive down, thinking about my own vanity. I'd given Skouras's machine another clue to my identity, telling them my father's name and that I was a bike messenger. It probably didn't matter. It wasn't like they couldn't find out where I came from, not if they wanted to know. Which now I was sure they would.

As we got into the Bronco, Serena hailed me: "Insula, do you read? Over."

"This is Insula. Mission accomplished."

"I'm looking at the three of you right now, man," she said. "I don't fucking believe it."

"See you on the main road. Over."

Even then, I'd probably known I was speaking too soon.

Serena was in Payaso's GTO. She'd driven it carefully off road and over field land to the surveillance spot because we hadn't had time to mount a sophisticated operation that would have entailed Serena hiking in from the distance that I had.

I turned the wheel and the Bronco trundled in a U-turn, and I headed back the way we'd come.

I told Payaso, "When we get down to where we left the guy driving the SUV, keep an eye out. He's unarmed, but if he got free . . . I don't know what he might try, just be looking."

"He didn't get free," Payaso said. "I did him up good."

But the danger rarely lies where you think.

There was about ten miles of long, lonely back road ahead before we'd get to Highway One south, along which we'd probably fall in behind Serena, or she behind us, depending on how fast we each were traveling. The single-lane road, shrouded on each side by pines and underbrush, was very lightly traveled. That was the reason I'd been able to lie by the side of the road in our ambush plan without first drawing the attention of some poor horrified local.

It was also why, when a sleek silver Mercedes carrying two people shot up the road toward us, I tensed. But that was all. It happened too fast. I was going about sixty, so was the other guy, and we were on top of each other right away.

The passenger was a man I didn't see clearly. The driver, whom I did, was Babyface. In that split second, I knew that he had time to see me, Payaso, and worst of all, Nidia.

"Oh, *fuck*," I said.

"Who was that?" Payaso said.

"*Enemigo*," I said.

Maybe he didn't see. Maybe he didn't. Maybe he didn't. Eyes glued to the rearview, I willed the Mercedes to keep going.

Its brake lights flashed red, and I knew it was going to turn around. I pushed the accelerator to the floor. With my right hand, I grabbed the radio. "Warchild," I said, "we're being pursued. It's a silver Mercedes, California plates."

"Insula, I'm two miles to Highway One. What's your twenty?"

"About five miles out," I said. "Just stay clear of us, okay? I'll catch up with you when I can."

He was gaining fast. I had less than a quarter mile on him when I gained Highway One, braked hard, and swung the Bronco into the southbound lane at about thirty miles an hour. That might not sound like a lot of speed, but it is for a right-angle turn, when you're carrying a pregnant woman. In the rearview, I saw Payaso wrap his arms protectively around Nidia.

I jammed the accelerator down again, picking up speed.

I should have listened to Serena. I should have gotten the fastest goddamned car CJ's money would buy. I was an idiot.

If I stopped, could we win in a shoot-out? Who was the other guy in the car? Was that guy armed? That Babyface was strapped was a given.

We were both doing 110 miles an hour, and I was glad that we were passing through a quiet stretch of Highway One. Peace, privacy, and not a lot of cross-traffic: convenient for those rare times when a white homegirl needs to blast through at a high rate of speed, pursued by a mobster's henchman in a Mercedes.

I wondered if I could lose Babyface just long enough to dump Nidia out somewhere. Not only would this mean she and her baby would be safe, but I'd also kind of decided that she was my bad-luck charm, because every time I was in a car with her, shit like this happened.

Then I was distracted by a blur of motion in the bushes off the road, a flash of red lights. It was a highway patrol car, all lights and siren, coming out of his speed trap.

Payaso cursed in Spanish, then apologized to Nidia.

The highway patrolman fell in behind Babyface, who at this point was right behind me. Neither of us was showing any sign of stopping.

After the first initial flash of anxiety, I was wondering if this couldn't work to our advantage. If I pulled over, Babyface almost certainly wouldn't. It wasn't like he could explain to the cops why he was chasing us. And if I complied and Babyface kept going, surely the patrolman would chase Babyface, wouldn't he? Maybe the cop had even decided that I was simply trying to outrun a nut job who was chasing me.

That was it, then. I would pull over like a nice white college girl, Babyface would keep going at a hundred miles per hour, the cop would chase the Mercedes, and I'd bang a U-turn and haul ass. Perfect.

I took my foot off the gas and hit my turn signal, showing my intent to pull over.

"What are you *doing*?" Payaso said.

"Trust me," I said as the Bronco bumped onto the rough shoulder of the road.

Babyface raced around me and kept going. The patrol car did not pursue him. It was slowing, pulling over behind me.

Shit. This was not going according to plan.

We'd both stopped, but the patrolman was still in his car. He had his hand to his mouth, and I thought he was talking on the radio, calling his buddies to chase Babyface. This would give me a moment to think.

I looked down at my hands. Unless I was very charming and very convincing right off the bat, this was going to go sour fast. We were carrying two guns, a switchblade, pepper spray, a ski mask, and duct tape. We couldn't afford a search.

A pickup truck rambled past, heading north, and I had time to notice the dog, a Dalmatian, that pressed its face against the glass as if curious about our situation. The cop was still inside his cruiser.

"Payaso," I said, "whatever happens, we're not shooting a cop, okay? Worse comes to worst, if Nidia's in custody, she's safe, right?"

"Bullshit," Payaso said. "*La jura* isn't going to protect her. The old man will send his lawyer to bail her out and that'll be that, he'll have her all over again. We'll never find her this time."

"*Payaso,*" I interrupted, meaning, *Stop scaring her.* "I'm going to talk our way out of this. Make sure your gun's not showing, okay?"

The patrolman was at my window. Young and blond and starched and ironed, nothing out of place. I smiled at him and rolled down the window.

"Thank God you came along," I said, making my voice breathless and relieved. "That man was chasing us."

"Yeah, the Mercedes, I noticed that," he said. "Why?"

"I didn't mean to, but I cut him off," I said. "He pulled up alongside us, waving a gun. I accelerated to get away, but I guess that was the wrong thing to do. He started following us, and I guess it just got out of hand."

"I guess," he said. "Where were you headed?"

"To a doctor," I said. "My friend is pregnant. She was having some abdominal pains, and I offered to take her and her boyfriend to the ER."

Sure. Just a nice white girl, chauffeuring a *vato* and his girlfriend to the ER, pursued by a psychotic Mercedes driver. Who *wouldn't* buy it?

"Am I going to get a ticket, Officer?" I said, trying for an abashed smile. "I swear, I was just trying to get away from that guy. Please, do you think we could just let this go?"

His eyes narrowed; he was looking down at my clothes. "Is that blood?"

Oh, hell. I'd abandoned the jacket we'd stained with stage blood, but in all the excitement, I hadn't noticed getting that guy's blood on me, though it had been practically inevitable. "Uh, yeah," I said. "It's, uh, hers. She had a nosebleed as well as the stomach—"

Too late, the patrolman wasn't buying it. His voice froze over. "Miss, step out of the car. Now."

That was when I heard the safety click on Payaso's gun, and I felt the cold ring of the barrel pressed just below my ear. The young cop's mouth dropped open.

"Officer," Payaso said, "take your weapon out of your holster and drop it on the ground, or I promise, I'll shoot her dead right now."

Falling into my role as cowed carjacking victim, I put both hands on the wheel and tried to make them tremble. "Please," I said. "Please, Officer, he'll do it."

I had to hand it to the kid: He was probably still a rookie, and in this part of the state, I doubted he'd dealt with much more than heavy sarcasm from speeders he'd stopped, but he had backbone. He didn't immediately comply. Looking at Payaso, he said, "Sir, that's not going to happen. Put down your weapon now, before you do something I think you really don't want to."

Then I heard the sound of a car approaching us, powerful engine rumbling.

"Orale," Payaso whispered, looking through the windshield.

I thought first of Babyface, but it wasn't the silver Mercedes. It was Payaso's GTO, in the wrong lane, bearing down on us like a bull in a matador's ring. Serena had arrived.

The patrolman looked up, too, and his mouth fell open. A minute ago, he'd thought his situation couldn't get any worse, but now it had. I knew the feeling.

"Run," I said.

He scrambled and dove behind the car. Serena blasted past us, so close I didn't believe the side mirror would survive it, the Bronco shuddering in the wall of air the GTO displaced. Then Serena drifted into a beautiful sideways stop and wriggled up to sit sidesaddle in the driver's window, watching the patrolman scramble up the hillside at the edge of the road. She braced her arms on the roof of the car, gun in her hands, and fired.

She was too far away to hit him with a handgun, which was why, for a minute, I didn't call her off. I just wanted to do what Payaso and Nidia were doing, which was staring in awe. This was not Serena. This was Warchild.

She fired twice more, and the rounds made dirt fly up from the hillside, about eight feet from the cop. He was on his feet now, running in an evasive zigzag.

I threw open the Bronco's door and leaned out. "Warchild!" I yelled. "Stand down! He's running!"

She turned and looked at me.

"It's okay!" I reiterated. The cop had gained the tree line and disappeared.

She nodded, understanding. I made the shape of a phone with my thumb and little finger against my cheek, then pulled myself back into the car and picked up the radio from between my feet.

"We gotta get out of here," I told her, without preamble. "Here's what we'll do: Payaso's gonna drive the cop's car up the road a mile, so that the guy can't get to his radio right away. Then I'll pick him up again." I looked at Payaso, who nodded assent. "Then we'll follow you. Just get us off Highway One. Find us a back road out of the county."

"Ten-four," she said. "What if we see the *enemigo*?"

"I hope we won't," I said. "The Highway Patrol is gonna be looking for him; maybe they'll find him and hang him up for a while."

"But if we see him?"

"Shit, I don't know. Let's not get ahead of ourselves."

So Payaso got out of the car. In a minute, he was behind the wheel of the patrol car, heading south.

In the back of the car, Nidia was sniffling. I glanced backward and saw her fighting tears.

Shit. I rubbed the bridge of my nose, thinking hard. "Hey, don't do that," I said. "Really, the worst is over. You're in good hands."

She didn't say anything to that or look reassured, and I couldn't entirely blame her. I spent another second or two trying to think of something else to say, then gave up and pulled out onto the highway. My mood, whether it was warranted or not, was on the rise. In a moment I caught myself whistling and realized it was Simon and Garfunkel: "Feelin' Groovy."

thirty-eight

"We should've got a car from Chato instead," Serena said for the third time.
The four of us were at a pizza restaurant. Payaso, who had taken instantly and seriously to his role as Nidia's guardian, was at the salad bar with her, watching her select fresh vegetables and cottage cheese and pineapple chunks. Serena and I were at a table. I had just washed down a pair of Advil with Mountain Dew for my aching finger. It should have been healed by now, except that I'd reinjured it in the fight with Serena's girls, my jumping-in. And now the scuffle with Skouras's guy had aggravated it. At this rate, it'd never be healed up.

Serena's face was dark, and I knew what she was going to say next.

"You spent nearly six thousand dollars on that SUV and now it's gone," she said. "You had it for what, a week and a half? What a waste."

I agreed with her. I'd already said that I agreed with her. The Bronco was in a picturesque abandoned barn where no one would find it for months. Maybe years. Because unless the highway patrolman we traumatized hadn't followed procedure, he'd radioed in the make, model, and license of our car before he'd gotten out and approached me. Given that a routine speeding stop had turned into an armed attack on a law-enforcement officer, the Bronco was now hot as hell, and I'd had to abandon it.

Now we were all riding in the GTO, which was safe. I doubted the highway patrolman even remembered the color of that car. In moments of trauma—like a speeding car bearing down on you—the mental videographer usually doesn't capture many details.

Serena said, "If you'd had a stolen car, you wouldn't be out any money when you had to dump it."

I said, "I know. But I've been driving all over the damn state for ten days. If I'd had a stolen car all that time, some enterprising meter maid would have run the plate by now, and I'd be arrested, and then the mission would never have happened."

She said, "Maybe you could have driven around and done the research and the reconnaissance in the SUV, but then taken a stolen ride to get Nidia."

"Yeah, maybe," I said.

So this was leadership, being the goat when things went wrong, even small things. It wasn't like our mission had failed, overall. But Serena was wound up, frustrated over what hadn't gone well.

I said, "We're hitting over five hundred, you know. We have Nidia."

"Mmm," she said, a noncommittal sound.

"What?"

She looked across the tables, toward Nidia and Payaso. "You've got a choice here," she said. "You wanted to rescue her and now she's rescued. Are you sure you want to keep babysitting her?"

I sipped a little of my Mountain Dew. "Yeah, I do," I said. "Skouras isn't going to say, 'Win some, lose some,' about this. She can't handle this herself." Then I said, "If you're not in—"

"I'm not saying that," Serena said quickly. "I'm sorry, *prima,* I'm just nervous. It's just that we're out in the middle of nowhere, the old man and his crew are gonna be looking for us all over, and Jesus, I left *Trippy* in charge back at home." She frowned. "We probably weren't even around the corner in the car before she rounded everyone up and started a war with Tenth Street. She hates their asses."

I nodded in sympathy, but my thoughts were elsewhere. I looked over to where Nidia was, still slowly choosing from the salad bar.

In the shady confines of the old barn where we'd hidden the Bronco, Serena and I had done a short debriefing with Nidia. We'd sent Payaso away, outside, so she could speak freely, and then Serena had begun firing questions at her, in rapid Spanish: *Are you okay? Did they hurt you? Touch you? Did they mess with your head?*

Nidia had shaken her head, saying *no, no*. Serena hadn't seemed to believe her. *Are you sure?* she'd demanded.

Serena, I'd cut in, *stop tripping. They were under orders from Skouras. They wouldn't have done things like that.*

I'd been worried that she was going to get Nidia upset, as Payaso nearly had earlier, in the car, with his rant against the American law. I'd also been surprised at Serena's depth of concern for the girl she'd dismissed as a "little vic" earlier. But some things were women's concerns; they transcended petty differences.

When I'd gotten Serena to shut up, Nidia had told us the story. Most of it confirmed what we'd already guessed. The baby she was carrying was Adrian Skouras's, and Tony Skouras knew about it and wanted the child. Nidia's family, likewise, had known. They had thought that a tiny village in Mexico, if Nidia disappeared quickly and completely, would be a remote enough place to hide from him. I'd been right about all that.

I'd been wrong about how Tony Skouras had learned about his grandchild. Adrian had not revealed it to his father on his deathbed. Instead, when Nidia had missed her period, she'd asked the help of his home-care nurse with arranging a pregnancy test. The nurse had known even before Adrian had. After Adrian's death, she apparently told the old man about the joyous life-in-the-midst-of-death fact of Nidia's pregnancy.

Just days before his death, Adrian had warned Nidia that his father would want the child and would use any means necessary to get sole control of it. Nidia had kept her pregnancy a secret for that reason, never guessing that the nurse would use the information to her advantage.

"That fucking bitch," Serena had said, as if personally affronted.

After Adrian's death, Skouras Sr. and his lawyer came to the house with a rich financial offer for Nidia to give up the child, and Nidia had realized that if she didn't take the carrot, she'd get the stick. She didn't want money. She wanted her child to be safe from its grandfather. She'd pretended to feel ill and fled out the back door of Adrian's house.

She'd stayed with her family only a few days. They had known Skouras would be looking for them. As I'd thought earlier, their very anonymity had protected them. If they'd been a middle-class suburban family, he could have found them in the phone book. But her family had wisely fled to another part of the state, while Nidia went to stay with an old friend of her mother's in Oakland.

Nidia also told us that after she'd been taken from the tunnel, Skouras's men had driven her to a rented house where a doctor had checked her out for signs of shock after the traumatic events of the day. Then they'd taken her to the airport and brought her back to California by private plane.

Nidia had been under guard in Gualala ever since, treated courteously, fed a healthy diet with plenty of prenatal vitamins, and checked out regularly by a doctor whom the big man—I assumed she meant Babyface—brought up to the house. I'd wondered if the doctor had been the passenger in the Mercedes today.

Payaso and Nidia came back to the table, and in a few minutes, a waiter came out with a pizza that Payaso, Serena, and I would share, and a chicken sandwich for Nidia.

Nidia was quiet, but then, she'd always been quiet. I believed her, though, that Skouras's men hadn't mistreated her. That lined up with what I'd told Serena: They wouldn't have physically or sexually abused the mother-to-be of Mr. Skouras's grandchild. I didn't know what psychic scars Nidia was carrying, but she was functioning, and that was going to have to be enough. I'd learned to do a lot of things the hard way in the past few months, but I wasn't going to learn to be a therapist.

"It's a good thing we didn't bring Deacon," Payaso said, pulling a slice of pizza free of the pie. "My car would be way too crowded."

"Yeah," I said. "We've got a lot of driving ahead of us."

"Back to L.A.?" Serena said.

"No," I said. "We're going east."

thirty-nine

The McNair sisters, Julianne and Angeline, had been the most beautiful girls in their high-school class back in West Virginia. As with many pairs of sisters who turn heads, the key to their appeal was their contrasts. Angeline, the older of the two, had seraphic red-gold hair and pale blue eyes that her sons, Constantine, Cletus, and Virgil, all inherited. Julianne had glossy dark-brown hair, and her eyes were a deep iris blue. Angeline was engaged by her senior year of high school, to a funny shade-tree mechanic named Porter Mooney. Julianne drank and danced and remained uncommitted through graduation, when she left West Virginia with a girlfriend to see America.

Julianne was both pretty and smart. She was quick-witted to the point of cruelty, but people forgave her easily, because she illustrated why people call intelligence "brightness." She drew the eye and held it. In photos, you can see that she knows exactly how to lean out for a man to light her cigarette, in a way that is fetching but not too accommodating. He still has to reach. She is the object.

She met a young Army private in a bar just off the base where he was stationed in Texas and married him six months later. Henry Cain was her emotional opposite—simple, hardworking, forthright. To this day, I still don't know what their marriage was really like. Part of that is because he died when I was very young. But part of it's probably deliberate obtuseness on my part. I had loved my father; I didn't want to believe he was unhappy for twelve years. I did know that in conversation, Julianne had used her brains and verbal quickness to chase him around rhetorically like a jay harries a hawk. He'd never openly expressed anger with her. Sometimes, when she would excoriate him for small things, he would shake his head and say quietly, "Why do you have to be like that, Jewels?"

I suppose she did love him, because she loved men in general. After his death, there had been plenty more. Air Force men and guards at the prison, then a switch to artistic blue-state New Men in Santa Barbara and Ojai, where she lived after I went east for school. She'd followed the latest one to Truckee, nearly on the Nevada line. Pretty soon she'd tire of the quiet Sierra life and move to a city, where the lights were brighter and the dating pool bigger.

She had always worked—she couldn't have afforded not to—but through it all, and between drags on a cigarette, she declared that the world was a man's world, ambition a joke. Sincerity was anathema to her, a form of submission. Her dislike of authority and sincerity found its natural enemy in her husband's employer, the Army. Drilling with rifles, starting and stopping and turning when you were told, snapping your hand to your forehead every time you approached someone who outranked you—she thought it was Boy Scouting on steroids. It was not coincidence that I told nearly a dozen people my plans to apply to the United States Military Academy before I finally told Julianne.

"I despair of you," she'd told me. "You could do anything, and this is what you want? The Army?"

"It's not just the Army," I'd said, not once but many times. "It's West Point."

In her way, Julianne thought she was a feminist, just by virtue of being smart and having casual sex, of mocking supermodels and cheerleaders. For that reason, she could never admit that being beautiful was important to her. She hid it so well that I was into adulthood before I realized how much she liked it that I wasn't as good-looking as she was.

She was subtle. She was careful to reassure me that my port-wine birthmark wasn't "disfiguring" and gave my face "character." I never noticed how often she brought the subject up even when I wasn't worrying about it. She sighed, too, about the shallow "California ideal" of the blue-eyed blonde. "It's too bad you didn't inherit my eyes instead of your father's," she'd say. "Californians are *so* hung up on that."

I was mostly okay with not being as beautiful as my mother because I'd long ago realized that it was the reason we got along even as well as we did. If I had been better-looking, our relationship would have been a lot nastier. And had I been beautiful *and* my father still alive for Julianne and me to compete over—I didn't even like to think about that.

As it was, I spent my youth being her foil: poor, sweet Hailey, who'd inherited her father's plain brown eyes and his ass-aching sincerity and went east to play soldier girl in a touching attempt to emulate him. If Julianne "despaired" of me, she privately enjoyed doing so.

I'd called her from the road, told her I was coming up to her little trailer on a half-acre of land outside Truckee. I hadn't told her that I was coming up with a ganged-up entourage. All in due time.

I'd explained the logic to Serena and Payaso: "It's not traceable to her, and thus not to me. The land and the trailer both belong to this guy she nearly married. When their relationship fell apart, she started paying rent, but everything's in his name."

Now it was about ten in the morning, and we were ascending her driveway. We'd driven all night, taking turns behind the wheel, Nidia sleeping on Payaso's shoulder. Awake now, Nidia was looking out the window. She didn't look too happy to see more forested land outside, just like Gualala. I suspected she was probably more homesick for city light and fast food than Payaso and Serena and I were. She'd been without those things a lot longer.

Julianne came out onto her front steps, cigarette and lighter in hand. She lifted the cigarette to her mouth, then stopped when she saw that there were four people, not one, in the car.

Payaso killed the ignition. I said, "You'd better let me talk to her first."

Serena said, "She doesn't know who we are?"

"I'm easing her into this," I said.

I got out of the car. My legs felt shaky, and not just because I'd been riding for so long. My mother hated being told what to do, and I'd never had to try before.

I walked up to the front steps.

"Well," she said. "Hello, darling."

"Hey," I said. "You're looking good."

"Thank you," she said. It was true.

"You didn't say you were coming with friends," she said.

"No," I said. "Sorry, I didn't."

She lit the cigarette, the better to give me a narrow-lashed look through the cloud of start-up smoke. "So who are they?"

"The woman in the backseat is Serena, an old friend of mine from L.A.," I said. "The guy behind the wheel is Payaso. And the girl in the passenger seat is Nidia. She's six months' pregnant and needs a place to hide until her baby is born. That's why we're all here."

Julianne said, "Where, exactly, do you mean by 'here'?" It was clear from the pointedness of the question that she already understood.

I pointed to the ground. "Right here."

"Is this a joke, Hailey?"

"I think we should go inside to talk," I said.

She opened the door and I followed her into her low-ceilinged living room. I said, "This girl, Nidia—it's hard to explain, but it's my responsibility to take care of her. I don't have a home of my own to take her to. This is the only place I have."

Julianne said, "They can't stay here, Hailey. It's out of the question."

I'd anticipated that answer, and pulled out a roll of ten fifty-dollar bills. It was part one of two tactics I thought would persuade her.

"I think you should go to Nevada and stay with Angeline and Porter until we're gone," I told her. "This is for gas money and expenses. You could stay here, but I think you'd be more comfortable at your sister's. Plus, I'd feel better about it. There are men looking for Nidia. I came here because this is someplace they can't trace us to, but if somehow they did, there's going to be a firefight, and I'd want you safely away from here."

Her eyes narrowed. "A 'firefight'?" she echoed. "I don't know what you're up to, Hailey, but maybe you should get some kind of therapy. I don't think it's healthy for you to be getting involved with criminals and playing soldier to assuage your feelings over West Point not working out. I—"

Part two: I crossed my arms, pulled my sweatshirt over my head, and stood in front of her in just my bra. As Julianne stared, confused by my behavior, I touched the corrugated, dark-pink scars from where I'd been shot. "Do you know what these are?" I asked.

She knew, I thought, but just couldn't process the information.

"I got shot," I told her. "Twice."

"Jesus Christ," she said.

I pulled the shirt back on. "I know this is hard to take, but I was never 'playing' soldier, not back east and not now," I said. "When I do something, I'm serious about it. Nidia is my responsibility because I've made her my responsibility. And it's also my responsibility to protect you. Take the money and go to your sister's."

She was still staring at me. I wondered if my father had ever talked to her that way.

Then she took the money from my hand. "Is it too much to ask," she said, "for you to ask your friends to go into town for an hour until I'm packed and out?"

forty

Julianne's trailer was pretty nice: double-wide, two bedrooms, a little porch in back. There wasn't much food in the refrigerator; my mother apparently shopped day by day. Naturally, there was a whole carton of cigarettes in the cupboard above the refrigerator. I could imagine Payaso's happiness at seeing them, but they'd probably be going with her.

I'd sent Serena and the rest into town, as Julianne had asked, and since they left, I'd been avoiding her. Now I went into her bedroom. Nothing I was going to say was likely to help, but I couldn't help myself; I needed to smooth things over.

The bedroom decor was clearly picked out by Julianne's ex, still the nominative owner of the whole place, because it was dominated by masculine hues: hunter-green and rust red, with inexpensive pine furniture.

Julianne was in the little bathroom. I watched through the open door as she threw things into a makeup kit: eyelash curler, tweezers, nail clippers, lipstick. She glanced at me in the mirror.

I sat down on the bed. "I'm sorry about this."

"No, you're not. If you're going to be a bitch, Hailey, don't be a half-assed bitch. It undermines the whole point." She fished a deep-red lipstick back out of her makeup kit and rolled it gently onto her lower lip, then her upper.

She came to stand in the bathroom doorway, studying me. "There's something you don't know, Hailey. When you were fourteen and I'd gotten back on my feet after your father's death, I wanted to move to Santa Barbara or Ojai right away, someplace nearer the ocean, with more culture and more people." She paused. "But you told me you wanted to go to West Point, and I stayed because of that.

A metro area would have had a larger student body, more standout athletes and kids with 4.0's. You would have been a smaller fish in a bigger pond. I never told you, never made a big deal of it, but I stayed in Lompoc for four years so you'd have your best shot at getting in."

I looked away, repressing an irritated comment, which would have been this: If she'd tried to stir up any interest in my potential Army career, she'd have known that such a sacrifice wasn't necessary—as the child of a dead serviceman, I'd already had a significant edge on the other candidates. Sons and daughters of personnel who died while in active duty are given special consideration.

But there was no point in embarrassing her. I played along.

"I'm sorry," I said. "I didn't realize."

"Lot of good it did, in the end," she said.

Ah, there it was, the sharpened-dagger point to that little story.

She walked out of the bathroom and placed the makeup tote into her packed suitcase, zipped it up, and looked at me. "Why do you even think Porter and Angeline are going to open their house to me on such short notice?" she asked.

"Because they're Mooneys," I said.

She gave me a sharp look, but this time there was more than pique in it. If there was one legitimate grievance Julianne had with me, it was that in my younger years, I'd made no secret of how much I'd envied CJ and his siblings their settled home life, a jealousy that had clearly implied that Angeline had been a better mother than her sister.

"Oh, of course," Julianne said. "You've never forgiven me for making you move out of the paradise of your aunt and uncle's house. If you'd had your way, you'd have been there until the day you left for West Point." She paused then, chambering her next thought like a shooter chambers a round. "Probably in bed with your cousin Cletus, too."

It was unfortunate that Julianne had such contempt for the Army. She would have excelled at planning missions: She always knew where the weak point lay.

"That's a sick thing to say," I told her tiredly.

forty-one

The next few weeks were uneventful. That was almost a problem in itself.
Serena and Payaso did not take well to mountain life, finding the
blackness and the silence at night unnerving, and the days boring.
Julianne's little home would have been spacious for two, but not for
four. There always seemed to be someone in the single bathroom. The
TV got only a small selection of channels, and there was no sound
system to speak of, just a clock radio that would also play a CD.

Relief came in the form of Bravo and Deacon, who drove up from
L.A. to put in some bodyguarding time. A grateful Serena and Payaso
jumped in the GTO and headed south for a fix of *tacos mariscos* and
city light, as well as to check in with their respective lieutenants,
Trippy and Iceman.

They came back in five days like a supply dogsled from Nome,
laden with DVDs, magazines, a deck of playing cards, a box of Krispy
Kreme doughnuts, groceries from a Mexican *tienda,* and several
ounces of marijuana. I had to put my foot down about that.

"We're guarding Nidia, and everyone who's here needs to be clearheaded, which means no drinking and no drugs," I reminded them.
"I know it seems like Skouras's men have no idea where she is, and
they're never coming for her, but that's what the two guys in Gualala
thought, right before Payaso and I walked through their front door
and took Nidia away from them."

That didn't have the desired effect. "Motherfucking Trece style!"
exulted Trippy, who'd come with them, throwing Trece's sign. Deacon
and Bravo threw it back, all of them focusing on the last part of what
I'd said and ignoring the first.

It turned out that nearly everyone wanted to come up and do guard duty. While I'd have liked to believe it was esprit de corps, there was an ulterior motive, and not one I'd ever have thought of.

"Snow," Serena told me. "Most of them have never seen it. They all want to be here when the first fall comes."

Soon there was a regular rotation. Not only did Payaso's home-boys come up to be security, but the sucias came, too, providing company both for their guys and for Nidia. Despite the glaring surface differences between the sucias and Nidia, Serena's girls were natural and easy with her, playing cards and chatting, brushing and braiding her red hair. The guys, meanwhile, followed Payaso's example, showing Nidia an excess of courtesy, cleaning up their language when she was around, holding doors for her.

Of all of us, I was the only one to stay with Nidia day in, day out. I dealt with mountain life by reaching back and tapping a little of my old West Point discipline, deciding to get my body back into its pre-coma shape. I got up early and ran for miles on the fire roads, coming back to do push-ups and Russian twists on Julianne's little porch. In the evenings, I played more kinds of poker with Serena and the guys than I'd known existed. One afternoon, Serena and I took our guns out into the hills and shot at soda cans, sharpening our skills. Nidia and I went into town to get cold-weather clothing. Everyone else had a chance to get things from home, but I'd come to Truckee with only the clothes on my back, as had Nidia. Skouras's guys had bought her a few things in Gualala, but in her haste to get out of there, naturally, she hadn't thought to grab anything before leaving.

The snow came in mid-November, turning everyone into giddy children except two of us. Me because it reminded me, soberingly, of the pristine fields and quads of West Point, and Nidia because she was Nidia, with the weight of the future in her belly. So she watched from the steps as her friends pelted one another with handfuls of snow, put it down collars, and tasted it cautiously. Meanwhile, I put snow chains on our cars, laboriously, with reddening fingers and a little cursing.

December came, and Truckee put on its Christmas finery, white lights glittering along every storefront in the town's Old West–style retail district. Skiers and snowboarders overran the town, the streets full of muddy SUVs with loaded roof racks. Had she wanted, Serena could have had her pick of the college boys who appraised her from the windows of their Tahoes and Denalis. Winter clothing suited her, the gunmetal-colored trench coat and boots and the long hand-knit scarf I'd bought for her at a downtown boutique.

After the initial adjustment period, Nidia's confinement proved an oddly peaceful, settled time for all of us.

One day, though, I overheard Payaso and Deacon in a discussion of whether an icicle would make a good impromptu weapon in a fight.

Innocence never lasts.

forty-two

One chilly night I found Serena outside, looking up at the night sky.

"What a trip," she said, breath clouding in the air. "Look at all those stars. That's too many, man. That's just wrong."

I looked, too, seeing the dusty backbone of small stars that formed the Milky Way. I said, "You know, when the Northridge Quake hit and the lights were out all over Los Angeles, people called the media, saying that they could see a river of dust kicked up by the quake. They said the dust was hanging in the sky, glowing white from city lights elsewhere. What they were seeing was the Milky Way, for the first time in their lives."

"I bet they were scared."

"Scared?" I said. "Why? It's beautiful."

"You really like it out here?" she said.

"Sure. It's not so different from where we used to live. It used to get pretty dark and quiet out there."

"Yeah," she said. "And you grew up and hauled ass for the city, L.A. and then San Francisco. But you get up into the mountains and you go all white on me: 'Isn't nature beautiful?'"

"That's not a white thing," I said.

"Maybe not, but—" She shrugged. "I keep thinking of this girl I knew, she was from Lennox but she never got ganged-up. She stayed in school, became an inner-city schoolteacher, that whole trip. So she takes these girls from the hood to the ocean. Some of them have literally never seen it, even though they've grown up just about ten miles inland. She thinks this is going to be a beautiful life-changing thing for them. But they get out on the beach, and they start freaking. It's

205

windy, their hair's getting messed up, they're afraid the gulls are going to shit on them, they think the kelp smells funny. They want to go back into town, go to Taco Bell." Serena grinned. "She gave up and took them."

"Thanks for telling me that," I said. "It was so uplifting."

"I'm just saying, maybe your parents were white, but somewhere along the way a homegirl breast-fed you. You don't like it up here any more than us."

"It'll be over soon," I said.

"No, it won't."

"Sure it will," I said, confused. "Nidia will give birth, and then at least she'll be safe. Once Nidia and her child are two separate units, Skouras's men won't have any reason to chase her."

"Insula," Serena said, "have you really talked to Nidia about that? Giving up her baby?"

I said, "The baby's going to have to be hidden somewhere, under a whole new identity. It can't be living with Nidia. As long as they can find her, they can find her child."

"That doesn't answer my question. Point blank, have you told her that?"

I was silent.

"That's what I thought."

I looked out into the black shapes of the woods. "Why is it so hard to talk to her?" I asked.

"This is a difficult subject," she said.

"No, I mean about anything," I said. "Since we got her back from Gualala, you and me, we've both avoided being alone with her. Your girls like to kick it with her, but you and me, we avoid being one-on-one."

Serena lifted a shoulder. "I just don't think I have anything in common with her," she said.

"None of us do," I said.

When we'd rescued Nidia in Gualala, when I'd opened the bedroom door, I'd said, *You're safe,* but beyond that I'd said and done nothing to reassure her. I'd tried to get her to kick the bound Skouras soldier in the ribs. Later, after we'd narrowly gotten away from the Highway Patrol officer, I'd spoken only briefly with her about her ordeal in Mexico and then Mendocino County, when Serena and I had reassured ourselves that she hadn't been sexually mistreated or roughly handled, that she was basically okay. At least that's what we told ourselves.

The truth was that what had happened to Nidia was difficult to think about, no matter how she'd been treated in Gualala. The extent to which Nidia had lost control of her own life, living with only Skouras's guards for company—if I let myself think about it too long, it'd sicken me. I couldn't stand to ask her how she felt, how she'd gotten through it. Because some part of my own psyche feared that I could still, despite all my training and toughening, be like her. It was as if victimhood were a catching illness and I couldn't afford to get too close to it.

I didn't have to ask Serena if she felt the same way. I knew she did. It had been Serena, before she'd even met Nidia, who'd called her a "vic," or victim. I didn't think either of us was proud of the way we felt about Nidia, but we were in a unique position. The guys felt comfortable around her because they'd always been guys; they'd simply never had to think about being hurt in such a deep psychological way. And the sucias, well, to them this whole thing wasn't real. It was a movie: Serena and Payaso and I had walked into *enemigo* territory and taken Nidia back, *motherfucking Trece style!,* and then we'd made a fucking cop wet his fucking pants, applause, roll credits.

Nidia probably needed to talk to someone about what had happened to her, someone other than Serena's homegirls, but apparently it wasn't going to be Serena, and it wasn't going to be me, either. I'd nearly gotten killed for her, and I'd gotten her back from Skouras, and since then the extent of my commitment had been to assure her that we'd keep her safe.

Somewhere along the way, I'd come to understand that there was no way that Nidia and her baby could live together, not for many years, at least. The baby was going to have to disappear into safe, anonymous hands. Skouras's men were never going to be able to find the baby, not if they'd never laid eyes on it. Nidia was different. Her they would recognize. As long as they could find her, her baby wasn't going to be safe in her care, and the opposite was also true: As long as she had her baby, she would be a target.

And now, as Serena pointed out, I had to make that clear to her.

"All right," I said, "let's go talk to Nidia."

"Right now?"

"It's not going to get any easier. I might as well get this over with." I got to my feet. "Come on."

"Me?"

"Yeah," I said. "Please, even if it's just for moral support, do this with me."

One of Serena's girls, Cheyenne, was in Julianne's bedroom with Nidia. Serena said to her, "Insula and I need to talk to Nidia for a while." She always referred to me by my street name in front of her sucias. She added, "In private."

Cheyenne switched off the CD player and got up. Serena and I stepped into the room to let her pass.

Nidia looked from Serena to me and said, *"Todo esta bien?"* Is *everything okay?*

Serena sat on the bed. *"Por ahora,"* she said. *For now.* "It's really Hailey who needs to talk to you."

Nidia looked to me. Stalling, I moved over to the low pine dresser and lifted my hips to sit on its upper edge, putting my legs out and my feet on the edge of the bed.

"We really haven't talked about what's going to happen in the future," I began.

"The future?" she said.

The easiest way to do this, I decided, was to make her do the reasoning. "What exactly do you see happening after you have the baby?"

Her green eyes were uncertain. "I don't understand."

"With Skouras, I mean."

She didn't exactly wince, but I saw his name prick her, like a dart. She said, "I don't know."

"You don't know?" I was playing amateur therapist, making her do the emotional and logical heavy lifting. "I'm not trying to be unkind here, but you have to think about it. Your baby is due in about a month. Then what? Skouras's not going to stop looking for the two of you."

She said, haltingly, "I—I have to hide, with the baby."

"Where?" I said. "They know about your mother's village. That's off the table."

She looked down at the deep-green bedspread. I waited.

"Hailey," Serena interrupted. *This isn't working,* her gaze said.

"Okay, look," I said. "Nidia, I've been thinking about this a lot, and I just don't think your baby is going to be safe from Mr. Skouras unless you're in separate places, and even you don't know where the baby is."

"Como?" she said, her eyes wide and shocked.

Quickly, I explained to her the reasoning that I'd shared with Serena. Nidia listened, but I could see she wasn't accepting it.

I finished by saying, "We'll find your baby a good foster home. The best, I swear. And it's not forever. Mr. Skouras's an old guy. He's already had one heart attack. He doesn't have close family that'll pursue this after he's dead. After that, the two of you can be together, I swear."

But Nidia said, "No." She laid a hand on her stomach. "This baby is my responsibility. No one else's."

"I understand," I said, "but making sure your baby is safe is the biggest part of that responsibility. I know it seems backward, but living separate from your child is the best thing you can do for it, until Skouras is dead."

Falling silent, I waited for her to respond, but she didn't, looking down, not meeting my eyes.

I was about to speak again, to push harder before she could think of another argument for keeping her baby. But Serena beat me to it. She leaned forward and said simply, "Hailey got shot."

Nidia's green eyes flickered, closed and then open, with an expression that looked like guilt.

Serena went on: "She took two bullets and nearly died down there in Mexico. It wasn't your fault, but it was because of you and this baby. And after she got better, Hailey didn't run the other way like most smart people would. She went and fucking found you and got you someplace safe."

"I know that," Nidia said softly, her green eyes nervous.

"Yeah, you know that, but what are you doing about it? Nidia, grow up, be a woman. Do what's gotta be done."

These were hard words, but I didn't jump in with anything to soften them, because Nidia's face was clouded, uncertain, and I thought she might finally be relenting.

Finally she nodded. "Okay," she said. "I understand."

"And you'll let Hailey find your baby a safe place to live?"

Nidia nodded.

"I'm sorry," I said. "I wish there was another way."

Outside the bedroom, I went immediately to the refrigerator and stood looking at the drinks inside, the RockStar and Red Bull, orange juice and milk, and wished that I hadn't laid down the law about no drinking or drugs on the mountain. I closed the door without taking anything out.

"Thanks for doing the heavy lifting in there," I said.

"You weren't gonna," Serena said. "You're too soft, *prima*."

Alcohol would have helped me sleep less fitfully that night, so it was probably a good thing there hadn't been any in the trailer. My light and restless sleep ended a little after midnight, when I raised my head with a sense of the noise that had awakened me: the soft click of the front door being pulled to.

I reached for my SIG, but already I could tell that there was no one in the darkened living room who shouldn't be: me on the couch, and

Serena in a sleeping bag on the floor. Payaso and Iceman had taken the extra bedroom. I wasn't sure where Cheyenne was: maybe in the master bedroom with Nidia, maybe with Payaso and Iceman. Sleeping arrangements between Trece and the sucias were fluid—except for Serena, of course, who never sexed the guys.

If no one had come in, someone had gone out. I sat up and pulled apart the blinds to look out the window. Outside the trailer was a moving shadow, a slight female form carrying a shapeless bag. Nidia. I should have known she'd given in too easily to Serena's browbeating.

I sat up and put my head in my hands for a moment. I was very tired, like lead was braided through the fibers of my muscles. But I got up, very quietly so as not to wake Serena, pulled on my sweat-shirt, jeans, and boots, and slipped out the door.

Now I knew where Cheyenne was: with the guys. She couldn't possibly have slept through Nidia's getting up, packing her things, and leaving the bedroom. Unless, of course, Cheyenne had known that Nidia planned to run away and had become a silent accomplice.

The time it had taken me to get dressed had slowed me down. Nidia was halfway down to the main road when I caught up with her. In the moonlight that filtered through the treetops, I could see that the bag she was carrying was a pillowcase into which she'd stuffed her few possessions.

She heard my boots crunching in the snow and gravel when I was about ten feet behind her, and she turned, raising a gloved hand to her eyes when I switched on my flashlight.

"Go away," she said, eyes narrowing in a mix of resentment and defensiveness at being caught. "Go back. Leave me alone." She turned and started walking faster.

I broke into a jog, closed the small distance, and grabbed her arm to stop her.

"You've got to be fucking kidding me," I said. "You're running away from the only safe place you have, by yourself, with no money? Nidia, where do you think you're going to go?"

"I'll find someplace," she said, pulling her arm from mine.

"How?" I demanded. "The only reason we've been able to get you this far is because we had a plan and resources. This is crazy. Come back up and we'll at least talk about this where it's warmer."

That last part was only half a negotiation attempt. I really was cold. She had the long parka and gloves that I'd bought her. I was in a sweatshirt and bare-handed.

"No," Nidia said. "Not until you promise to help me protect my baby, not give it away."

I stood still, thinking about my options. If I made that promise, I didn't know how I was going to keep it. If I didn't promise, I couldn't just grab an eight-months'-pregnant woman and muscle her back up the hill. And if I let her go, my mission was over and I'd have failed.

I rubbed the bridge of my nose, trying to understand. "What's going on, really, Nidia?" I asked. "Did you love this guy, Adrian? Is that what this is about?"

Her face was pinched, as though I'd touched a sore spot. "No," she said. "Johnny was the only one I ever loved. But he would understand this. He would want me to stay with this baby and take care of it."

She'd told me as much back in El Paso, when she said that Johnny would have wanted her to go to Mexico. Because I hadn't known she was with child, I hadn't understood what she was really saying.

Now I thought I did. Nidia wasn't delusional. She knew the baby she was carrying wasn't Johnny's, yet in some way it represented the children they were supposed to have had. She'd loved Johnny and then he'd been killed. Then she'd felt something for Adrian, if not love, and he'd died, too. Nidia had suffered a lot of loss. In her mind, this baby was the universe's gift to her to make up for it. She wasn't letting go of that.

I wished I didn't understand what she was feeling, but I did. I knew how powerful love could be when it came at an age little greater than childhood. I'd been first introduced to my cousin around the same age Nidia was when she'd first seen Johnny Cedillo. That was how I knew that if CJ had died, leaving me with the only child who would carry a piece of his soul into the world, I would not let that baby out of my hands. No matter what the cost, I'd find a way to keep it with me and protect it. And with that realization came the unwelcome corollary: *If you could do it for yourself, why can't you do it for Nidia?*

"Okay," I said, capitulating. "I'm going to help you."

"You are?" She hadn't expected to win me over. Her hand was on her stomach as though her child needed physical protection from me.

"Yeah. Come back up, and I'll think this through all over again. I'll think of something."

Nidia relaxed, and her hand moved away from her stomach.

We began the walk back up. I blew on my bare fingers to warm them. Nidia noticed and said, "Do you want my coat?" It was the only way she knew to thank me.

"No," I said. "I'm fine."

When we reached the mobile home, Serena was sitting on the doorstep, smoking a cigarette, its red cinder glowing. Nidia's steps faltered, as if she were expecting a tongue-lashing from Warchild, but I said in a low voice, "It's okay, I'll handle her."

When we were in speaking distance, Serena said coolly, "Out for a walk?" But she clearly saw the pillowcase in Nidia's hand. She understood.

"Not exactly," I said, and then to Nidia, "Go on inside."

For a girl as heavily pregnant as Nidia was, she almost ran up the steps, then slipped through the door and closed it softly.

Serena dropped her cigarette into the snow. "What's up, Insula?" she said.

I drew in a deep breath and released it in a long plume of steam in the air. "This is about Johnny Cedillo," I said, and explained the conclusions I'd come to.

Serena scowled. "This girl used to want to be a nun, and now her whole life's about being a mother?" She shook her head.

"I know it's hard to understand."

"She's not being realistic, either," Serena said. "No matter where her heart's at, she's not gonna be able to defend her baby from the Greek and his whole machine."

"She expects me to do that," I said. "She thinks like a child. She was mad at me for not being able to handle everything with no compromise from her. That's what a kid expects from a parent. And if I can't, she'll run away again with no plan, like a kid, and she'll get herself killed."

"And you can't let her do that," Serena said.

It wasn't a question, but there was a question inside it, and after a moment, she articulated it. "Hailey," she said, "why are you doing all this? Some pretty heavy shit has happened to you since you first met this girl. Nobody could have known those guys were going to shoot you in Mexico, but since then . . . that guy broke your finger, and then you and Payaso did the rescue mission up north, going into the gangster's house, and you could've got hurt there, too—"

"But I didn't."

"But you *could've*. Don't argue with me for the sake of arguing," she said. "Why are you going all the way for this girl? She seems totally oblivious to the shit that's come down on you because of her. It's like she doesn't care."

I couldn't dispute that. I said, "You're here, too, protecting her. Why do you do it?"

"Not the same thing. I didn't get shot. I didn't get my finger broken."

She was right. I sighed. "Would you believe I didn't have anything better to do?"

"No."

"That was only partly a joke," I said. "My life in San Francisco, even my life before that in L.A., it wasn't about anything."

"Whose life is?"

"Mine was supposed to be," I said. "I was supposed to have a commission by now, troops to command. I was working toward that, and I thought I was doing everything right, but I still got reassigned to Fort Livingroom. This is the only operation I'm ever going to carry out." I rubbed my arms against the cold. "It might seem extreme to you, the risks I've taken, but that's how I was taught. You don't protect yourself when there's a civilian ass hanging out where it'll get shot. And if Nidia doesn't fully appreciate what I've done, well, civilians rarely do."

Serena nodded slowly. Then she said, "So what happens next?"

"Tomorrow I have to make a phone call."

forty-three

The next day dawned quite warm, and everywhere snow was thawing into translucent puddles. Serena and I waded out through it at about ten in the morning, walking out to a quiet place, an empty, slushy meadow at the edge of a ranch.

I stopped and took out my cell phone, leaning on an old-fashioned split-rail fence.

I'd explained it to Serena the night before. "Negotiations," I'd said. "They may not work, but you've always got to try talks before committing to a shooting war."

She had assumed that I'd want to place this call from a pay phone, but I'd said no. A pay phone, however anonymous, might show its number with an area code on caller ID. My cell phone had an L.A. area code. That was the one I wanted to show up on the screen.

"Then he'll have your phone number," Serena said.

"That's fine with me," I said. "If you're thinking he can track my signal, he can't. The cops could, but not a private citizen."

I climbed up on the fence and Serena got up next to me, close enough to hear. I pulled up my directory of saved numbers on my cell and found the one for Skouras's lawyer.

"Good morning, Costa and Fishman, how may I help you?"

"I need to speak to Mr. Costa immediately," I said. "My name is Hailey Cain, and it's urgent."

"He's in a meeting right now. Can I get your phone number?"

"I'm afraid not," I said. "Listen, no matter how important his meeting, if you walk in there and say Hailey Cain is on the phone and wants to talk to him about Tony Skouras's grandchild, I guarantee you he'll get up and walk out of that room."

There was a beat of silence, then her voice was stiff as she said, "Please hold."

And I did, for quite a while. A horse whinnied in the distance. Sweat started to trickle along my spine, under my shearling-lined jacket. Truckee's part of the Sierras had wide dips between its frigid nights and warm days, and besides, Serena and I were in full sun.

"Miss Cain, this is Nicolas Costa," a man's voice on the line said. "You've been leading everyone on quite a chase."

"Had to," I said.

"Actually, that's not true," he said, his voice more animated. "That's the funny thing about all this. Nobody on our end can figure out how you got involved. You have no discernible link to Nidia Hernandez or anyone else in this matter." When I didn't say anything, he prodded, "You have no response to that?"

"It wasn't a question," I said. "Mr. Costa, I'm calling to ask you a question: What's it going to take for Nidia and her baby to be allowed to live together? She's the mother. She has a right to that. There has to be a way that can happen."

When he didn't answer right away, I added, "This line's not tapped, and I'm not recording this conversation for anyone, if that's what you're worried about."

"I never thought you were working with law enforcement," Costa said. "Your unorthodox methods make it clear that you're not. In fact, I think you have no better position here, in terms of the law, than we do. You came into a private home with guns, assaulted one of our employees, and took a defenseless young woman away with you. And then, if I'm reading news reports correctly, you tried to kill a California Highway Patrolman."

"That wasn't me."

"Let's stop wasting time here," he said. "You called to find out what it's going to take for Skouras to give up on having his grandchild. The answer is, nothing. Our position is completely nonnegotiable. We will call with instructions for where you can bring Miss Hernandez, and in exchange, you and she will be allowed to live. If we have to track her down ourselves, Miss Hernandez will be killed, as will you. Quentin, the young man you unwisely taunted in Gualala, has expressed some interest in spending some private time with you, and Mr. Skouras has already given his approval for that."

Next to me, I felt Serena stiffen.

Costa said, "You do understand the implications of the words 'private time,' don't you?"

"Yeah, it's a rape threat," I said. "Excuse me if I don't worry about it too much. He and I spent a little time together that day in Gualala, and he came out of it second best."

"Spare me the youthful bravado. You're in over your head, firstie. I'll call in twenty-four hours with instructions. If you don't accept them on receipt, the mother's survival and your survival are off the table."

He hung up.

"Holy shit, Insula," Serena said.

"Yeah." I jumped off the fence. "Well, we've got a little time to think."

As we were heading back down to Julianne's trailer, she said, "Why'd that guy call you thirsty?"

"He didn't," I said. "He was calling me a 'firstie.' It's a fourth-year student at West Point, or a cadet first class. It's a good thing I didn't wash out in my third year. I'd be stuck at 'cow.' "

forty-four

"No fucking way," Payaso said.

We were back at the trailer, on the porch, and I'd just let him in on my conversation with Costa, including the callback in twenty-four hours with further instructions. Payaso's face was again a mask, but an angry mask, not the least bit clownish. Iceman was sitting nearby. It was another war council.

"We're running out of options," I said. "Nidia wants to keep her child; Costa says Skouras will never stop coming after her, and furthermore, if we don't at least agree to give up the baby when he calls back tomorrow, the stakes go up. Nidia's life and mine are going to be forfeit."

Payaso was still shaking his head. "He's not getting the kid."

"My question, though," I said, "is how we're going to deal with him. We can't just throw Nidia and the baby on a Greyhound and hope for the best. She's not capable of protecting herself and her child." My throat felt dry from so much talking, first with Costa, now here. "And we can't keep guarding her and the kid around the clock, long-term."

Everyone was silent. We could hear the faint throb of music from inside Julianne's bedroom, where Nidia was with Cheyenne, like yesterday. I said, "Nidia should be a part of this conversation."

"No," Payaso said. "She's pregnant and under a lot of stress. I don't think she should have to think about things like this."

Serena said, "It's her baby and her life. If Nidia shouldn't have to be in on this, who the hell should?"

Payaso ignored her. "You said that she and the baby would have to be separated until the old man dies, right?" he asked me.

"Yeah," I said. "And who knows, that could be soon."

"What if it was really soon?" He smiled slyly. "Like, extremely soon."

Iceman smiled. Before that, he'd been as impassive as an Easter Island statue.

I had to swallow before I could speak. "You mean an assassination."

"You saying he doesn't deserve it?" Payaso asked. "You know he does. If you want to keep your hands clean, Trece and I can TCB on this. You wouldn't have to be involved, except in the planning, like you did with finding Nidia. But not in the actual—" He made a gun of his thumb and finger and mimicked shooting.

He was making a good point, in his way. If Trece went after Skouras and succeeded in killing him, it wasn't like the old man wouldn't have brought it on himself. Everybody knew what happened when you lived by the sword.

But there was a problem. "I doubt you could get near him," I said. "He knows a Hispanic gangbanger was involved in the mission in Gualala. He'll spot one of your homeboys a mile away. You guys aren't gonna blend in, not in Skouras land."

"Guys? Maybe not." Another sly smile. "But a nice innocent Mexican girl, dressed like a maid or a janitor? One of Warchild's home-girls could walk right up to him and blast away. Some of them are as good with a gun as my homeboys."

Serena shot me a look that, in anyone else, would have appeared to be mild consternation. In her, it was alarm.

I said what she was undoubtedly thinking. "They could get in to do that, sure. But could they get out?"

Payaso didn't look like he had considered this, but he lifted a shoulder. "Under the right situation, yeah, I bet they could."

Finally Serena spoke up. "She'll have other kids."

"What?" Payaso said. "What are you taking about?"

"Nidia will have other kids," she repeated. "And the old man doesn't want to kill this one, he wants to *raise* it."

Payaso started to speak, but Serena didn't let him: "Listen to what we're saying. We're talking about *killing* someone, with one of my homegirls doing the shooting, and maybe not coming back, and for what? All so Nidia can raise this kid instead of giving it up? It's too high a price." She jumped off the porch railing. "I'm going to get her. I want to hear her say it's worth one of my homegirls' lives for her not to have to give up her baby."

"No," Payaso said. "She doesn't need to be in on this decision. This is gang business."

"No, it's not, Payaso," she said. "That's what we've been pretending so that we can tell ourselves we can handle this, but it's not. In case you didn't notice, we're like five hundred miles out of our territory, the *enemigos* are rich white guys we didn't use to ever have to think about, and she's"—Serena gestured toward me—"not really even one of us, like Trippy was saying. This isn't just Trece business, and Nidia needs to be in on it." She headed toward the back door of the trailer.

When Payaso stepped in front of her, I thought it was just to block her way, until his hand whipped out and he slapped her face.

I understood why it had happened. Serena was as tall as Payaso was, five-nine. She was smart. She used to run with the guys. She wasn't like the other females, whose anger and opposition he could have blown off as girlish pique. A challenge from Warchild was a challenge. He couldn't have backed down and not lost face in front of Iceman.

So he hit her. Not a hard slap, just enough to remind her of how things were. In case she'd forgotten. Which I guess she had, because she was staring at him in shock, and he was looking back at her with a cold, impassive expression, not moving out of her way.

I said, in a low voice, "Let's take a break, okay? This isn't getting us anywhere."

They were still staring at each other.

I went to Serena's side, playing the soothing girlfriend. "Let's go into town, okay? Everyone needs to cool off, and we didn't really eat a lot of breakfast. We'll get something to eat, all right?"

"Yeah," Serena said, her voice muted. "Okay."

I looked at Payaso. "Can we take your car?"

forty-five

We'd barely gone two miles, me driving, when Serena leaned forward, head in her hands lowered almost to the dashboard, and started to cry.

"God damn him," she said, sniffling.

I recognized what a good time this would be not to say anything glibly comforting, and didn't.

We were silent the rest of the way into town, except for Serena's brief spasm of tears, which dried quickly. We went to a diner and ordered garlic fries and cream-cheese jalapeños and Cokes and found a table in the back, where we could talk without being overheard. The infusion of sugar and grease seemed to have a calming effect on Serena. She watched through the window as a stellar jay splashed and bathed in a parking-lot puddle. I watched, too, but I was thinking of the problem at hand.

By the time we'd finished our food and were sitting idly sipping our Cokes, I said, "I think you're right."

"About what part?" she said dully, sitting with her chin in her hand.

"Skouras has to die," I said.

She raised her head. I'd surprised her. She wasn't used to hearing me sound so bloodthirsty, and in so flat a tone.

I explained: "This isn't going to be over until Skouras's got the baby or he's dead. I'd say that it's okay for him to get the baby—hell, I'd offer to *bring* the baby to him, except that Nidia will never stop trying to get the kid back. Maybe she'll go through the courts or even go to the media, but somehow she'll make an annoyance of herself, and he'll have her killed. He might have her killed anyway, preventively, and Costa's warning about '*if* you don't cooperate' was bullshit from the start. For all I know, if I arrange a meeting to hand the baby over, he might have his guy say, 'Thank you very much,' and put a bullet in my head, just for knowing about the whole thing. And for wasting his time and punking his guys."

Serena said dully, "You want us to do what Payaso said, have one of my girls dress up as an office cleaner and get close to him?"

I shook my head. "I'm not letting one of your homegirls do this," I said. "That wouldn't work very well, either. The problem with an assassination in his home or his office, for one of your sucias, would be getting out safely. But there's another option. Skouras has to get around, and San Francisco has horrible traffic. That's why bike messenger services are so successful there. Bikes cut right through the traffic."

"Are you saying *you* want to do it? On your bike?" Serena said.

"It's a variation on a drive-by," I said. "They do it a lot in foreign countries, on motorcycles. I'd be almost unrecognizable as a bike messenger, dressed like one, wearing a helmet. If I pull my hair down low enough, it'll obscure a lot of my birthmark. And I could probably even dye my hair dark." The details were coming to me fast. "I'm wearing a half-open jacket over a shoulder holster with the gun under it. I pull up alongside Skouras's car, blast away, I'm gone. One of you could be waiting for me somewhere nearby. I cut through an alley or a parking garage, dump the bike and the helmet, get in a car with you, and we're gone. Skouras's guys will know who it was afterward, but they already know who I am. No one's at risk who wasn't before."

Of course, it was possible that it wouldn't work, that Skouras's guys would kill me, either on the spot or later. That possibility was part of my calculations. I do X, he does Y, I get killed. It was still weird to me that I could think so dispassionately about my own death. I'd learned not to talk about it that way, though, not even in front of someone as jaded as Serena.

"I don't like it," she said.

"We'll refine the details as we go," I said.

But she was shaking her head, looking out at the hills and the horizon. "This is a detail that can't be refined away," she said.

I hesitated, grasping her meaning. "An assassination is unacceptable to you?"

"*You* doing it is unacceptable to me," she said. "You're not a murderer, Insula."

I pulled my food basket toward me and picked up one of the few remaining french fries, even though I wasn't hungry. "In a way, I'm avenging my own murder. His guys shot me to death in Mexico, or at least that's what they thought. They dragged me off the highway so no one would find me. It doesn't absolve Skouras that I didn't actually die. He wanted me to."

"But you didn't, *prima*."

"We haven't got a world of options here, Serena." I was frustrated.

We were silent a moment. Then I said, "Look, we're not going to throw this plan together in twenty-two hours, anyway. When Costa calls back, we'll stall. I'll try to work out a deal in which Nidia stays with us until the baby's born. I'll tell him we'll work out a handover then."

"He won't go for that."

"He doesn't know where we are. He'll have to go for it or stick his thumb up his ass."

"No, he's going to stick a *gun* up your ass when he finds you, that's what he said on the phone," Serena said.

"Well, it's the best plan I can come up with," I said. "We just need to stall while I go back to San Francisco and do enough surveillance on Skouras to get his routines down. Then I do the hit, and Nidia and her baby are safe."

"You sure about that?"

"Yeah," I said. "The baby's value to Skouras is strictly personal. Once he's gone, there's no reason for his soldiers to keep this quest alive. They're just hired guns. If no one's paying anymore for the baby to be found, that'll be the end of the search."

"Hired or not, the Greek's guys might take his murder kinda personal," Serena pointed out.

"They won't blame Nidia for that."

"You mean they'll go after you."

"I'll be the one who hit Skouras," I said. "They'll know that."

Serena said, "I'm still in unacceptable-losses territory with this."

I pried the lid off my drink and stirred the sepia-colored mix of Coke, water, and the remnants of hollow ice-machine cubes. "I don't know anymore who started this," I said. "When I drove into that tunnel, I was a civilian noncombatant, and those guys shot me point blank. But then we took the fight back to them when we went after Nidia. We didn't have to do that. But however you look at it, we're engaged now. It's a war. And if someone's got to die before it's over, I think it should be Skouras rather than Nidia or one of your homegirls or me. Can we agree on that?"

She nodded.

I crumpled my napkin and threw it into the plastic basket. "Come on, then, let's head back."

On the drive back to Julianne's place, I said, "So what was Trippy saying about me?"

Serena looked blank.

"You know," I prompted, "that I'm not really one of you guys?"

"Oh, that. Don't worry about it. She's young and insecure. She's my lieutenant, but then you came back to L.A. and took your beating, and suddenly you're at the center of the biggest mission we've ever done. She feels pushed aside. She'll get over it. When we get back to L.A., I'll do some Trippy maintenance."

"You should," I said, braking for a stop sign, then pulling through. "What she's saying wasn't wrong. I'm not really one of you. I've said that all along."

She shrugged, not wanting to relive the argument we had on the phone.

"Hey," Serena said, "slow down, you're gonna miss the turnoff."

She was right. I braked as hard as I dared on the snow-wet road and turned, steering us up through the gauntlet of trees.

When we got to the trailer, Cheyenne came out to meet us. She looked shadowed and worried.

"What's up?" Serena said.

"Nidia isn't feeling good," she said. "She's having cramps."

"Cramps?" Serena asked. "Or contractions?"

forty-six

The one advantage to Nidia going into labor early was that it blew away our previous, half-baked theories about jacking a doctor to attend the birth. Nor did Payaso bring up his idea that Nidia could give birth to the baby alone. Instead, he did the guy thing: He turned the whole situation over to the women. Serena and I quickly decided to take Nidia to a hospital.

I did the driving. Nidia was in the passenger seat, which was pushed back to accommodate her belly and also reclined into as comfortable a position as possible. She'd gathered her hair into a loose ponytail off her face, which was faintly beginning to shine with perspiration. But she didn't seem to be in any distress, just tense and inwardly focused.

Serena and Cheyenne were in the backseat. No one was talking. I was concentrating hard on the road ahead of me. The day was still warm enough, yet I imagined a rogue patch of ice causing me to slide the GTO disastrously into a ditch. The sun was low enough now that I had to fumble for my sunglasses.

At the hospital, the parking lot wasn't even half full, a good sign that Nidia wouldn't have to wait long to be seen. I parked us in a space that said AMBULANCE ONLY and cut off the engine. Cheyenne and Serena climbed out of the backseat, noisily closing the doors behind them. I didn't open my door, because I would have to find a more permanent parking space for the GTO. That's when I felt Nidia's small hand clamp around my wrist. I glanced over, and her alarmed eyes met mine.

"You're coming in, aren't you?" she said. "I only trust you."

This was something new. I'd never heard her say anything like it before.

Serena opened the passenger-side door. "Ready?" she prompted Nidia. "Let's go in."

I said, "Give us a minute."

Serena shrugged and gently closed the door. I struggled to think of the right response. "Of course I'm coming in," I said. "It never occurred to me not to."

She didn't take her hand off my arm, the knuckles slightly pale. She said, "Back when I thought you were dead, when I was in that house in the hills, I prayed for your soul, every day. That God would take it into heaven."

Maybe she was frightened because of the difficult hours of labor that lay ahead of her. Or maybe she was just emotional because her baby was finally hours from being in her arms. But I felt certain that she wouldn't lie about this. And I would have been lying if I tried to pretend that the knowledge didn't touch me, somewhere I hadn't known I was still vulnerable.

"Why didn't you tell me this before?" I asked. "Like, last night, when you nearly ran away and I stopped you?"

She said, "I thought you would laugh."

"No, I wouldn't have," I assured her. "Go on inside now. I'll be along as soon as I park the car. Things are going to be okay."

Payaso and Iceman drove down a little later, and we slept in turns. Around three A.M., I was in a quiet, dim waiting room on the hospital's top floor, stretched out along a row of linked chairs with padded seats.

We had ten hours, roughly, before Nicolas Costa would call. There was nothing to be gained by telling him that Nidia was giving birth—or, by that time, maybe *had* given birth—to the Skouras grandchild. I planned to go through with the plan I had come up with that morning. We'd need to stall for time if I was still going to hit Skouras.

That had become my word, *hit*. That was how I sanitized it to myself. That and reminding myself, over and over, that he'd done it to me first, or tried to. In Mexico, Tony Skouras's men took me to the limits of my fate, and it had been no thanks to them that those limits stopped short of death.

Soon I was going to repay them.

If I succeeded—and that wasn't a given—things would change once again as drastically as they had after Trey Marsellus's accident. Another flight, another new home. I had yet to think about where I'd go.

Closing my eyes, I remembered CJ's offer to lend me enough money to open a little bar and restaurant on the Gulf Coast. I'd never take him up on it, of course. I'd already taken ten thousand dollars from him that I could almost certainly never repay.

But for the moment, on a chilly December night, it was too comforting to slip into a fantasy of faraway warmth, and I did. I imagined a place in a small Louisiana town, down on the end of a pier, where I'd string white lights along the roofline and keep cold Jax beer in the cooler. At night I'd sweep up and wash dishes and watch the lightning out over the water. CJ would come visit me. I'd mix him up dirty martinis and cook Cajun food like he asked. He could play his guitar for my customers.

Sure, the good times. The ones you know are never really coming.

forty-seven

When I slept, I didn't remember my dreams, but I woke up paranoid, my hand twitching for the SIG.

"Hey, Insula, take it easy," Serena's voice said.

I rubbed sleep from my eyes. Serena was bundled into a heavy flannel shirt, and she looked cold. At least that was my first impression. Then I realized that there was something wrong with her face, a guarded apprehension that had nothing to do with physical discomfort. I thought of Babyface and Quentin and the rest of the tunnel rats, that somehow they'd found us despite every precaution we'd taken.

"What's up?" I said. "Did she have the baby?"

She said, "They're still getting the baby out."

Serena wasn't a sentimental person, but *getting the baby out* was not the way she would refer to a mother giving birth. *Getting the baby out* meant something was wrong.

"What's going on?"

"Nidia must have had an undiagnosed heart condition," Serena said. "A weak heart. It gave out during labor."

"Is she going to be all right?"

"She's dead."

"She can't be *dead*, Serena."

"I'm sorry, but it's true," Serena told me. "They've got to get the baby out now, because I guess there's no oxygenated blood without the mother breathing, and . . . I thought you should know."

People in TV and the movies were always breaking bad news to people by saying, *You'd better sit down*, but as soon as Serena told me this, I thought, *I've got to stand up.* So I did. My legs were a little shaky, and once I was up, I didn't know what to do.

I said, "Do you know what practically the last thing I said to her was? 'Things are going to be okay.' What a fucking idiot."

"No," Serena said flatly. "Of all the things you could have looked out for, this wasn't one of them. You did everything you could for her, *prima.*" She paused. "That probably doesn't help, right now."

Nidia's baby was a healthy boy. I wish I could say that he gave a lusty, life-affirming cry just as the first rays of morning light slanted through the hospital windows and Serena and Payaso and the rest crowded around to marvel at his little fingers and his little toes, and it was a great life-in-the-midst-of-death moment. Maybe some of that even happened; I don't know. I was outside, where the fresh, cold air and the light was almost assaultive after the stale recycled air of the hospital. It had snowed during the night, and most of it was still fresh. I walked over to the quadrangle of lawn and I sat on my heels to touch it.

The first time I saw snow, we'd been based in Illinois. Like this one, that snowfall had come in the night. I had been afraid to touch it until my father did. In that memory, I can't see the features of his face, just his big bare hands, picking up the snow, showing me how it melted as he rubbed it between his fingers.

Like he'd done, I got my fingertips wet from the snow, then painted that wetness onto my eyelids. My eyes felt dry and bloodshot from poor sleep, and I felt the relief as the water sank in and stung my eyes, then ran down onto my cheeks like the tears.

Since I'd first heard her name, Nidia to me had been a series of imperfect motivations. I'd driven her to Mexico for some cash and maybe drugs, plus for a break from my daily life in San Francisco. Then I'd tried to find out whether she was alive or dead, because I'd needed to understand what happened in the tunnel and why. Finally, I'd taken on the job of rescuing and guarding her to prove to myself that, given the chance, I could have been a good officer.

Nothing I'd done had been because I'd known who Nidia was or cared about her, and now it was too late to try. Somewhere inside that religious, distant person had been a real girl who'd loved a real man, and later had a sexual indiscretion with another one, a man with whom she'd known there was no future. I'd never known that Nidia. Serena and I had both held her at arm's length for fear that her victimhood was some kind of catching illness.

Should that matter to a soldier? Wouldn't such personal feelings simply be an encumbrance? If so, why did I feel guilty for not having them?

I straightened up and went back into the hospital. We had things to think about, Serena and I.

But when I got to the neonatal unit, Cheyenne was sitting in the waiting room, her eyes reddened. Payaso was stretched out along several hard plastic chairs like I had been, sleeping with his head pillowed on a rolled-up sweatshirt. Iceman was doing the same, but sitting up with his head tipped to the side.

No Serena.

I turned to Cheyenne. "Where's Warchild?"

She frowned. "We thought she was with you."

I walked the corridors, looked into other waiting rooms, checked the women's restrooms. No luck. But by then I had an idea about where she might have gone.

It wasn't difficult to find the morgue. No one was around to stop me, to ask to see my ID. There was a sign above the double doors that read AUTHORIZED PERSONNEL ONLY, but Warchild wasn't one to let the rules stop her.

The morgue wasn't that different from the rest of the hospital. It had the same vaguely synthetic smell of recycled, conditioned air, the same sound-absorbent flooring. Only the sound of the climate-control system was different here, louder. It was here that I found Serena, sitting with Nidia's body. She was crying.

Serena, *Warchild,* crying for the little vic she'd claimed to disdain. This was a private moment. I decided to slip out the way I'd come in.

Except then my cell phone rang. Serena looked up. When she saw me, she knew who was calling. I did, too. Costa. Our deadline had arrived.

Serena watched with wet eyes, both of us silent, as the phone rang a second, then a third time. Once more and it would go into voice mail. We couldn't afford that, no matter how ill-equipped I was to deal with the situation at the moment.

I connected the call. "Hello?"

"Good morning, Miss Cain," Costa said. "I've conferred with my client. We've come up with an arrangement for you to bring Miss Hernandez to us."

He went on about how Nidia had been well cared for physically and medically before, and how that would continue. Then he started to tell me about the meeting place they wanted me to bring her to. I cut him off.

"That's not going to happen," I said. "She's staying with us until the child is born. That's nonnegotiable. We'll be in touch afterward about a hand-off."

"What makes you think any of this is negotiable?"

"You want the baby," I said. "That's your only reason for doing any of this."

"For someone in your bargaining position, you strike me as almost arrogant," he said.

"My position's pretty good. I've got what you want and you're the one calling me to get it."

"You know, when I said yesterday that no one understood what was motivating you, that wasn't entirely true," he said. "I think I understand the root of your reckless behavior. Miss Cain, I know the reason why you had to leave West Point."

I hung up on him.

forty-eight

"*Did you hang up?*" *Serena said.*

"We were getting nowhere."

"What did he say to you, at the end?"

"Nothing."

"He said *something*."

"He was just messing with me. He thinks he's smart." I put the cell phone away and walked to Serena's side. The sheet covering Nidia was pulled back to reveal her face and shoulders. Her eyes were closed, but she didn't look asleep. She looked diminished, lifeless.

Serena said, "You stalled him."

"That was the plan."

"I know, but things have changed," she said. "You could've told him what happened. You could've arranged to hand off the kid and get yourself off the hook."

"I know."

"So you're still doing this?" Serena said. *This* meaning the war with Skouras, protecting Nidia's baby even without Nidia alive to know about it.

She had prayed for me, Nidia, even though she'd believed me to be dead. As far as I knew, no one had ever prayed for me alive. I owed her something.

"I am," I said. "Are you in?"

Serena nodded. "I'm in." She slid off the stool. "Come on. We've got some planning to do."

"Go on without me," I said. "I'll be there in a minute."

Her footsteps receded, the door closing with a faint gust of air. I stood a moment longer, looking down at Nidia.

"Pray for us, kid," I said.

forty-nine

Three days later, we were at a rest stop off Highway 101: Serena and I,
Payaso, and the baby I'd come to call Henry. I sat on a picnic table,
holding him. He was freshly diapered and had had as much formula
as I could get him to take. Now, content, he regarded me with milky
eyes that hadn't decided on a color yet.

Indecision marked all our lives today. We had no idea what we were
going to do about Henry Hernandez. Serena and Payaso were looking to me to make that decision, as they had with most of our choices
thus far. Most, but not all. They'd made a crucial one late yesterday
that had changed the game.

Serena came out of the restroom, shielding her eyes against the
sun, finding us. She walked over. "It's on the radio," she said.

"We knew it would be," I said. "Infant son of adolescent Mexican
single mother, taken at gunpoint from a maternity ward by a *cholo*
and his girl . . . Yeah, Skouras's gonna know whose baby that was."

Serena said, "I was doing what I thought was right." It wasn't the
first time she'd said it.

"I know," I said.

Yesterday, Serena and Payaso had, in essence, kidnapped Henry
from the hospital nursery. I had been back up at Julianne's trailer,
getting some badly needed sleep after the restless night in the hospital. They hadn't called to consult me. They'd made an executive decision.

There would have been some difficulty in getting Henry out
otherwise. None of us were legally related to him, and the county

foster-care service had been about to step in. Serena and Payaso, with their deep-seated distrust of the system, weren't about to let that happen.

"For Skouras's men to take him out of a foster home, that'd be child's play," Serena had told me afterward. "You think some skinny white do-gooders are going to be able to protect him? He needs to be with us."

She and Payaso had recounted it for me. Cheyenne had been the third party, the getaway driver. They'd taken Payaso's GTO to the hospital, Cheyenne waiting in Iceman's Taurus two blocks away. Serena had gone up to the maternity ward and signed in as Encarnación Hernandez, aka Teaser, Nidia's now-deceased cousin. It was an ID that would only lead back to Nidia Hernandez and family, not to any of us. Serena had gotten permission to hold the baby and strolled with him as close as possible to the exit. Covertly, she'd texted a single character to Payaso, an exclamation point.

That had been the signal for him to fire two gunshots in the stairwell before running out a ground-floor exit to the GTO. With the hospital's security officers headed toward the sound of the shots, Serena had escaped with Henry. She'd jumped into Payaso's car, and they'd driven two blocks to where Cheyenne was waiting in the Taurus. Serena had lain down out of view in the backseat holding the baby, while Payaso had gone the other way in the GTO, both cars slow and careful.

When I'd stopped yelling at Serena for taking such a big step without me—this after making such a big deal of setting me up as the leader of this whole endeavor—I'd realized that she and Payaso had been right about Henry not being safe in the foster-care system. And their plan, however audacious, had worked. The news reports had only the color and model of Payaso's car, not the specific make, and no license number. And nothing at all about the Taurus. I had to admire both the nerve and the planning.

But what they'd done had meant that we'd have to leave Truckee. As soon as the news went out, Skouras's men would come. Truckee was not a big place, and our East L.A. crew didn't quite blend in, and Julianne's place, while set back from the road, wasn't a cabin in the middle of no-man's-land. It wasn't safe anymore.

I'd gone into town to buy a car seat and other things the baby would need, and then I'd simply driven us both out of town in the Taurus. White woman, white-looking baby in a car seat, unassuming domestic car: Sometimes plain sight is your best option. On the streets of Truckee, I'd passed several police cars, but if the whole town was in an uproar over a baby's kidnapping, it had been taking place behind closed doors. No one made any attempt to detain me on my cool, law-abiding way out of town.

"They can't stop every car with a baby in it," I'd told Serena and Payaso. "What kind of proof could they demand from me that Henry is mine, anyhow?"

They'd gotten away shortly thereafter, taking fire roads outlined on my area map. It was only now, about two hours north of L.A. on the 101, that we'd finally felt safe hooking up again.

"Have you heard anything from Iceman and Cheyenne?" I asked.

Serena shook her head. "They'll be all right," she said. "Don't worry."

They had stayed behind an hour, in order to clean the trailer— well, maybe not Iceman, but Cheyenne probably had. I'd insisted on that. When Julianne came home, I didn't want it to be to cigarette butts in the ashtrays and hairs in the shower drain.

I said to Serena, "Pretty soon we've got to call Lara Cortez, so she can get in touch with Nidia's family. I don't want her in a morgue cooler indefinitely."

Serena nodded. "I'll get a phone number from Lara and call them myself," she said. "It's a death notification. Believe me, in *la vida*, I've seen this news dumped on *mamis* and *papis* in really screwed-up ways. I want to handle it myself."

"Sure," I said.

"Can I hold the baby?" Serena asked.

There was nobody nearby who looked remotely official, so I judged it safe for Serena to be holding the baby. The nearest people to us were a young Latino family who piled out of a green minivan. The kids jumped out, racing for the water fountain. The parents, a man in a straw cowboy hat and a woman in jeans and a warm-up jacket, got out at a more leisurely pace.

I handed Henry over into Serena's arms, and she held him adeptly, supporting his downy little head. "Hey, Enrique," she cooed. "*Que pasa,* lil' homey?"

She seemed quite at ease, and it was worth considering that if Henry lived at Casa Serena, he'd have a dozen or more experienced babysitters. Most of the sucias had grown up diapering and coddling little brothers and sisters, and many of her former homegirls had babies of their own. But I also thought of Herlinda Lopez's death and my own shooting down in Mexico. Adrian Skouras's baby was four days old and innocent as rain, but he had an unwanted gift for bringing terrible trouble into the lives of people around him.

Who the hell could I have given him to? Who would I wish that on?

One answer would have been for me to become his guardian myself, keeping the lightning always potentially poised over my own head. Noble, but not practical. I was inextricably linked in Skouras's mind with his grandson. Like Nidia, I would serve to identify him wherever we went.

The woman next to me called her children, and they ran to the table, where she'd laid out a lunch of sandwiches and boxed juice, a Tupperware container of apple and orange chunks, and vanilla cookies. The kind of lunch I remembered from my childhood: inexpensive, balanced, charmless.

The best thing would be for Henry to disappear into the anonymous hands of strangers like this, into the heart of mundane working-class or middle-class life. Of course, this family was Mexican, and while I tended to think of Henry as Mexican, he was only half. Henry might grow up to be easily taken for white.

There were infertile couples everywhere who would, in theory, leap at the chance to adopt a healthy, appealing infant like Henry, only

four days old. But in practice, most of those couples would ultimately shy away from a dark-alley, extralegal adoption, if I even
knew how to set one up. Which I didn't. It was too bad, really. So
many childless couples, wanting—

Wait.

An audacious idea had come to me.

No way. Put it out of your head, Cain.

"What are you thinking?" Serena asked.

"Nothing," I said. "Come on, let's go. It's probably not smart for
you to be standing around holding him like that. We should keep
moving."

Serena handed the baby back to me. "See you soon," she said.

I walked back to the Taurus and strapped Henry into his car seat,
backed carefully out of my space, and drove toward the freeway.

But on the road, I couldn't stop thinking about the idea that had
come to me at the rest stop, and by the time I was back in L.A., I
knew what I was going to do.

fifty

At Casa Serena, an informal vote overwhelmingly suggested that baby "Enrique" live with the sucias, like a mascot, a baby boy with no mother but a dozen loving, devoted older sisters. The girls passed him around among themselves so much that Serena finally had to intervene.

"He's fine," Heartbreaker pleaded as Serena carried him away. "Babies need stimulation."

"Not that much," Serena said. "He's four days' old, for God's sake."

Deprived of the baby they'd quickly come to consider a living toy, the girls turned to the night's second form of unexpected entertainment, the cable news channels and the latest on the baby-napping. To the sucias, this was the latest exploit of *la leyenda* Warchild, and they devoured the media reports with a mix of pride and derision. They jeered when Payaso's GTO was reported as "possibly a Chevy Nova" and laughed outright at the police sketch of Serena.

"That could be fucking anybody!" Teardrop exulted.

Escaping into the privacy of Serena's room, where she'd made a makeshift cradle from a dresser drawer and blankets, I gave Henry a bottle. Serena followed me in, holding a pair of cold, wet Corona bottles by their necks, then expertly cracked them open using the edge of the dresser and her hand.

When Henry rejected the rest of the formula, I set it aside and turned him upright, jouncing him gently. In a moment, he burped, a loud and healthy sound. Serena giggled, and I did, too.

This was the moment where most girls our age would have asked one another, *Do you think you'll ever want a baby of your own?*

Serena and I didn't. We'd already implicitly asked and answered that question. We already knew.

She handed me a beer and said, "Have you thought any more about what to do with him?"

I had—more than that, I'd decided—but couldn't say so. "Tomorrow we'll brainstorm."

She nodded. "Sounds good." She set her bottle down. "Can I hold him again?"

I handed him over. Serena took him in her hands and bounced him gently. "Don't you worry," she said to him. "Your Auntie Warchild and Auntie Insula aren't going to let anything happen to their littlest homeboy." She kissed the top of his head. I snickered.

"What?" she said.

" 'Auntie Warchild and Auntie Insula,' " I said. "We've gone crazy."

"A long time ago," she agreed.

We put Henry in his makeshift bassinet to sleep. I lay back on Serena's bed, my head at its foot, and took my first sip of the Corona, felt it trace a cold path down deep through my chest. "Ahhh," I said, eyes half closed.

"No shit," Serena agreed.

I opened my eyes again and looked up at her print of Halong Bay. It was an image so clean and pure I imagined Serena willing herself to touch it and suddenly be there.

"Warchild?"

"Eh?"

"Have you ever thought about going to Vietnam?"

She gave me a quizzical look. "To do what?" She rolled the neck of her beer bottle in her palms.

"To see it. It's a tourist destination. The war's been over a long time," I said.

"Are you saying you believe me now, about my dreams? You never did before."

"What I believe doesn't matter," I said. "You're interested in Vietnam; you ought to go someday."

"You mean, like, on vacation?"

"Yeah. Not a big fact-finding mission. Just walk around, see the people, eat the food."

"Homegirls don't do that shit," she said. "I mean, Jesus, it's on the other side of the planet."

I rolled over onto my stomach. "For God's sake, think of the things you do every day. You're a shot caller in a gang, for crying out loud. You're telling me you couldn't make a reservation, get on a plane?"

"And the money's coming from where?"

I shrugged. "The usual ill-gotten gains. Start a jar, stuff a couple tens and twenties in it every time you have a particularly good week."

She took a hit off the beer and studied me, her eyes hooded and speculative. "Would you come?"

"You don't need me," I said. "I'm not ruling it out, but Vietnam's not my deal, it's yours. Whether or not I could go with you, you should go."

"You always got this crazy shit on your mind, stuff that no one else thinks about," Serena said.

A little after midnight, Henry's crying woke me. I told Serena, "Stay here, I'll get him."

" 'Kay," she said, burrowing back down under the covers.

I got up and went to the bassinet, sat on my heels and scooped Henry up, blankets and all. I picked up his bottle on the way out of the darkened bedroom.

Serena's girls were used to sleeping through nearly anything. The two in the living room didn't stir as I turned on the light over the stove and, one-handed, poured water into a pan, topped off Henry's bottle with formula, and put it on the stove to heat. All through this, he cried. Pettish little sounds, not loud wails. I bounced him and made clicking noises with my tongue.

When Henry was fed and quiet, I composed a note.

> *Serena,*
>
> *I'm going into the city. I think I know*
> *a place where Henry will be safe. I know*
> *you've got enough cojones to go*
> *with me, but it's best I do this alone.*
> *I'm taking the Honda that Trippy*
> *stole earlier today, sorry. I love you.*
>
> > *H.*

fifty-one

The streets were quiet, but nonetheless I obeyed all traffic laws, signaling my turns and staying within the speed limit, as was appropriate for someone driving a stolen Honda with a kidnapped infant. Even so, I was glad to get off the main roads and begin the climb up into the hills. I had one stop to make before I took Henry to what I hoped would be his permanent home.

CJ usually chained the corrugated-tin gate at the head of his rough dirt driveway at night, but I remembered the combination for the lock, drove through, and parked. Overhead, a black silhouette passed low: a hunting owl. A nocturnal creature, like me, and like my cousin as well. There was light on the dry grass behind the house, clearly coming from the back windows, and the faint sound of music.

I unstrapped Henry from his car seat and lifted him out, closed the car door, and walked up onto the deck. Then I hesitated. The music was clearer now, and I didn't think it was on the sound system; it sounded like the piano in the living room. The pianist was running lightly through bits of jazz, just pleasing his own ear.

CJ's relationship to the piano had followed a fairly typical arc. When he was a child, his mother had made him learn to play it. As a teenager, he'd rejected it in favor of the strap-on sex appeal of the guitar. As an adult, he'd come around to the pleasures of its rich nineteenth-century sound. And, of course, women loved to watch him at the keys.

It was this last part that gave me pause. It was possible that there was someone in there with him, a female someone. I didn't want to walk, uninvited, into the middle of that. But I'd come too far to simply leave.

I walked around to the sliding glass door. He was at the piano, and as far as I could see, he was alone, and so deep in concentration that I could have watched him indefinitely.

I tapped on the glass with my knuckles. The music stopped. CJ looked over his shoulder and did a double take.

"What the hell?" he said when he'd opened the slider. "I didn't know you were back in town. You should've called me. Come in."

I did. CJ, eyes on Henry, said, "Who's your friend?"

"Him? I'm just babysitting for a friend."

"Babysitting."

"Yeah."

It wasn't much of an explanation, but CJ didn't pursue it. He gestured toward the couch and said, "Can I get you something to drink? The bar's pretty well stocked up."

"Just water."

"You sure?"

"I'm sure, just water."

"What about him? Do you need me to heat a bottle or something?"

"No, thanks. He's fine."

CJ went into the kitchen and I heard him opening the refrigerator, then the rattle of ice. I waited on the couch. His living room was cluttered as always. There was a deck of cards on the coffee table and a girl's sandal half under the couch. A painting, apparently a recent acquisition, leaned up against the wall, waiting to be hung. It depicted the narrow, crowded street of a Chinatown. It could have been the work of someone famous, or the amateur effort of one of CJ's friends.

He came back with a bottle of Asahi in one hand and a tall glass in the other. It wasn't tap water. Bubbles crawled up the side of the glass, and it was stacked with ice, then a wedge of lemon.

"Pellegrino," he said.

I'd almost forgotten how CJ did things for the people he loved, always with a little extra touch of generosity.

He took a seat on the piano bench, sideways, with his long legs casually spread, and said, "How is it that you're down here again? Don't you have to work, up in the city?"

"I set my own schedule, remember? I've been taking some time off lately." I paused. "Look, if you're thinking about the money you lent me—"

"No, that's not why I asked. Don't worry about the money." He waved my concern off. "As long as you're down here, maybe you and I—"

"I'm going back north tomorrow morning," I said. "Sorry."

"Tomorrow?" He was casual about it, but I heard the veiled hurt in his words, that I would come and go so quickly, without making plans to spend any real amount of time with him.

"Sorry," I said again. This was where I should have said, *Please come up and visit me,* but I already knew I wasn't going to be in San Francisco.

I changed the subject. "You know, it's Saturday night. Why don't you have a date?"

He shrugged. "You can't always party," he said, then shifted position and started into "Lush Life" on the piano.

I leaned back and listened to him play. I wasn't optimistic about the days to come, that Skouras's men weren't going to catch up with me one way or another. That was why I'd come here to see my cousin. But I couldn't say anything important. If I launched into some reminiscence of old times or told him how vital his love had been to me, from my unlovely preadolescence to this moment, he was going to realize something was up.

Abruptly CJ got tired of his own talent, stopped playing, and stood, looking at Henry. "Can I hold him?" he said.

"Sure," I said.

"If he's sleeping, and it'll bother him . . ."

"No," I said, moving over to let CJ sit next to me. "He had his eyes open a minute ago. He's just being mellow."

I gave Henry up and CJ took him gingerly. He touched the baby's mouth with one finger, and Henry sucked at it, hopefully, opening his gray eyes again.

"I think he's hungry," CJ said.

"No, if he were hungry, he'd cry," I said. "He's fine. You're doing fine."

"What's his name?" CJ asked.

"Henry."

He took his attention off the baby to give me a curious glance. "Like your old man."

"You just saw me three months ago," I pointed out. "Do the math, CJ. He's not my kid. It's not possible."

CJ said, "I don't think the world has yet found the limits of what you're capable of, Cainraiser."

A little later, in CJ's spare bedroom, Henry slept in another makeshift bassinet while I stretched out in the graceful white iron bed. And failed to fall asleep. After some time, I gave up, rose, and padded barefoot into CJ's room.

The ambient light in there was a little better, because the uncurtained window faced the waning moon. In its dim light I could see my cousin lying on his side, his back to me, maybe sleeping, maybe not. Carefully, I lifted the covers and slid in behind him.

"Don't trip," I said quietly. "S'me."

"Knew that," CJ murmured.

I lifted the hair off the back of his neck and kissed the nape, the body's most unguarded area. He smelled of Ivory soap, like he had at age twelve, and that was one small point of continuity in our vastly changed lives. He didn't smell of anything *pour homme*. He never would.

"Hailey," he said, "I know something's up. Tell me. Maybe I can help."

"No," I said. "I don't want you worrying about me."

"I always worry about you."

I felt his weight shift, as if he was about to roll over and face me, but I put my hand on his shoulder and exerted a light warning pressure: *Don't*. We were Orpheus and Eurydice; if he brought us face-to-face, something was going to happen that shouldn't, even if it was just me breaking down and telling him the truth.

"Ask me something else," I said. "Anything."

"Say my name."

"CJ," I said obediently.

"No," he said, disappointed in my obtuseness.

I put my mouth close to his ear. *"Cletus,"* I whispered, and felt him smile.

"Better," he said.

I reached over his hip and took his hand. "Go to sleep. I'm right here."

"Never long enough," he said sleepily.

Like Serena, CJ woke briefly when I got up, again using Henry's crying as my excuse. Like Serena, he was asleep again by the time I left the house, Henry in my arms. It was dawn, and down the hills I could see a faint outline of the tall buildings of the real Los Angeles, the city I hadn't been to for over a year. Golden, godless, avoided, beloved: my Nineveh.

fifty-two

*Even in war, there are territories that aren't to be intruded upon, and reli-*gious sanctuaries are one of the most important. So, in the bright late-December morning that followed my long, interrupted night, I stood on the steps of the Baptist church that Luke Marsellus had re-built. I had only been inside as far as the narthex, where I'd politely asked one of the ushers to tell Mr. Marsellus, as soon as the service was over, that Hailey Cain was waiting outside to speak to him.

Henry was being good as gold. I only wished I had a hat for him. It was a nice temperature out, maybe sixty degrees, but I wondered if the full sun was bad for him, at his age. So I kept my back to the sun, putting Henry in my shadow.

The church service broke, and the parishioners emerged onto the church steps, into the sun. Then the usher appeared at the top of the steps. Next to him was Marsellus.

He was a very tall man, with large, lambent eyes and a physical gravitas that made people watch him covertly. He left the usher behind and came down the stairs until he reached my side. "You," he said.

"Mr. Marsellus."

"I'm told you want to speak with me." He had a low voice, like suede, and there was very little of South Central left in it.

I nodded. I couldn't read anything off his tone and bearing.

"About?" he said.

"Half of it's what you'd expect," I said, meaning an apology. "The other half's going to take a little explaining."

Marsellus looked into the distance and rubbed his chin with his hand, considering. Then he took a cell phone from his jacket. "I'm going to call someone to pick you up and take you somewhere we can talk. I'll be there later."

He didn't specify how much later and it wasn't my place to ask. But I said, "The baby's got to come with me, wherever I go."

"Yours?" he said. Marsellus was economical with language.

I shook my head. "My responsibility, but not mine."

He nodded and then moved a little bit away from me to make the phone call. I didn't try to overhear what he was saying.

Then he returned and said, "Wait here. Someone will be here in about fifteen minutes." He moved off into the dispersing crowd.

Not long after, a Lincoln Navigator pulled to the curb. There was a large black man in warm-ups behind the wheel, and another in the passenger seat.

"Miss Cain?" the passenger-side guy said after rolling down the window.

I nodded.

He got out and opened the back door for me. "You want me to hold the baby?" he asked. He had a soft, high voice.

"I got him," I said. Even so, the security guy took Henry's diaper bag, like the driver of a hotel shuttle, before I could reach for it. Then, after I'd settled in with Henry, he closed the door and we pulled away into traffic.

We made no conversation as the SUV made its way across town, and the SUV's good construction and windows kept a remarkable amount of city noise blocked out. All I heard was soft, throbbing beats from the satellite radio, set at a low volume. Henry slept in my arms, a warm weight, peaceful.

The driver downshifted, and I looked out the window to see that we were making an ascent. In a moment, I realized that we were headed up into Beverly Hills.

Surely Marsellus wasn't having me brought to his home? Maybe I'd been thinking of life as war for too long, because it seemed all wrong. Home was where you went to ground. You didn't bring your enemies there, even the ones who were no threat to you. Home was supposed to be a refuge.

Yet when the motorized gate slid back, I recognized the house. I'd read a lot of articles about Lucius Marsellus in my last days in Los Angeles, and some of them had pictures of his home.

The Navigator came to a stop and we got out.

I'd expected to be searched when we got away from the eyes of bystanders. That didn't happen. I considered remaining silent about the SIG I was carrying, but decided the wiser course was not to go into Luke Marsellus's home strapped and get found out later.

"I'm carrying," I told the guard when we were on the front doorstep. "You want to hold it?"

He paused and considered. "Lemme see it."

I pulled out the SIG and handed it to him. Expertly, he took out the clip, checked that there was no round in the chamber, and handed it back to me.

I followed him through the front door and into a tile entryway. I could see into a long, wide living room with a ceiling that was at least fifteen feet high. That was where the Christmas tree should have been, but it wasn't. There were no decorations of any kind, which suggested that there was no woman's presence in this house—that Marsellus's wife hadn't returned, nor had he met someone new.

"Which way?" I asked.

"Upstairs," the security guy said.

He led me up a curving staircase and down a long hallway, then opened a door. He didn't go in, instead motioning with his arm for me to enter. I stepped inside and looked around.

It was a bedroom, as I'd thought. There was a twin-size bed and a dry, empty fish tank and a toy chest. The walls were blue. God, this was Trey Marsellus's bedroom.

My escort set down the diaper bag. "Mr. Marsellus should be up soon," he said. "Does the baby have everything he needs?"

I nodded.

He withdrew, and the door clicked shut behind him.

I looked around. There was a stuffed bear on the dresser, a Dodgers pennant, a signed photo of one of the Lakers, personalized to Trey. But my eyes kept going back to that empty fish tank. It seemed emblematic of the room overall. Dry, because Trey's father couldn't bear to come into his room every day and feed the fish, but not gone, because he still hadn't been able to pack up Trey's room and make something else of it.

This was part of my penance, seeing all this. How much of my penance it was remained to be seen.

It was a good twenty minutes before I heard the door handle twist, like that moment in a doctor's office. I turned to watch Marsellus come in.

For a moment he just surveyed me, standing in the middle of his son's room, holding a baby. Then he pulled the chair out from Trey's child-sized desk and turned it to face outward. He gestured toward it, clearly indicating that I should sit. I did. Marsellus leaned back against the footboard of the bed, a position that was mostly still standing, and said, "Speak your piece."

I took a deep breath and did. "I came here to tell you that I'm sorry about your son," I said. "I went to the hospital the evening Trey died to say that, but your security men stopped me. After that, I was advised that you and your family might need some space."

"And then what happened?"

"I left town."

"Why?"

I knew he knew, but he wanted to hear me say it. It was as if Marsellus were handing me a shovel, wanting me to dig myself a deeper hole, but I wouldn't lie to him. I said, "Because it was suggested to me that you might not be able to forgive me." *Come on, Cain, say it all*. "And that you might have me injured or killed."

"Miss Beauvais suddenly being gone planted that idea in your head."

"Yes."

"Where did you go?"

"San Francisco."

"Not very far."

"I guess not."

He rubbed his long chin. "Now you're back. Why?"

"That's the story I came here to tell you."

"Go ahead, then."

"Do you know who Anton Skouras is?"

He considered and then shook his head no.

"Not a lot of people do. He's low-profile, but he's been called the biggest unindicted organized-crime figure in San Francisco," I said, borrowing Jack Foreman's phrase, because I couldn't put it any better. "And this baby is his only grandson."

I told Marsellus the story: Adrian and Nidia, my involvement, Herlinda Lopez's death, the tunnel, Gualala, and Nidia's death.

"Some of this can be confirmed by news accounts," I said. "Adrian's obituary was in the *San Francisco Chronicle,* for example, as was an account of Herlinda Lopez's disappearance. Henry's kidnapping from the hospital was statewide news."

"Good Lord," Marsellus said, recognition sparking. "This is *that* child?"

"Yes."

"You don't look anything like the sketch on the news, of the woman who took him."

"That wasn't me."

He shook his head. For the first time, I'd genuinely surprised him.

I went on: "Beyond the parts that were in the news, I can't prove the whole story. Although . . . can you hold the baby a minute?"

Marsellus looked taken aback, but then he held out his arms. I stood up and gave him Henry, who accepted the change equably. Then, as I had done with Julianne, I pulled down the neckline of my shirt, revealing the scar under my collarbone. I said, "This is what Skouras's gunmen did to me down in Mexico."

If he was impressed, it didn't show on his face, but then Lucius Marsellus had probably seen some shooting scars in his day.

I said, "Do you believe me?"

Marsellus was slow to speak. Then he said, "Yeah. Yeah, I do, but I don't understand what it has to do with Trey, or me."

I said, "Mr. Marsellus, it's fallen to me to look out for this child, but I can't, not in the long run. Skouras's men know who I am and what I look like. As long as Henry's with me, he can be found. And my resources are extremely limited. I can't start life over in Buenos Aires."

"Miss Cain, are you asking me for money?"

"No," I said. "I wouldn't do that."

It took him a moment, but then he understood. "You want *me* to take this child?" he said.

I looked him directly in the eye. "I can never repay what I took from you, however accidentally. But this child is the son of a genius father and a beautiful and virtuous mother. I think he might really be something, with the right resources and the right guidance. If Tony Skouras is allowed to raise him, he'll make this boy in his image, and Skouras is a monster."

Marsellus said, "Why take this child away from one gangster just to give him to another?"

"His mother would have done anything to keep him from being raised by Tony Skouras," I said. "Nidia could have gotten money from him for giving up the rights to her child. She could have been set for life. Instead, she fled to Mexico, to live in poverty in some village in the Sierra Madre. Obviously, Adrian told her very bad things about his father. If you read about this man and pay attention, that's borne out. A picture emerges of a guy who's spiritually poisoned, a trafficker in human lives, obsessed with money and with winning at all costs." I paced. "You, on the other hand, despite what you might do in the name of business, have never been impeached in your personal life. You seem to have a good relationship with your mother, your brother and sisters, your nieces and nephews. And you were said to be a devoted . . . a good . . ."

"A good father," Marsellus said.

I nodded. "And beyond all that, this is a good tactical decision," I said. "Your home is the last place Skouras would look for his half-white, half-Mexican grandchild."

"And I'm supposed to make it look legitimate how?"

"You have money and connections," I said. "You can make it look legitimate. Any good attorney could."

"You've thought about this," he said.

"Yes."

"But you're not scared."

"What?" It didn't seem to have anything to do with his line of questioning.

Marsellus steepled his fingers, tapping the tips against one another. He said, "Oh, you're polite enough, and respectful enough, but . . . I've lived a lot of life, Miss Cain, and I've seen a lot of fear in my day. It's not a feeling I'm getting off you." He paused. "Why is that?"

Before I could answer, Henry began to fuss, his face crimping and reddening. Marsellus looked down at him.

"He's probably hungry," I said. "I can give him a bottle."

"No," Marsellus said. "That boy's got a muddy diaper." He gave Henry back to me. "There's a bathroom down the hall where you can see to him. After that, come to the first room off the staircase. We can finish our conversation there."

fifty-three

The room Marsellus had directed me to clearly reflected a woman's tastes: pale Victorian striped wallpaper, an antique escritoire, wing chairs. When I got there, after changing Henry's diaper and washing up in the bathroom, Marsellus was standing by the window.

He said mildly, "You should have come and talked to me a year ago."

"I know," I said.

He went on: "Trey was a very active child. Almost hyperactive. Me, he'd mind, but I'd seen him disobey his nanny repeatedly, run away from her when she'd told him to stay close to her side. I'd seen him run out into the street before, though he'd been told repeatedly not to. My wife and I were thinking of getting a man to look after him, someone who could take a firmer hand. But Miss Beauvais was a nice girl, and Trey liked her, so we put off that decision." He paused, looking out the window. "When Trey died, I was very angry. Some of it was at her, and some at you. But a lot of it was at myself, for not doing something earlier.

"I have, like you said, a certain reputation in business. Some of that is deserved. Some of it is rumor and exaggeration. I don't always discourage that, since with fear comes respect. But a reputation like mine has unintended consequences. It was the reason Trey's nanny left town in the middle of the night. I assume she was acting on the same incorrect conclusion you later did, though to be fair to you, her disappearance gave you a little more evidence for it."

Then he said, "The hardest rumors to combat are the ones that are never printed or even spoken in your presence. I know that some people continue to believe I had Trey's nanny killed, and there's nothing I can do to fight that."

I nodded.

Marsellus said, "The advice you were getting in the days after Trey's death, to give me some space, was that from Cletus Mooney?"

Again I was surprised. He saw it and said, "I didn't learn about the connection until months after you left town. A business associate of mine used to see you two together in the clubs. You went to high school together, is that it?"

"He's my cousin," I said.

"Interesting guy," Marsellus said. "Lotta people curious to see what kind of work he'll be doing when he's thirty." He looked out the window again, then back to me. Finally he said, "This is a very big thing that you're asking me to do."

"I know," I said.

"What are you going to do if I say no?"

"Stay hidden as long as I can, fight if I have to fight," I said. "I know this is a big thing I'm asking, a lifetime, really. But I think this baby's going to be something special. I think he'll have things to give you, not just you to him."

Marsellus was quiet a long time. I resisted the urge to jump into the silence with more selling points.

Finally he said, "Trey is buried next to my father in Inglewood Park Cemetery. Go apologize to him, like you have to me, and then we're square."

"You'll take the baby?"

"Yes," he said. "I will."

*In the first-floor entryway, Marsellus's man took out the clip to my SIG and re-*loaded it for me, then handed it back.

Marsellus had accompanied me down, Henry in his arms. He said to me, "What are you going to do about Skouras? Do you expect to be able to hide from him forever?"

"I don't know," I said honestly.

"I won't protect you from his people. You and I are square, but I don't owe it to you to start a war with an organization like his."

"I know," I said.

"Good luck, then," he said. Then he turned to his driver. "Please take Miss Cain wherever she needs to go."

fifty-four

The quickest way out of state would have been to get to southern Nevada, or to Arizona. The roads in that direction were also more lightly traveled than those going north, which was a good thing when you were driving a stolen car, like I was—I'd had Marsellus's driver take me back to where I'd left it, apparently unnoticed and untagged. I'd get rid of it as soon as I could afford to.

All in all, I really didn't want to get on the 101 north. More than that, I didn't want to go into San Francisco. It was Skouras land. But I had to. Most of what was in my room over Shay's office I didn't need, but there was the small matter of my new driver's license, which I'd arranged to have mailed there; I wasn't going so deep underground that I wouldn't need that. Then there was my *Wheelock's Latin*, and inside that was my birth certificate and my only photo of my father.

So in Oxnard I got off the road and made a phone call. Shay didn't sound happy to hear my voice, but I had paid him his rent in full, so he didn't have a lot of grounds on which to act aggrieved.

"Has anyone been around looking for me?" I asked him, trying to sound casual.

In Gualala, I'd unwisely identified myself to Quentin as a "one-hundred-thirty-five-pound bike messenger." There weren't that many messenger services in the city. If Skouras's guys had wanted to, they could have narrowed it down.

"Looking for you? No," Shay said. "You're not in trouble with the cops, are you? Jesus, that's all I need."

"No," I said. "It's not that. But I'm thinking, can you maybe grab a few things, and I can meet you somewhere else? Like your place?"

It was hard to imagine Skouras's men staking out my place long-term, but as Serena would have told me, it's paranoia that keeps you alive.

"You can't just go and get what you want?" he demanded, irritated.

"I'm sorry," I told him. "I can't."

"Fine," he sighed, sounding exasperated. "Tell me what you need and I'll get it."

"Thanks. It's not much, I promise," I said.

fifty-five

Shay had given me directions to an address at the edge of the Haight. Parking was easier than it should have been, but then, it was two days until Christmas. Some of Shay's neighbors were likely out of town, traveling to visit relatives. The many darkened windows around me testified to that.

But at Shay's place, a tall, narrow Victorian, light glowed behind the closed blind of the front window. I climbed the front steps and rang his doorbell.

Shay answered his door dressed in jeans and a sweater.

"What's up?" I said. "Thanks for doing this."

"Hailey," he said, inclining his head for me to step inside. "Come on back."

I followed him across the smooth polished wood of a short entry hall. When we entered the living room, I saw figures on the periphery of my vision and turned sharply to recognize them: Babyface and Quentin.

I went for the SIG, but not fast enough. A third guy stepped out of the shadows and grabbed me, twisting me around into a rigid and painful hold.

Quentin swaggered forward. His dark-blond hair was freshly cut and his face was bright with enjoyment.

"Well, look who it is," he said. "It's Staff Sergeant Henry Cain's daughter, Hailey." He smiled widely. He'd been imagining saying that for some time now.

I looked at Shay. "You bastard."

I would have liked to think that Shay hadn't done this willingly, that they'd braced him and threatened everything he held dear, but he didn't have the strained look of someone whose home and life had been invaded. Instead, his eyes were hooded, the guarded expression of guilt.

"Was it money?" I asked.

He shrugged. "If you give these guys what they want, you'll come out of this just fine."

"No, I won't, Shay," I told him.

Quentin had called it, long ago in Gualala: *You'll be dead by Christmas.* That was two days from now, and all signs suggested I was not going to live that long. In the words of the first Bridge suicide: *This is as far as I go.*

Babyface said to Quentin, "Go get the car."

fifty-six

It was morning on the Gulf Coast, maybe around ten or so. My little bar and grill was out at the end of the pier. The waters of the Gulf looked a lot like the Pacific. A gentle breeze, which should have been tangy and salt-scented, jangled the clear glass bulbs strung along the roofline, the ones I'd light up tonight when we were open for business.

Right now I was at work at a big tin sink like you saw in fish markets, the kind with a white cutting board on the side. The surface of the cutting board had the shallow marks of many knives in it. I was cutting into a catfish with the boning knife I'd once held on Serena. Occasionally I washed away the catfish's blood with an extendable hose that could be pulled out from the faucet, but there was always more. The smell of blood obscured that of the ocean.

I scraped viscera over to one side, kept slicing. My hand hurt a little bit, the little finger that Babyface had broken. I'd thought it was healed, but now it stung.

"Hey, sugar."

CJ's long arms slipped around me, and he put his face down into my hair, the way he used to when we'd gone dancing together.

"Hey," I said. "I'm glad you're here."

"What are you making?"

"Catfish. You wanted me to learn to fix something Cajun for you. This was just caught." I nudged my chin at the choppy ocean. "Out there."

CJ said, "Catfish is a river fish."

My hand, holding the knife, shook a little. "Then it's swordfish," I said, and suddenly it was.

"Are you sure they catch swordfish around here?"

"Why are you making this so hard?" I demanded, slapping the knife down. "It has to be something, CJ. *I need something to explain the smell of the blood.*"

Scent was the hardest sense to re-create in memory or imagination. I wished I could create the smell of salt water for this, but I couldn't. I smelled only blood. This was a fragile fantasy, too ready to fall apart.

"I'm so sorry, baby," he said.

"I am, too," I said.

I turned around to look at him, the wind playing with his reddish-blond hair and the material of his loose white shirt. He was wearing undoubtedly expensive sunglasses with lenses that looked smoked, like something from the Victorian era. He seemed at ease, unhurt, and I was happy, too, because whatever happened to me, CJ was safe in his *vita felix.*

I put my arms up around his neck and drew him to me. "I've been so stupid," I said, murmuring against his neck.

"How?" he asked.

There was a chaplain at school who used to favor that passage from Ecclesiastes, with the refrain *All is vanity.* And it was, my whole life. Not just the past few months, running around pretending I could be the protector of innocent girls and newborn babies, imagining I could thwart Skouras and his whole machine, but even before that, my dream of being a second lieutenant in the Army, of commanding my own troops and making the world a little safer. All of it, vanity.

How many of the stupid, glory-seeking things I'd done had been to burn up the frustrated energy of not being able to have him? What a bloody fucking waste. So what if some of his genes were some of my genes? Who the hell cared? Now I was going to die, far away, having protected him but never fully loved him.

"I'm sorry," I said.

"Shhh," CJ said. "Baby, it's all right. I'm going to help you." He cupped his hands under my jawline and kissed me, then his hands went to my shoulders, gently pushing me down.

I went with what he wanted, kneeling and pushing up his shirt and rubbing my cheek against the skin of his flat stomach, then unhooking his belt and pulling his faded Levi's down. My hands left streaks of blood on his bare thighs but it didn't bother him, or me. I took him deep in my mouth.

"That's it," he said, leaning back against the railing of the pier. "Good girl."

CJ's hands, the ones that cupped my nascent breasts at thirteen, now spread through my hair and against the bones of my skull. "Everything's all right, baby," he said.

The lightbulbs swayed in the wind, and I closed my eyes and concentrated on his rhythm.

"*Hailey,*" he said, "Hailey, I love you," and his hands tightened convulsively in my hair as he finished.

And suddenly I was on the floor, my face against dirty, industrial-gray carpet, coughing and choking. The fantasy broke up because when Quentin finished making me give him head at gunpoint, he pulled me off him and shoved me unceremoniously facedown on the floor. I hadn't been able to break my fall because my hands were cuffed behind my back.

Jack Foreman had said that Skouras sold off his line of X-rated movie houses years ago, but maybe he couldn't get rid of all the holdings, because here I was, in the projection booth of a long-closed theater. There was a big rectangle of carpet missing where the projector had been wrenched up to be sold off. But there was still an editing table in the back. From my position on the floor, I could see the drying blood that had dripped off the edges of the table, and a little more on the carpet.

That was why, in the fantasy, my once-broken finger had been stinging so badly. I no longer had a once-broken finger. Babyface had taken it off with a pair of tin snips, while one of his two helpers held my arm in place. They hadn't bandaged it. It had clotted and stopped bleeding on its own, but that had been the main part of the torture: watching my hand spurt blood and not being able to put pressure on it. Humans are hardwired to do almost anything to keep our blood in our bodies where it belongs. The pain of losing a finger had been secondary to that psychological drive to do anything, *anything,* to make the bleeding stop.

I wasn't strong. I'd actually said, "Marsellus," while I was watching my hand spurt blood. None of them had understood it. Babyface said, "What?," and before I could repeat myself, I'd heard an inner voice say, *You got up. You got up and walked.*

And it was true. In Mexico, Skouras's men had taken me off the road to shoot me, far enough away that I wasn't supposed to have been found and helped. They'd left me there. At some point after, I'd opened my eyes and seen the rising moon, and somehow, with two holes in me, I'd gotten up and staggered to the road's edge, because that had been the only way I was going to live.

That memory gave me an inkling of pride. Just enough not to say, *The baby's with Lucius Marsellus.*

And when I didn't, they'd decided to try something else to break me down.

I thought I'd figured out the division of labor. Will, the short, dark-haired guy, was just hired muscle; his heart wasn't in any of it. Babyface was in charge, and it was he who wielded the compression shears. But Quentin had center stage now, and he was clearly relishing his role as the witty sociopath. If his erection was at half-mast now, his ego was at full mast.

He leaned over me. "I gotta tell you, considering the circumstances, that was *not* the worst blow job I ever had," he said. "You really got into that toward the end. Did you think it was gonna buy you some goodwill with me?"

He pulled up his trousers, got himself arranged. I rolled onto my side. The passages inside my nose were starting to swell, but I didn't think they were going to bleed. They'd toughened up from too many hits already.

All together and spruce again, Quentin said, "Okay, let's review what we've learned." He held up a didactic finger. "This hasn't been educational for you, actually, so much as it's been for *us*. See, we've done only two things to you so far, but they were important things. These"—he picked up and shook the tin snips—"and that really lovely knob job."

He set down the snips. "The thing with women is, they tend to fall into two camps. Some of them can take a lot of pain, but they can't stand anything sexual being done to them. Other women can let a whole freak show of guys ball them, so long as you don't hurt them physically." He sat on his heels, the better to look into my face. "So the first thing I do, with a woman, is see which group she falls into. You might not even have known which one you were."

He was having such a good time.

"Before I share my observations with you, why don't you tell me which one you think you are."

I didn't say anything. There was no point. They really were going to kill me. *Amissa mundo sum,* I was lost to the world.

The one person I'd failed to protect was myself. I understood why I hadn't, but it had also brought me to this, and this was a problem. I wasn't afraid, but I was in a lot of pain, and eventually, I'd break.

Maybe it was best that I crack under the pain and tell the truth. Just because Luke Marsellus had said he wouldn't start a war with Skouras didn't mean he wouldn't fight one if Skouras's men came after Henry. Maybe Marsellus and his men would have these guys for breakfast.

Or maybe Skouras's guys would wipe the floor with Marsellus's security detail and get the baby. Then Henry, or whatever Skouras named him, would grow up rich and well-cared-for, and become a monster like his grandfather. Maybe twenty years from now, in his late forties or early fifties, one of these men would work for Henry, and he'd see Henry so regularly that the sight of his young boss wouldn't remind him anymore of that chick he'd tortured to death for Tony Skouras.

"Hey!" Quentin poked my chest. "I'm talking to you. Which group?"

I licked my lips, still sickened by the taste in my mouth.

Quentin put his face close to mine. "You think we're just gonna give up if you don't talk to us?" he said. "Wrong, babe. This is fun for me. A job like this, it's like a bright spot in my week."

"Careful," I said. "On an MRI, a bright spot is bad news."

Behind us, Babyface was sitting with his legs out in front of him, elbow on knee, chin in hand. He looked bored with Quentin's antics, like a film director watching a B-talent actor overdo a monologue.

"This is taking way too long," he said, getting to his feet. "Get her back up on the table, I'm going to take off another finger."

Will hauled me to my feet and dragged me over to the editing table and pushed me down, bent at the waist, so I was half lying on it, like the catfish-turned-swordfish in my Gulf Coast fantasy, getting my own blood all over the mostly bare skin of my upper body. Babyface and the guys had stripped me down to bra and panties. Even in my current state of mind, I had to admit it was smart, as was starting with fellatio instead of outright rape. Babyface was taking things in stages, making sure I had things left to lose.

The handcuffs clicked loose and Will pulled my arms straight in front of me again, walking along the table to hold them down at full length in front of me. Babyface positioned himself with the tin snips in hand.

That was when I started laughing.

I know it's hard to explain. Babyface didn't understand, either. "I know you're scared, Hailey," he said.

"You don't know that," I said, still laughing. "You don't know that *at all*."

With his free hand, he stroked my hair. "Come on, Hailey," he said. "This doesn't have to happen. Just tell me where the kid is."

It was good cop, bad cop, all in one. Babyface was giving me some sugar.

"I can't," I said, trying to get myself under control.

Babyface straightened, his face turning cold. He looked at Will and said, "I'm going to speed things up a little, take off two fingers in this go."

He took my left ring finger in his hand and I felt the lower blade of the shears slide under it. That was the point at which I finally stopped laughing and took a deep, steadying breath. Even though I wasn't afraid, I knew the pain was coming and that it would be bad, and I closed my eyes tight. What came to mind, in that moment, was not Virgil or Marcus Aurelius but Jonah's prayer: *As my life was ebbing away, I remembered the Lord, and my prayer came to you.*

Then there was a deviation from the script. A clear female voice, from the doorway of the projection booth. "Mr. Laska," it said.

We all looked up, even me in my semi-prone chopping-block position with my arms being held out in front of me. It occurred to me to yell for help, but I didn't. The woman crossing the floor was too calm, and she knew Babyface by name. She had to be in on this. She was not going to help me.

Babyface said, "Yes?"

She said, "Please stop what you're doing."

She was near to my height, wearing a black cowl-neck dress and black boots. I thought she was somewhere around thirty. She had a heavy sheaf of bronze hair and brown eyes with half-moon lids, just a hint of gray shadow in the corners, or maybe that coloring was natural. A tall, heavyset man in a suit trailed her, like a bodyguard.

Babyface said, "Do we know each other? Jimmy I know"—nodding to the guy in the suit—"but I've never seen you before. I work for Mr. Skouras, and I'll stop what I'm doing when he tells me to."

She said, "I'm afraid that's not possible. You know Mr. Skouras had a heart attack two days ago, don't you?"

I raised my head slightly at this unexpected news.

"Of course I know," Babyface said. "He's getting better. They were going to move him to the step-down unit today."

The woman shook her head. "So I was told, but I'm afraid he had a second, more serious attack. He died several hours ago."

My limbs were starting to shake. I wished they wouldn't. The situation in front of me was so delicate, I didn't want to disrupt it by even breathing too loudly. I couldn't bring myself to believe that this woman in front of me was going to be able to back down these monsters. They'd never let me go on a strange woman's say-so.

She was going on: "I didn't answer your original question. I'm Teresa D'Agostino Skouras. Tony Skouras was my father." Her speech was so precise, it almost had a British clip.

"Mr. Skouras only had sons," said Quentin, thrusting himself into the exchange.

The woman said, "By his marriage, yes. But he's long acknowledged me, privately at least, as his biological daughter. He supported me financially when I was younger, and now, in the absence of his sons, he's left his estate and businesses to me."

Babyface said, "Mr. Skouras has mentioned you to me, but I never heard him say anything about leaving his estate to you, and—"

"I understand this all comes as a shock," she interrupted, her tone smooth and civil. "Here, call Mr. Costa's office. He can confirm everything—my father's death, the disposition of his businesses, all of it." She extended her hand, with a cell phone in it. Babyface looked at it a moment, as though he'd never seen a phone before. Then he said, "I have my own," and began to fumble in his pockets.

I didn't really believe this was happening.

Babyface walked a few short paces away from all of us. Unexpectedly, Teresa Skouras turned to Will. "For heaven's sake, do you think you could let go of her? In her condition, if she tries to run, I could catch her myself."

I didn't expect him to grant her any authority here, so when he actually did what she asked, I wasn't ready, and my knees gave out. I went down so hard my chin hit the edge of the editing table and my vision jolted like badly spliced film. I heard Quentin make a humorless snort of laughter.

Babyface was still pacing, saying, *Uh-huh, uh-huh, okay.*

On hands and knees on the floor, I felt and tasted blood, flowing from where I'd bitten my tongue, hitting the table's edge. I didn't get up. Teresa Skouras was right; there was no point in trying to run. I didn't believe this situation ultimately was going to go my way.

Babyface disconnected and said to the guys, "It's true."

Neither Quentin nor Will spoke, though Quentin glanced quickly at me as if to ensure that I wasn't already walking away.

Babyface squared his shoulders. "Listen, Ms. Skouras, I'm sorry for your loss. It's my loss, too."

"Thank you," she said.

"But this is important business we're doing here. It was important to Mr. Skouras that his only grandchild be raised a Skouras. I know you're new to the situation; you may not understand."

She nodded sagely. "If family weren't important to my father," she said, "he wouldn't have supported me so graciously in my youth. But sadly, he died before he could see his grandchild, and nothing will change that. He's gone, and any professional contract you had with him is now void. Including your commitment to"—she gestured at the bloody table—"this task."

"But Adrian's kid—"

"Is my concern, and I'll decide how I want to proceed on that."

Babyface stood for a moment, tin snips in hand, looking at the wall and the small dark window cut into it, the one that looked out onto the theater. Then he shrugged and said to Quentin and Will, "Let's go."

"What?" Both of them, in unison.

"Mr. Costa says she's in charge now. We're leaving."

Babyface walked over and nudged me with his shoe. "One thing, Ms. Skouras," he said. "Be careful with her. She's the only one we know for sure knows where the kid is, so you need her. But she's not the pushover she looks like she should be. I was thinking I was gonna have to take off all ten of her fingers, and even that might not have worked."

"I'll keep that in mind," Teresa Skouras said blandly.

"I'm saying," Babyface said, "that it's probably not in your interests to leave her alive when all this is over. If you don't have anyone for that kind of work, Mr. Costa has my number."

"Thank you," she said in the same dry tone.

With that, Babyface and his men walked past me and out.

I still couldn't believe this was happening. I listened for the sound of their footsteps receding, making sure they were really going, that they weren't going to come back, or wait just out of sight.

Teresa Skouras dropped to her knees beside me, lifting my injured hand to examine it. "Dear God," she said. "Miss Cain—"

I jerked my hand free of hers and staggered to my feet. "*No,*" I said. "Don't fucking *help* me."

She looked as though I'd slapped her, then she recovered. "You're in shock."

I stumbled backward until my back was against the wall and pressed my hands against my face to keep the rage from coming out. She didn't deserve it. She'd saved me. The fingers Babyface had been about to take, whatever else he or Quentin would have thought to do, this woman had stopped it, Skouras or not.

I lowered my hands, breathing raggedly. "I'm okay."

"No, you're not."

"I've been through worse than this."

"I doubt that very much."

"I just want my clothes. Then I'm leaving. I'll be fine."

Then I took two steps forward and collapsed.

fifty-seven

Even here, Latin.

Adeste fideles, laeti triumphantes, venite, venite in Bethlehem . . .

I opened my eyes in an unfamiliar low-lit bedroom done in cream-and-gold colors. The window curtains were open, and outside the sky was a dark blue. Someone was listening to Christmas music in another room, but it was instrumental, only my mind translating the old familiar words. A clock at bedside read 5:35. It was either before dawn or after sunset. A closer look at the digital face revealed a lighted dot next to the letters *P.M.* Evening, then.

I was sore all over, but in no immediate pain. Raising my hand above the covers revealed a lot of white bandaging, but my little finger was really gone. It stung, but not badly, and I wondered if I was on pain medication.

I kicked the covers aside, intending to check my body out for bruises and injuries, but instead I was drawn up short by the realization that I was dressed in pajamas with a fine orange-and-pink stripe, feminine and whimsical, like nothing I would have chosen for myself. I had no idea where I was, and now someone had undressed and re-dressed me while I was fully unconscious.

I got up, found my balance, and went over to the window. The darkened buildings outside appeared, for a moment, generic, then I saw the familiar shape of the Transamerica Pyramid and knew I was in San Francisco. I walked slowly, barefoot, to the bathroom. There, on the skirt of the double sink, was a basket full of toiletries. The labels bore the name of the Fairmont.

The evidence, at this point, indicated CJ. I must have gotten to a phone and called him, and he'd come up and brought me here. He would have needed a place for us to stay, and no one else I knew had the financial resources that made a suite in a five-star San Francisco hotel the logical choice.

I closed the bathroom door and urinated for what seemed like a small eternity, then got cleaned up as well as I could: washed my face and rubbed toothpaste inside my mouth. Then I walked out to the doorway of the suite's main room, where the Christmas music was coming from.

I was disappointed not to see CJ, but not very surprised to see the person who was sitting on the couch: Teresa Skouras, reading papers spread out on a low coffee table.

I cleared my throat and she looked up.

"Well," she said. "How are you feeling?"

"I'm not sure," I said, speaking carefully, because my tongue was still a little swollen where I'd bitten it.

"Would you like to sit down?" She gestured to a chair covered in the same material as the couch.

I did so. "How long have I been sleeping?"

"Nearly a day," she said, "but not straight through. You're in San Francisco, by the way. We're at—"

"The Fairmont, I know," I said. "It's on the shampoo bottles. I can read."

She glanced down, perhaps taken aback by my rudeness. I was a little surprised by it myself.

She went on: "I looked in on you several times, checked your hand for signs of infection and changed the dressing. There was no serious inflammation and you were never running a fever, so I let you sleep."

"Are you a nurse?"

"No, but I did some volunteer medical work overseas, right after college."

"Well," I said, "what's Christmas without a saint?"

I wasn't sure why I was giving her such a hard time. She had saved my life, after all. I cleared my throat and tried to start over.

"Look," I said, "I think we should talk. Miss Skouras—"

"Tess," she corrected me. "And my last name is D'Agostino. Using his name last night was dramatic license."

"Miss D'Agostino, I don't know how else to say this: You are the last of the Skourases and I am the only person in the world who knows where the Skouras grandchild is. Are we going to have a problem?"

She smiled a deeply curved smile, like a Valentine heart. "That statement contained a rather large contradiction in logic," she said. "The 'last of the Skourases' part. If there's a grandchild, then—"

"Don't play games with me." I leaned forward. "Are we going to have a problem?"

She sobered. "About the baby . . ." She picked up her cup of tea. "You allowed yourself to be tortured and maimed for that child. I'm fairly sure you didn't do that after abandoning him in a cardboard box somewhere."

"But—"

She interrupted. "You tell me, then. Is he safe?"

"Yes. More than safe. He'll be loved, and he'll never want for anything. But for me to get him back would be difficult. Making the arrangement that I did was . . . fraught, to say the least."

"That sounds like an interesting story," she said.

"It is."

"Maybe you'll tell me someday."

"That's it?" I said, disbelieving. "You're satisfied with that?"

"I haven't decided if I want to take over my father's businesses," she said. "But I do know I'm not ready to be a mother."

I sat back, still baffled, but silent. I wasn't sure why I was even arguing the point.

She interrupted my disordered thoughts. "Are you hungry? I can't imagine you wouldn't be."

When she said it, I realized that I was.

She said, "I'll get you something to wear."

"I thought you were going to say 'something to eat.'"

"We can get room service here," she said, "but first, I'm very particular about coffee, and I have a favorite place for cappuccino. You've said you feel well. You might as well get out and stretch your legs after lying down for such a long time."

When I didn't move to get up, Tess said, "You're from San Francisco; you must know how lovely North Beach is on Christmas Eve."

"I'm not really from here," I said, "and no, I haven't been in North Beach at Christmas."

"Then you should see it."

That was how I ended up walking around North Beach on Christmas Eve with a mobster's daughter. I was wearing lost-and-found motley, things Tess had sweet-talked the hotel staff into surrendering: a big fisherman's sweater and brown wool trousers and leather ankle boots. Everything was slightly too big for me, but comfortable. Tess's clothes wouldn't have fit. I'd realized that she was inches shorter than she'd appeared in the projection booth. I supposed it was both my literal and psychological perspective on the situation that had made her seem taller.

Although it was Christmas Eve, Tess had assured me that many of the shops would be open until six for frantic last-minute purchases, both by traditional *nonnas* and non-Italian yuppies. And, she said, there would be a café or two open late.

As we walked, me navigating carefully in my slightly-too-large borrowed boots, Tess greeted and was greeted by people on the sidewalk. She seemed to invite the courtesy of passersby. They were clearly looking at her, not at me. She wished them *Buon Natale,* and something lovely and Italian happened to her voice when she did.

"People like you," I said.

"You don't," she said mildly.

"That's not exactly true," I said. "It's just that—"

I broke off then, because we were standing at the doorway to Café Puccini, and a pair of tourists, chatting in German, held the door for us to go in. We did.

At the counter, Tess ordered herself a cappuccino. I opened my mouth to second it, when she interrupted, speaking directly to the man behind the counter. "She'll have a steamed milk."

"A what?" I said.

To me, she said, "You haven't had anything to eat or drink in over a day. You're not starting with coffee."

I thought of objecting but realized I didn't feel legitimately indignant enough to do so.

She came back with two paper to-go cups, handed me mine, and then added a packet of raw sugar to hers. As she stirred it in, I sampled the milk cautiously.

"Is it okay?" Tess asked.

"I don't know," I said. "I've never had hot milk before, not even as a child." I tried it again. "It doesn't taste anything like cold milk."

"It's not supposed to," she said.

"Listen, Miss D'Agostino—"

"Tess," she said.

"Tess, what I was saying outside was, the past few months have not paid a good return on faith in my fellow man. And I really don't know anything about you."

She sealed a plastic lid onto her cup. "Would you like to?"

As we walked back toward the hotel, she told me her life story.

She was from a small Italian clan of fishermen in Bodega Bay, who later ran a bait-and-tackle shop on the water, with a small deli inside. Soon the deli was the heart of the business, with tourists and working fishermen alike coming in for espresso and cappuccino and her grandmother's sandwiches and pasta salads. Her mother, Anna, worked at the store in her teenage years.

That was how she met Tony Skouras, who had a second home and moored a pleasure boat in Bodega Bay. He seemed like the perfect gentleman. Anna knew he was married, but she was young and swept away.

Skouras supported his illegitimate baby financially until Anna married a nice working man, a roofer. After that he sent several checks a year anyway, for extras, nice Christmas presents, and piano lessons. Teresa always knew the roofer wasn't her real father, but she loved him. And when she met her biological father in her last year of high school, she was as charmed, in a very different way, as her mother had been. Skouras was mannerly and interested in her. He was willing to pay for whatever higher education Teresa could win through her grades and aptitude testing. She went to college back east, then to grad school in London. Tess, as she became known in England, stayed in touch with Skouras. She sent him notes and small gifts on holidays. Of course, she'd become aware of who this man really was, where his success in business came from. But like many middle-class civilians, she had a romanticized view of organized crime. She never stopped writing him notes and sending small gifts on holidays. She revered him.

"The truly ugly side of that, I didn't see that for a long time," she said. "My father made it possible for me to become who I am, and not just financially. I love my mother and her family, but they were simple people. None of them had any success in school, or much in business. It was my father who gave me my intellect. I wasn't brilliant like Adrian, granted, but my mind . . . it was a good deal more than my stepfather could have given me."

I realized I'd been thinking of her as Tony Skouras's daughter, not Adrian Skouras's half sister, but clearly that was equally true.

She added, "I briefly considered taking his last name, but my family in Bodega Bay . . . they were my home. I'm part of them."

"Tess of the D'Agostinos."

"Are you commonly this acerbic, or is it your way of making yourself feel unscathed after everything that's happened?"

She'd nailed me. I lowered my face to my steamed milk. Actually, I'd decided I didn't like it, and had been scoping for a trash can in which to discreetly deposit it behind Tess's back, but now it made a good diversion.

She went on: "I know it'll be particularly hard for you to sympathize, given what you've been through at my father's hand, but an inheritance like that . . . your very genetic material, the stuff of who you are, that's a big gift, and hard to reject outright." She reconsidered. "I mean, it's hard to reject outright the person who gave it to you, no matter what you've learned about his private life."

"After last night," I said, "do you think you're any closer?"

Her gaze went to my bandaged hand. She said, "When I walked into that room . . . Hailey, I never saw anything like that before."

"You seemed very calm."

"I was acting," she said. "I didn't feel it."

"How did you know where we were, anyhow?"

"My father was lucid in the hospital, between the first and second heart attack," Tess said. "He must have suspected he didn't have much time, and he was unusually honest with me. About the baby, everything that was going on. I think he hoped I'd understand, that I'd see that this was about family, about our line continuing."

That brought up an interesting point: "You're his daughter, and you're obviously young enough to have children. Why didn't he hold out hope that you'd give him an heir?"

Tess smiled, a private, interior smile, and lifted a shoulder. "I'm thirty-two and never married," she said. "I suppose he'd simply given up on that option." She paused. "At any rate, I knew the overall situation because of my father, and then Mr. Costa was able to tell me where they'd taken you, because Joe Laska had been keeping him apprised."

Babyface. Joseph Laska. I filed that name away for future reference.

"Are you really thinking of taking over your father's businesses?"

"I'm considering it."

"Tough line."

"I know," she said.

"What about you, what are your plans?" she said. "If you don't mind my asking. I'll understand if you still don't feel comfortable enough with me to have me know where you are."

"Miss D'Agostino—"

"Tess," she corrected again.

"I've learned something from all this," I said. "I'm not the kind of person who can hide much of anywhere. I have a birthmark on my face and a nickname in Latin tattooed on my back, and now"—I held up my hand—"only nine fingers. Not to mention, my fingerprints are on record and my DNA is in the Pentagon's battlefield registry. For good or bad, I've got to live my life out in the open."

"The battlefield registry?" she echoed. "You're a veteran? At your age?"

"I was at West Point."

"And then what?"

"I left."

"That's obviously not the whole truth, Hailey. A West Point cadet represents a substantial financial investment by the U.S. government. They don't just let you walk away from that."

"No," I told her. "They told me to walk away."

"Why?" she asked. "Oh, I see it on your face already: It's another story you're not ready to tell me."

"Don't take it personally," I said. "I don't tell anyone."

We had reached the Fairmont but stopped outside, as if the conversation was too important to carry inside among other people and their light and noise.

"I'm just trying to understand you," she said. "I meant what I said earlier. When I walked into that theater, I've never seen anyone behaving the way you did before."

"I wasn't behaving any particular way. I was being held down on a table."

"Don't be flippant," she said. "You went to great lengths, and let yourself be tortured, for the son of two dead strangers. You weren't even saving the boy's life; he was in no physical danger from my father. You nearly died to preserve his moral and spiritual welfare."

"But I didn't die," I said. "Look, I don't know if I can explain my behavior in a way you can understand. Have you read the Book of Jonah?"

"Jonah?" she repeated, her brown-gray gaze curious on my face.

"Yeah," I said. "Even if you have, read it again. That's the best I can do."

epilogue

Two days later, I was up on the Golden Gate Bridge. It was a bright morning, December cool. I wasn't looking for jumpers. In fact, I wasn't sure I'd ever be up on the bridge, looking for jumpers, again. Tomorrow I was going home.

If I'd cared to make a list of the things I'd lost in the past six months, suffice it to say it would be extensive. Every piece of paper that documented my identity—driver's license, passport, even my birth certificate. Two guns, the Airweight and the SIG. Two cars, one of which I didn't even own. And, of course, my finger.

What hurt most was the loss of the things I'd asked Shay to get for me, the *Wheelock's* with my birth certificate and my only photo of my father tucked inside, my unworn red dress, my West Point class ring. On Christmas night, I'd gone back to get them, only to find the room bare except for the furniture it'd had when I moved in.

That had been too bad, really. Not just for me, but for Shay. If only I'd found the stuff I'd gone back there for, I could have let his betrayal slide. As it was, I'd had to pay him a visit.

Christmas night was a good time for a break-in: quiet and dark, half the houses on any given street standing empty, police patrols few and far between because of skeleton-crew staffing. I'd taken my time with a crowbar on Shay's back door.

The crowbar had also helped Shay to be cooperative and forth-coming when he'd come in around eleven from wherever he'd had Christmas dinner. Conveniently, he'd been alone, or at least he'd thought he was alone until he flipped on the lights.

Nothing he had to say had surprised me much. They'd paid him fifteen thousand dollars to give me up. Shay insisted that Babyface had told him I'd walk away from the situation; that I'd owed a lot of money, and they were just going to slap me around some.

"Bullshit," I'd said. "You cleaned out my room. You knew I was never coming back."

I'd heard it before but never really believed it, that there were people like Shay in the world, who looked good and acted normal but had necrotic tissue where their conscience should have been. I understood Babyface and his crew; what they had done to me was their job, and I was nobody to them. Shay was different. He'd known me, even if we hadn't been close, and I'd certainly done nothing to earn anything like animosity from him. Shay had simply wanted the money and he would have believed anything they'd told him to get it.

It wasn't really a hell of a lot of money, not for a human life. "Frankly," I'd told him last night, "I would have held out for more."

I didn't very often have an opportunity to give full rein, without remorse, to the rage that sometimes seized me. Last night had been a rare exception.

Blood makes the grass grow.

He was fine, he'd heal. Me, I hadn't left empty-handed. Shay had kept my cadet sword; no one throws something like that in a Dumpster. And the balance of the Skouras money, a little more than thirteen thousand dollars, had been stashed in a flour canister in the pantry.

Already, ten thousand was on its way to CJ, the repayment of my debt. The rest was starting-over money, already covering the inexpensive Powell Street motel room I was staying in, and the Greyhound ticket I'd bought.

Tomorrow I was going home. I would spend New Year's Eve in L.A., probably with CJ.

My cell rang and, for once, I answered it without even looking to see who was calling.

"Hailey Cain," I said.

"Hailey, good morning."

"Tess," I said. "What's up?"

"You sound like you're somewhere outdoors."

"I'm on the Golden Gate Bridge."

"What are you doing up there?" she asked.

"Just making some plans."

"And what have you concluded?"

"I'm going home."

"I thought San Francisco was your home," she said.

"No," I said. "L.A. is."

"I see," she said. Then: "Hailey, there are very good doctors up here."

When she said it, I had two conflicting thoughts at once. First, that I couldn't have heard her properly; second, that I knew I had.

She said, "I found out why you left West Point. It puts a great deal of your behavior in context."

"Reading Jonah might have done the same thing," I said.

"I did that, too," she said. "Jonah inexplicably fails to feel fear when it's clearly called for. His actions show no regard for consequences."

"Yeah."

"That's behavior very consistent with having a tumor in the amygdala region of the brain, the center of fear, rage, and aggression. Patients sometimes go off into unexplained fits of anger. Others aren't afraid even when the situation calls for it."

"Yeah."

"And it would make a person, even one otherwise in the bloom of physical health, unfit to serve as an officer in the United States Army."

"Yes, it would," I agreed.

It was so funny, looking back. . . . In my yearling and cow years, and into my final year, I had been so proud of my reputation for being hard to scare. In the boxing ring, jumping out of planes . . . other cadets used to ask me, *Why aren't you scared?* They'd thought it was because I was brave. I had been content to believe that, too. No one saw it as a problem.

That I even got diagnosed was a fluke. The tumor was so small yet that I was nearly asymptomatic. But one day, in my firstie year, I was helping plebes learn to rappel. They were going down a bluff, and I was too close to the edge, sitting on my heels, and my ankle turned the wrong way and I fell. That was it.

The only injury I had from it was a broken wrist, but they checked me out pretty thoroughly, including an MRI for head injury. When the results came back, my company tactical officer came in with the doctor. My TAC said, *There's nothing from the fall, you're going to be fine out of that.* There'd been an unusual tone to his voice.

Out of that, sir?

The doc saw something else he'd like to biopsy.

All right. When?

The doctor and my TAC had exchanged glances, and the doctor said, *You do understand that when I say biopsy, I mean we're looking for cancer, right?*

I guess so, yeah, I'd said.

My TAC gave the doctor a hell of a look, and the doc said, *That's fairly typical for this region, the amygdala. Patients understand that something frightening is going on, but there's no emotional weight attached to it.* He'd seemed a little excited, like he was seeing something rare.

It was so goddammed stupid. I could have stood in Michie Stadium with my graduating class. I could have been a second lieutenant for a brief time, at least, if only I hadn't been diagnosed. Meaning if I hadn't fallen, meaning if I hadn't been so close to the edge of that bluff. Which I wouldn't have been if my fear hadn't been suppressed. It was like the goddamned tumor wanted to be found, had pushed me into unmasking it.

That was the thing Serena and I did at the Beverly Center, the thing the rest of the world wouldn't have understood: We had bought our funeral dresses. Me because of the tumor, her because of *la vida*. She'd chosen a white silk sheath, making up for the wedding she was already sure she'd never have. I'd chosen a scarlet party dress, to spite Julianne, who'd always told me that red lit up my birthmark.

"Hailey? Are you there?" Tess said.

"Sorry," I said. "I'm here."

"It's inoperable, I take it?"

"Yeah," I said. "It's not just location, but proximity to blood vessels and other such things . . . I tuned out after hearing the word *inoperable*. I said, Doc, I'll take your word for it."

"What's your prognosis?" Tess asked.

"It could be years, and I could be healthy for most of those. Tumors aren't necessarily a day bigger with every day that passes. The tumor could stay at its size for a while, then one day it'll get curious: 'I wonder what it's like in that region of the brain? I think I'll spread on over there and find out.'"

"And it's never occurred to you to walk into UCSF Medical Center and see what they might be able to do for you? They have an excellent neurology department."

"So does UCLA."

"But there might be a much higher class of work for you up here," Tess said. "I'm leaning toward taking over my father's businesses rather than selling. I could use a lieutenant who never knew my father and his ways of doing things, a lieutenant who I know can respect a woman, and who is, for all intents and purposes, fearless."

"I didn't say I'm *never* afraid."

"That's probably for the best. Hailey, you're not leaving town today or tomorrow, are you?"

"Tomorrow."

"Promise me you'll think about it a little today? We can talk again."

I looked across the water at San Francisco, which seemed very bright and promising in the December midday.

"All right," I said. "We can talk again."

about the author

JODI COMPTON is the author of the acclaimed novels *The 37th Hour* and *Sympathy Between Humans*. She lives in California.